Scorched Fury

THE DARKWORLD ORIGINS

Pyros (Logan)
Ailuros (Kailin)

~

THE DARK SIGHT SERIES

Dark Sight
Cursed Sight
Vissarion
Shadow Sight
Dark Prophecy
Cursed Prophecy
Shadow Prophecy

~

THE APSARA CHRONICLES

Immortal Bound
Gods Ascendent
Dominion Falling
Vengeance Born
Last Legion

~

A SEASON OF ASH AND BONE

Heartfyre

~

Adult Sci-Fi

HANDS ASSASSIN

Death Dealer

Death Mark

Death Strike

Hand's Assassins Series

❧

NEW ADULT CONTEMPORARY THRILLER W/A TONI VALLAN

Beautiful Collision

Beautiful Conviction

❧

PSYCHOLOGICAL HORROR W/A TONI VALLAN

Dark Shadows

Splinter

Scorched Fury

A SkinWalker Novel #5

Cover art by Eduardo Priego

Editor: J.C. Hart

ISBN-13: 978-0995112568

Scorched Fury

USA TODAY BESTSELLING AUTHOR
T.G. Ayer

I remember my parents taking me to see the Great Tree for the first time when I was four years old.

I remember thinking at the time that the tree was an incredibly wondrous thing. How was it even possible that any living thing could grow to be that big? For a kid, most things seemed enormous by comparison, but I recall marveling even then at the very size of it, even then understanding that I was witness to something incredibly special.

The Great Ash Tree; mystical, magical, symbol of hope to all supernaturals in the EarthWorld.

Decades ago, after a black night in which lightning storms and bitter rain fought like embattled gods, the tree had taken silent root. At the edge of the inner city, where the skyscrapers of the concrete jungle gave way to older, more staid architecture, a whip-thin seedling appeared as if by some inexplicable magic.

Even to a paranormal like me, such a beginning encompassed that which a normal mind cannot unravel. And the people watched in wonder as within mere months the seedling rose to the skies, and little branches reached further and further out.

Not long after the tree had gained its majestic height, it had dwarfed even the tallest skyscrapers in Chicago. With its pale, almost ivory bark, and gigantic branches that spread out hundreds of yards from the base of the tree, and leaves whose colors ranged from deep emerald to dusky brown, the gigantic white ash tree towered over the city, reigning supreme, albeit in such a serene silence that it became an accepted, welcome sight. And one that we soon became so used to that it drifted into the background of our thoughts.

Not taken for granted, but rather accepted as part of our lives.

No season affected the tree, no leaves fell when winter came, no branches stripped bare as the snow fell. The Great Ash bloomed all year round, decade after decade.

Until now.

Sixteen years after that first visit, I found myself standing, again, in front of the Great Ash Tree, without a parent holding each hand, and with awe and wonder the furthest emotions from my mind.

The Ash had been turned into a monument of sorts, and people regularly came to visit. The city had ensured an entire block was dedicated as grounds around the tree were manicured, and planted with seasonal flowers which tended to confuse the gardeners by blooming all year round.

I stood still, squinting up at the tree, the sun high in the sky and casting little shadow. To the other visitors who milled around the grass at the base of the tree I'd appear to be just like them. I'd dressed in black jeans, a gray long-sleeved tee, rugged biker boots and a leather jacket that was warmer than it looked, though not warm enough. I didn't exactly blend in with the humans around me, but neither did I call unwanted attention to myself.

I shivered, pulling the lapels of my jacket closer and giving the ruddy-cheeked woman to my right an answering nod and smile. The weather had turned colder, with four weeks to Christmas, and the volume of tourists visiting the tree had thinned, with only one group of gawkers here today besides me. A gust of icy wind encouraged the woman and her party of three to return to the warmth of her car.

Leaving me alone to inspect the tree.

I was here as an agent of the Supreme Elite; Kailin Odel, agent for the Elders' newly instated investigative arm. The Elders were the most venerable, most respected of all supernatural races. Some say they preceded all races and were even older than the gods. Some even made whispered suggestions that they were the last of God's first children – the Angels.

Whoever they were, to us they were the lawgivers and the lawkeepers. They oversaw the laws across all the planes, acting as a respected senate of sorts. All the High Councils answered to them, no paranormal would dare to defy them.

Not that there were never factions who disagreed with the old ways. Such dissatisfaction spawned Omega, an agency which rivaled that of the Supreme High Council's Sentinel.

Until recently both Omega and Sentinel had worked under a banner of inter-agency cooperation. But with Omega under investigation, charged with crimes against supernaturals – some of which I'd seen with my own eyes – Sentinel's agents had trouble coping.

The Elders put together a cadre of high-level agents known as the Elite, using only the best, most powerful supernaturals from around the world to handle the most sensitive cases. Logan, Saleem – our djinn friend who also happened to be a prince - and I had been recruited a while back. Only now, Logan was in a coma, and Saleem was on a personal mission.

That left me to perform my role, alone.

In the human world, I'd be the equivalent of the CIA or sometimes even the FBI. I even had a license to kill. Just like good old Bond himself.

A suspicious call had come through on the Elite's hotline an hour ago from a concerned citizen: the Tree is dying. That was it.

Had the call been traceable, and had the voice not been digitally masked, the call center might have ignored it. They didn't.

My boss Horner's demeanor on the phone was the first sign that something was wrong. The tight edge of his voice as he'd left his message had me on alert because Supreme High Councilman David Horner was never flustered, never stressed.

I could picture him, all geeky, thin and bespectacled, his face seriously bland, his voice controlled and neutral. Flustered and stressed were two words so not in his repertoire.

Despite his obvious concern, I'd spent my entire ride here unconvinced that it was a legitimate problem. How could anything bad happen to the Great Ash, anyway? It didn't make sense to consider the tree as vulnerable. I'd never known the Chicago skyline without the silhouette of the Tree.

So, any suspicions regarding the health of the Ash were easily brushed away as some madman's ramblings, or a crazy Shaman's mixed-up prophecy.

But now, I stood a scant foot from the pale bark of the tree, my boots carefully placed between desiccating roots that rose from the ground like curling waves turned instantly solid. The smoothness of the pale bark was marred by dozens of ragged gashes, as if someone had taken a broken hatchet to it, long thin jagged slashes penetrating deep into the wood. Where the surface lay split open, a dark ominous substance pooled.

The trunk of the Great Ash cried ebony tears.

I had to force myself to move, to loosen the stiffened muscles in my arms. No matter how shocking the tree's condition, I had work to do. From my satchel, I withdrew two small tubes and a narrow wooden spatula - one of those tools that resembled an ice-cream stick but had a much loftier purpose than aiding in refreshment.

Scraping off an equal amount of black ooze from each gaping wound, I deposited them into the tubes and sealed them with red rubber stoppers.

In the last few weeks, evidence had become an increasingly important part of my daily work. A few months ago, I would have barreled in, eliminated my target and left, happy the job was done. These days, with Elite cases taking me across, and beyond, the continent, there were rules to abide by.

And one of those rules was the preservation of evidence. The agency currently had a whole forensics department devoted to crime scene investigation and research. Which meant that evidence had to be preserved so Forensics could do their jobs.

And though, in the past, I'd had very little respect for CSI work, I was now well aware of the volume of information that the biology of an item could contain. And how much each bit of data could help solve a case.

All Elite agents were supplied with the necessary tools to retrieve evidence. Tubes, spatulas, boxes, plastic bags, gloves. The whole thing was straight out of a crime scene TV show.

I was about to stow the vials into a small cardboard box when something moved at the corner of my vision. I turned to my right, searching for the cause but found nothing. Pausing, I studied the area around me, looking harder, beyond any glamor that may be hiding an interloper.

But I saw nothing untoward.

Still, I remained wary as I craned my neck, peering into the dense shadows above. Within the tangle of branches once-green leaves hung lifeless, dark and sickly, as if painted with a macabre shadow. Every single leaf on the tree now an ailing replica of its once vibrant and beautiful past.

I felt sick.

It wasn't a surprise now that someone would assume that the tree was dying. I wanted to think that it was merely ill, afflicted with some kind of magical or ethereal disease. But two things told me that whatever was killing the tree was not natural.

One was the hard, heavy feeling in my gut.

The other the putrid stench that rose at every wound where

the black substance met fresh air. I refused to imagine what the inside of the tree looked like considering the awful odor.

Was I kidding myself by retaining some tiny hope that the tree could be saved? But it wasn't just *my* hope that was important. The tree stood for so much more than met the eye. It represented the existence of the nonhuman species.

Normal humans had little idea what the Great Ash truly meant. But the tree had risen when the supernatural community had finally decided that they would no longer hide, when they at last decided to choose a new form of invisibility. What better way to stay under the radar than to live right next door to the humans?

And it seemed that the Great Ash had agreed.

Around the world, in cities where the concrete jungle had long overtaken the spirit of the citizens, ash trees took root, growing fast, and strong. In some cities, citizens were concerned by the sudden appearance of the pale tree. A tree that defied attempts to remove, kill, poison or damage it in any way.

But here in Chicago, the tree was revered immediately, accepted as something special so much so that a fringe cult had emerged, dedicated entirely to the tree and its apparent representation of life on earth. It surprised few that the group believed firmly that should the tree die, then so would the world. Wonder what they'd do if they saw the tree in its current condition?

Nausea burned within my gut as I sensed the ebb and flow of the dark energy that seemed to run through the root system of the tree, and rise within its gigantic trunk all the way to the sky.

As I stepped away from the tree something shifted in the branches. Just as I lifted my eyes to scan the canopy, three tiny leaves floated down toward me, drifting back and forth on an invisible breeze. I lifted my palm and the leaves found their way onto the center of my hand.

My stomach twisted into a rock-hard knot. Here was more proof that this was indeed bad. That maybe there was no reversing the rot that had taken up residence in every cell of the ash tree. I cupped my hand carefully, praying that I wouldn't destroy any of the leaves, so fragile that a mere gust of wind would render them to dust.

With my left hand I dug into my satchel, and withdrew three plastic bags. Sealing each leaf in its own separate bag, I gave them a firm nod, bidding them to reveal all their secrets, give us some information to go on.

I placed the bags and the vials carefully into the cardboard box, then filled in the details on the white label on the top of the box. Case name and number, names of the items, the name of the agent who procured said evidence, the tests required, and any suspicions the recovering agent may have.

I smiled as I scribbled my signature at the bottom of the label, wondering what Logan would think should he awaken today and discover how much I'd begun to follow the rules.

With one last look at the Great Ash, I turned on my heel and headed for my motorbike.

Technically the Ducati belonged to Tara. It had been just one more thing that I'd appropriated from my Fae friend in her absence. My only justification was that it served her right for not being around to prevent me from taking them.

I frowned, thinking about Tara and the Fae creatures. All Fae were closely connected to the Elemental Planes. Tara and her mother Gracie, being Fae royalty, were far more powerful.

I'd gone to Tara's store a few weeks back, intending to use it as a base because I was tired of having everyone coming in and out of my apartment. Pretty sure Grams didn't enjoy our home doubling as Grand Central when stuff hit the fan, which they tended to do where we were concerned.

I needed a place to hide, to relax away from the mayhem of my life.

To my surprise, the abandoned shop had gifted me with the bike which I'd found inside the back room, covered with an old red tarp. The shiny black helmet had been safely stored on the top shelf of a metal cabinet, right above Tara's collection of obsidian, mercury and platinum. I'd had little use for the metals, but the bike and its peripherals were another story altogether.

I turned the key and listened as the machine growled beneath me. How had I never understood the satisfaction of riding such a beast before? I now understood Grams' obsession with her own Ducati. For an older woman she rode like a born biker.

As I gave the great tree one last sad glance, I gunned the engine and took off down the brightly lit street. I knew that the only person that would be able to help us right now was the very person who may not appreciate the intrusion on her privacy. The rot taking hold of the great ash tree, while probably not biological in intent, was likely biological in origin. And poison, biological or not, was the forte of the Fae.

Tara and Gracie had helped me with species-related poisons before so I was certain they'd be able to help me now.

I just had to find them.

CHAPTER 2

"Holy shit, where the hell did you come from?" Lily's voice broke on a high-pitched squeak as she stared at me, frozen in place. She stood on the threshold of the inner doorway that led into the apartment behind Tara's shop-without-a-name. It was a Fae thing, from my understanding, and I wasn't about to start complaining.

I rolled my eyes and pulled my satchel over my neck, placing it on the glass countertop as I slipped behind it.

In recent weeks Lily had taken to coloring her golden hair every shade of purple possible, from pale to mauve to indigo. And oddly they worked for her, the hair going well with her shit-kickers, black tights, and fingerless net gloves. With her clothes and dark eye makeup, she looked almost goth, but just a little too cute to go all the way.

"You can't be seriously telling me that you didn't hear that great big bell on the door." I glared pointedly at it. The bright metal bell now sat silent, but a moment ago it had clanged annoyingly, loud enough to wake the dead.

When Tara had been here, she'd needed loud, especially when

she'd been busy in the back room working on her weapons. Today her absence prodded me like a hot poker. Had she been here we may have already solved the problem of the dying Ash Tree.

Tara's weapons and ammunition shop was the other thing that I'd appropriated in her absence. I sighed and sank onto the stool behind the main counter, then stared at the empty, dust-covered display shelves around the shopfront.

She'd been here one moment - Greer's funeral - then left the next. Sent her clients to other manufacturers, and left her friends behind. Without an explanation, or even a goodbye.

She had her own responsibilities, likely related to her royal bloodline, or something to do with the Fae Council or the Court of the Fae. Stuff I didn't ask about because the business of Fae royalty really wasn't any of my concern. So how could I blame her for not being there for me, not being there to see how badly Storm had betrayed us, to sit with us and mourn the loss of Anjelo at Storm's hand, to help us try to find a way to save Logan?

But right now, sitting in her shop, surrounded by our memories, I felt her absence keenly.

"Seriously, Kai." Lily shook her head as she stared at me from the threshold, her voice pulling me out of my thoughts. "If the bell had rung I'd have heard it. I'm not deaf, you know." She sounded annoyed, and a little distracted.

Her distraction may have been attributed to the sticky bun in her right hand, or to the smears of sugar around the thin annoyed line of her lips. But I knew better. There was a sadness, a murky shadow in her eyes, that told me that Lily was still deep in mourning.

Which was the reason I'd chosen to stop off here first. Lily enjoyed ferrying stuff to Forensics for me. It gave her something else to do besides mope around all day. Took her mind off stuff.

Not that she didn't deserve to nurse her broken heart.

I did too, only in silence.

We both grieved for Anjelo.

And me, I nursed both grief and guilt. I'd failed to save Anjelo Alvarez, my friend, my clan. The boy had followed me from Tukats to the big city, emulated me in my search for freedom.

And where had that gotten him?

Killed.

Killed by someone he'd trusted. Someone who'd mentored him, even helped him to get into bursary programs. A snake who'd masqueraded as a father.

Storm, an Immortal, the fallen God Ares hiding amongst humans and supernaturals, had not just betrayed *me*. He'd betrayed Anjelo and Lily, and every other youngster and home-less person who'd come under his care.

Worst of all, we had no idea how he'd been punished. How he'd paid for his sins. Jacinta Carnarvon, the Titan who'd been at Logan's side for years, who'd claimed to be here to look after Logan because he was special, had taken Storm to the Immortal High Council weeks ago and had not returned.

She assured us he'd be punished according to the Law of the Immortals and though nobody had been satisfied, we'd had little choice as the Immortals were, other than the Elders, the most powerful, and most revered of the paranormals. Now, in the aftermath of Storm's ultimate betrayal, I watched Lily struggle to put herself back together.

Despite every instinct to ask how she was coping, to ask how she was feeling, I had to give her space. She'd talk to me when she needed to. When she was ready.

I wasn't sure how that worked when it was my turn to need someone to talk to. It seemed that suddenly there was nobody to complain to, to sound off with. Mom's services had been employed by Sentinel to investigate Omega's off the books jobs, and Grams had been investigating the Walker High Council's shenanigans in between her other Sentinel cases. Lily was busy with her broken heart, and my father was busy tending to Logan.

And Logan, well, he was busy trying to recover from whatever the hell it was that Storm did to him.

Storm who had gained our trust. Storm who had hurt us more than we realized. We were still grasping the extent of the damage he'd done.

I moved off the stool and reached into my satchel to withdraw the evidence box. Handing it to Lily, I tried not to roll my eyes as she hurriedly licked her lips and wiped her wet fingers off on the back of her tights. She took the box carefully, her expression almost devout.

"I need to get that to Forensics, like yesterday."

Lily nodded, her expression now serious as it was Elite-related. My suspicion that Lily wanted a job with the Elite was not unwarranted. It was merely unacknowledged.

"Was it as bad as we thought?" she asked, the worry darkening her already shadowed eyes.

I gave a tiny nod, reluctant to commit formally. But Lily knew me too well. She narrowed her honey-gold eyes, piercing me with a look that said she was sure to rip the truth out of me if she wanted it enough.

"That bad huh?" she asked, watching me as I gave a soft sigh and followed it with a stiff nod.

She gave the box a pointed look and said, "I'll take this over to Forensics myself."

Before I could say anything in response, she turned and disappeared into the apartment leaving me alone in the storefront.

Being alone had never been a problem for me. But right now, alone was a place that I didn't prefer to be. It was probably because I'd glanced down into the glass counter, now bare when it would have once been filled with weapons and ammunition of every kind.

The grime had built up so much on the windows that the light had a difficult time finding a spot to penetrate. Only a handful of rays had braved the dirt, striping the empty room with golden lines, enhancing the abandoned, ghostly feel of the store.

I thought about the black ooze on the tree, and accepted what I'd known the moment I'd seen the rot. I needed the help of the Fae.

Only, Tara hadn't left me a contact number. At the time I'd assumed she was returning to the Faelands. Cell phones and other mobile devices wouldn't work across the reaches of the Veil.

But there were ways that I could get in touch with her. I knew enough jumpers who'd help me should I need them, but though I'd wanted to contact her in the past, I hadn't allowed my feelings to get in the way of my respect for her privacy. Tara had left for a good reason, of that I had no doubt. And I respected that.

But right now, the Great Ash Tree was far more important than our personal relationship, or anyone's right to privacy.

I got to my feet and slung my satchel over my shoulder as I headed into the apartment at the rear of the shop. Tugging my cell phone out of my jeans pocket, I tapped out a quick text to Mel Morgan, neighborhood tracker, and good friend. Mel had come to my aid many times, and through the past few months we'd forged a solid friendship.

She'd recently said she wished she could help me out in a situation which didn't result in me losing something important. She'd helped me bring Logan to safety, but she'd also been there to bring Anjelo's body back home.

Asking for her help now, where the Great Ash was concerned, would give her just such an opportunity.

My cell pinged; Mel would meet me in three hours.

That gave me enough time to make one important stop.

I left the building through the back entrance, locked the gate and slung a leg over the seat of the Ducati.

Flipping the kickstand, I gassed the engine and headed slowly up the alleyway.

Running in shifter speed would have gotten me to Tukats faster, but I needed the drive. I needed the time to think.

CHAPTER 3

I stood on the threshold of my old bedroom, watching Logan lying unmoving on the bed. The sight of him still scared me more than I will ever admit. Beneath his closed lids, his eyes shivered, shifting left and right, the movements sudden, sharp, as if he was caught within his dreams, desperately needing to escape.

My childhood bedroom had been transformed into a hospital room. The old double bed remained though, accommodating the patient and offering visitors like me a place to sit. Around the bed, my father had gathered more equipment than any patient could possibly require.

Dad being overzealous in his care, or proof that Storm had damaged Logan in worse ways than I could imagine? Storm had frozen Logan, placing him into a cryogenic chamber, keeping him on ice for Ailuros knew what reason.

I tiptoed further into the room, scanning his pale face, the tan long gone, his skin now a lifeless alabaster. I sat beside him and took his hand, holding it carefully between mine. Once-strong fingers which had hurled balls of fire, now appeared so weak and so fragile, that it seemed all I had to do was squeeze and they'd disintegrate into ashes and flutter to my feet.

Three weeks had passed and Logan's condition remained unchanged. Sure, my father had murmured positive things every few days, well-meaning assurances that were not as assuring as he'd meant them to be.

It wasn't that I didn't trust my father to take care of Logan. It wasn't even the fact that I'd had no idea that my father was a scientist before he'd taken over the reigns as Alpha, or that he was just as skilled and educated as his brother Niko. In spite of the fact that he'd refrained from telling us all these years, I still trusted him to do whatever he could to help Logan.

No, what brought me to my knees was that I didn't trust that Logan would recover.

I hoped, yes.

Prayed too.

It was just the sight of Logan, a man always doing whatever it took to keep supernaturals safe from harm and from doing harm, lying there so still and unmoving, and so lifeless. With not even a sign to indicate that he'd come back to me.

There were traitorous moments in which I was unsure that anybody could save him. And I was so afraid Storm would finally get what he'd wanted.

A sudden beeping snatched my attention from Logan to the machine beside me that measured heart rate; it had spiked. Was it me? Was my presence upsetting him?

But he hadn't opened his eyes. He wouldn't have seen me.

I watched his face, taking in the rapid movement of his eyes beneath his lids. He was still caught within his troubling dream, and even though I squeezed his hand in comfort, it didn't alleviate his distress.

He tossed his head from side to side, a low moan escaping his cracked lips. His fingers clutched mine harder, the desperation clear in the white knuckles, his other hand grabbing onto the sheets just as tight.

Logan moaned again, then cried out, the sound sharp, cutting through the air, filled with hysteria. His pain tore through me, wildfire scorching its way through my heart. But I could do little else other than hold his hand and pray that my touch would be enough to pull him free from whatever demons sought to control him.

Suddenly Logan's muscles tightened, his head and torso lifting off the bed, as if a shock of electricity had surged through his body. His lids flickered then opened wide, eyes staring blindly. He shouted unintelligible words that made my heart twist with fear.

I held on as tight as I could, part of me wondering if my presence was necessary, if I even helped him at all. I held onto him as his body bounced against the bed. Once, twice. And then, as if nothing had happened at all, the beeping machines ceased their cries, and Logan fell back against the pillows with a soft sigh.

The only evidence that he'd been through anything stressful, were the beads of perspiration that coated his face and neck. And the tight grasp of his fingers around mine.

He let out a soft sigh, his head moving frantically left to right.

"I'll find you," he whispered. "I promise I'll find you."

I stiffened. Who was he talking to? Was it the girl – maybe his sister - that had haunted his dreams these past months?

I scanned his face, relieved that he was still in deep sleep. He'd complained so many times of bad dreams, and when he'd slipped into the coma, I'd been terrified those dreams that took hold of him, would control him.

Now, it seemed that I was right to be worried. He was deep within his unconscious. His subconscious. He'd see the little girl, the one he didn't know. The one who'd faded from his memory as he'd grown older.

I'd asked him to speak to Darcy, to ask for help to unlock his memories. And he'd agreed. I'd been relieved to hear that he was willing to try. But that was before Storm had taken him. Before Storm had reduced him to this paralyzed creature that I had no idea how to help.

I got to my feet, my muscles tightening, and stood beside the bed, staring down at our still entwined fingers. I hadn't lost Logan, not really. He was still here. There was still hope that he'd wake up, still hope that my father would bring him back to us.

We hadn't lost Logan.

Not yet.

CHAPTER 4

A sound at the door drew my attention, and Justin Lake walked through the doorway.

I stiffened at the sight of him, the memory of his proposal still fresh in my mind. I let go of Logan's hand, and tried to ignore the loneliness that blanketed me the moment his fingers left mine. I focused my attention on Justin, where he stood in silence, his golden eyes gleaming brightly, a thin smile curving his lips.

Forcing my feet to move, I went to him, to do the hostess thing and greet him. He held out his arms, drew me into a hug and when his lips touched the skin of my cheek, a traitorous shiver ran through me.

I wasn't naive. I knew I probably would never be rid of my feelings for the Cougar Alpha. Justin Lake had been my first love, my first kiss, the boy I'd harbored dreams of marrying and having the requisite 2.5 children and the perfect life with. But the weight of Alpha responsibility had been enough to nix those dreams.

"How are you, Kai?" asked Justin, smiling down at me, his expression tender, edged with concern. I could never accuse him of not caring.

I gave him a tight smile and moved to the seat beside the window. Somehow it felt wrong to have any sort of discussion with Justin while in Logan's presence, even when Logan himself had no idea what was going on around him.

But I didn't have anything to hide. Nor did I want Justin to think I did.

I took a seat and knew I should offer him something to drink, but I didn't. Justin took the seat beside me and shifted to face me, his legs taking more space than necessary.

I ignored the ripple of awareness that ran through me, and said, "If you're here to see Iain, he's in New York."

Justin shook his head. "Actually, I'm here to see your father."

"He's somewhere around the house. Probably pottering around in his new lab."

I used the word lab as if it was a drop of poison on my tongue. Anything to do with biological research reminded me of my uncle Niko, and it still bugged me that my father had kept his own past from me.

Not that I was about to look a gift horse in the mouth. If he was able to save Logan, who was I to question him on one omission?

"Fine, I'll find him. But first, I want to know how you're doing." He tilted his head studying my face, concern in his eyes.

I offered a short nod. "I'm fine. I'm doing okay."

"The Elders keeping you busy?" he asked, giving a wry smile.

Another nod. "In fact, they're keeping me far too busy."

Justin frowned. "You know you don't need to do everything by yourself, right?"

My eyes narrowed as I stared at him, bristling. He wasn't in my life. He didn't have the right to question me. Just because he'd proposed marriage, didn't give him any rights. But I tamped down my annoyance. No need to lash out at him just because he was concerned.

"There's a lot to do. I just wish that the things I need to facilitate my job would happen faster."

He laughed softly, his voice low, conspiratorial. "I know exactly what you mean"

Clearing my throat and straightening I asked, "Any news on the Walker Council issues?"

Justin nodded, although his expression clouded. "Ivy and Celeste were able to identify the Alphas who were feeding the council information. Gerald Bartlett and Sofia Morgan. There's a surveillance team on them twenty-four-seven in the hope that we can catch them in the act."

I shrugged. "Just because they're talking to someone on the council doesn't make them guilty of anything."

"We're well aware of that. Which is why we're just watching them for now. Our other leads have confirmed that the two newest members of the council have grown astronomically in their influence over the rest."

"Who?"

"Neil Trapper and Delia Wade. They joined the council two years ago. Seem to be the ones in charge despite Joseph Marsden's seniority."

"At least I know that Mom and Grams have been busy."

"No kidding." Justin laughed, his admiration obvious. "Those two seem to be the best investigators around."

"Just be thankful that they're actually on your side." I smiled.

Justin burst out laughing, the sound reverberating around the room and enveloping me. Reminding me of time spent on the back porch as the sun set and the fireflies came out. Long conversations with intertwined fingers, Justin's arms around me, keeping me warm and safe.

"Too bad they were needed elsewhere." He sounded regretful.

"I'm sure you'll all manage," I said as I pulled myself out of the past. I scooted forward on the seat and got to my feet. "I really have to go."

I gave him a tight smile, realizing too late that moving from the chair had been a bad idea because I now stood an inch from Justin, hemmed in by his well-muscled thighs.

And he knew it. He moved his hands and rested them on my hips. Although I stiffened, they didn't fall away.

"Have you thought about my proposal?" asked Justin, his voice low as he watched me intently.

I nodded. "Yes. I have. And my answer is the same. I don't think it's a good idea. I'm in a relationship, and I don't believe in personal relationships for political reasons."

"You can't seriously be telling me that you don't feel what we have. You and I both know that a relationship between us would definitely not be for political reasons."

I let out a short laugh. "The last time we had anything going on between us I was seventeen, and very naive. Going to Chicago was the smartest thing I could have ever done. It taught me a lot about who I was."

"But I already knew who you were." His voice was soft, and I suspected he was right.

I'd been torn in so many different directions that I'd failed to see my own strengths, whereas to those around me they were obvious.

The silence hung between us.

When I didn't respond, he said, "A person's feelings don't change overnight, Kai. You found love again, but that didn't happen for me."

I let out a sharp laugh. "I may have been all the way in Chicago, but people still felt the need to inform me of your rampant love life."

"I never said I was a monk." Justin laughed, completely unaffected. "Look, all I want is for you to give it some serious consideration."

I raised my eyebrows. "Do you seriously think that I'm so fickle that I'd leave the man that I'm with while he's in a coma and probably dying, to run off and marry somebody else?" I shook my head. "I wouldn't think you'd want to be married to someone like that."

"That's not what I was asking you to do." Justin cupped my face with both of his hands. "We still have something special between us. That's something that can never die, no matter how hard you try to kill it. Right now, Logan is lying there in a coma. He may die. He may live. Either way you still need to make a decision. All I'm asking is for you to think about what we have together, to consider who it is you want spend the rest of your life with."

But I was already shaking my head. "You asked me this question before. When Logan was fine. And I told you then that I wasn't interested. What makes you think I'd be interested now?"

Justin didn't answer. He bent down and placed his lips on mine giving me a soft, tender kiss. Nothing passionate, just a gentle butterfly kiss. Then he took a step away and headed to the doorway. "Just think about it. And I mean really think about what you want out of life, who you want in life."

Before I could answer, he was gone, leaving me standing by the window, alone with my thoughts.

CHAPTER 5

The Supreme High Council did things their own way. Likely due to centuries of doing just that. Their Chicago Elite headquarters was located in an old two-storied colonial home, its red-brick exterior, little white porch and black window shutters elegant and respectable to a fault.

Likewise, their forensics division was located nearby, in an equally regal residence, making my regular trips between the two divisions pleasant and short.

Fresh air was better than canned elevator music any day.

Elms and oaks guided me toward the forensics building, and I headed up stairs swept clean of the debris of shedding blooms from the ancient jacaranda that dominated the tiny courtyard. The beautiful purple blossoms gave the house a friendly and welcome feel.

I slipped my key card out of my pocket and swiped it through the reader. The door opened with a soft click, and I entered, quickly closing it behind me.

The tiny front hall was silent and claustrophobic, and I placed my helmet on the floor and swiped my card again, eager to get inside. The second level of security was important given the importance of evidence on site. Hence the need for key cards and fingerprint scanners.

The black square panel gleamed, backlit by a neon green light that intermittently scanned the panel from top to bottom. On the off-chance that both key cards and thumbprints were of the stolen variety, the cameras guarding the door were manned by twenty-four-seven security who were authorized to capture and contain any intruder.

Overkill, maybe. But you just never knew.

The reception desk, usually manned by stern-faced Gerda Charles, a level 1 Mind Mage, was empty, but the steaming mug confirmed she wasn't far off.

The inner hall was silent, and smelled overpoweringly of lilies and furniture polish. Furniture wax I could handle, but a mere whiff of the pungent fragrance of lilies was always enough to give me a headache. I held my breath as I scurried across the entryway and up the stairs, making a quick left at the landing. Two doors down I opened the glass door to Dr Archana Gupta's office without knocking.

With her rich copper skin, black hair that hung to her waist and exotically shaped, almost feline eyes, she looked more like she belonged on the big screen than behind a microscope.

Ash looked at me as I entered, excitement flashing in her black eyes despite both being distorted by a pair of thick goggles. She slid the protective eyewear up, and rested them in the dark hair that framed her heart-shaped face.

"Perfect timing." She crooked a finger at me, then rose and walked to a microscope on a long table against the back wall. She pointed at the eyepiece and said, "Take a look."

I obeyed, unsure of what I was supposed to see.

When I straightened and frowned at her she clicked her tongue in annoyance. I'd known the technician only a few weeks, and been unapologetically impressed with her supernatural forensics skills. She used more than just her expensive equipment to study the samples I sent her.

Often she'd insist on checking out the scene herself, and I'd accompany her just to see if her extra sensory skills were as good as I thought. We'd passed the early friendship stage almost instantly, moving on to relaxed sibling bickering within seconds.

"That is a sample of your black gunk, and if you look closely-"

"Nice to see *you* gracing us with your presence, Odel." An icy voice drifted toward me from the open doorway and I stiffened.

"I do work here, Sean." I murmured without turning. One of the reasons I'd always preferred to work alone was I never had the need to deal with people like Sean Martin. I had no time to entertain overly ambitious backstabbers either inside or outside of my job.

Sean snorted. "If what you do can be called work."

Sean was a Level 6 Air Mage – I'd learned the rankings of supernaturals quickly, with 1 being lowest and 10 being unclassifiable - who, as far as I knew, had been recruited two months prior to me, when the Elders had decided it was time to up the ante.

They'd selected Sean for his air magic, and I was fine with that. He, on the other hand wasn't fine with me. My very presence had irked him from the moment we'd met. His strawberry-blond hair was pulled back into a tight, low ponytail, giving him a deceptively casual air. Not a hair was out of place, not a thread marred the surface of his dark suit.

For some odd reason Sean seemed to think that belonging to the Elite meant he was required to dress like an FBI agent, all tailored black pants and jacket left open to reveal a crisp white shirt. Right on cue, his gaze drifted over me, taking in my low-heeled leather boots, black skinny jeans and white tank. He even spent a moment studying the leather jacket I held on my arm.

I very much regretted having left my helmet in the front hall. That at least would have gotten a much higher lift to his currently curved left eyebrow.

He gave a long sigh. "You know, I'm kind of glad you don't care much for image. Means I have less competition in that department."

I shrugged. "Image doesn't matter jack if you can't get the job done."

His black eyes flashed, as if I was criticizing his case successes. I knew very little about his cases, or whether or not he'd achieved a one hundred percent success rate.

"I'll have you know the only reason I don't have one hundr–"

"Look Sean, this isn't a race for me. If you want to compete against me, go right ahead. Just know that I'm not running."

He sniffed, then tugged the edges of his suit jacket before smoothing down the front seams of his pants. "Doesn't make much of a difference does it?" His mouth curled, the bitter sneer so slight I would have missed it had I blinked.

"What's that supposed to mean?" He was finally beginning to piss me off.

"What it means is being favored by the higher-ups gives you an edge. Only the best of the best are selected for the Elite. And somehow you made it on board. I wonder why that is? Maybe it's your Alpha status, because you certainly don't have the track record to prove your merit. Or maybe there are other reasons." His gaze settled pointedly at my chest.

The nerve of the guy.

I bit back a much-deserved selection of profanity and said, "I think you're deluded. There is no favoring."

Sexist bastard.

Then I stopped speaking. Trying to reason with Sean was like trying to coax a starving lion from devouring a fresh kill. That, and I didn't care for office politics. Sean's brother Tate had missed out on a place with the Elite and he'd held it against me from the moment we'd met.

Seems he's holding it against my boobs too.

I bit back a laugh. I'd have to keep one eye on my back at all times when it came to Sean.

Now, I met his gaze steadily. "I have work to do. If you want something, do tell."

This time both his eyebrows rose, his gaze drifting toward Ash. "Do you have my DNA results?" The condescending tone he used made me want to strangle him on the spot. Sean could pick on me all he wanted but I didn't care because it was competitive, if a little misogynistic, but his prejudicial attitude toward Ash set my teeth on edge.

My fingers closed into a tight fist and Ash cleared her throat, giving my hand a pointed look. Okay, so the girl can fight her own battles. But she'd better know I was right there if she needed me.

Ash gave Sean a blank smile. "I apologize, Agent Martin. I'm only following protocol and Kai's evidence takes precedence given the importance of her case."

Wow. Okay, so looked like I didn't need to save her. Her clipped, formal English made her little dressing down all the more cutting and I enjoyed the pink spots that bloomed on Sean's pale cheeks.

So, tough guys do blush.

He straightened then turned on his heel to face me. That he completely ignored Ash didn't go amiss. Sean pointed a manicured finger at my nose. "This is exactly what I mean about *you* running roughshod over everyone else's cases. Nobody jumps the line, and yet *you* suddenly get to?"

I gave a nonchalant shrug. "If you have a problem with it, speak to Horner." I looked at her over my shoulder. "You need my help with anything while we wait for the Fat Lady to be done?"

The Fat Lady, aka Ash's mass spectrometer, whirred in the background and I could have sworn the machine had mumbled something about being done when she's done.

She nodded as Sean headed for the door, and tipped her head at the folder. "Plant morphology just confirmed your report is ready. You can grab it from the printer."

I ignored the sound of Sean's raised voice in the corridor outside as I stalked to the printer in the corner. Ash was explaining the report to me when Sean re-entered the room. "So what's your next move?"

"I beg your pardon," I asked with a scowl. I'd hoped we'd gotten rid of the guy. But I should have known better.

Most of my cases were top secret, which pissed Sean off even more because he couldn't poke his nose around in my business.

"Horner gave me the low down on the Ash Tree case." Sean sounded very sure of himself. Too sure. "What's your next move?"

"What does it matter to you?" I asked, sharing a glance with Ash who proceeded to tap away at her keyboard, sending me copies of everything with a written explanation. She understood that I wouldn't want to discuss anything further about the case in front of Sean.

"Odel, there is no I in 'team'. Keeping your cards close to your chest doesn't help you in the long run."

"I don't need your help, Agent Martin. If I do, I'll be sure to let you know. And besides, you don't have clearance."

Sean smiled, his face an icy mask. "But Carter just told me about the case. No need to hold anything back." He gave an encouraging smile.

I shifted and faced the air mage, caring little that he could freeze every single liquid cell in my body with a flick of his little finger. "You need clearance to be involved in this. And I know for certain that neither Carter nor Horner want the details of the case to be common knowledge. When I get informed that *you* are on the list, then I'll be happy to share. Until then, I'm sorry."

Sean grumbled, and muttered something unintelligible under his breath. He shoved past me and rounded Ash's desk. "Show me those reports."

"I apologize, Agent Martin. Each of those reports require a security code and only those agents working on the case have access."

"Then access it," Sean snapped pointing at the keyboard.

She shifted in her seat, swinging around enough to allow her knees to nudge Sean's legs, making him recoil instinctively. "You are welcome to access the files whenever you wish, Agent Martin. All you need is your security code."

Sean leaned over and tapped his agent number into the little box but when he pressed enter, the computer complained, "Error. Incorrect Security Code."

He swore, then straightened. Again, he gave his jacket a firm tug then stalked from the room. "We'll just see about this. Security clearance my ass."

Ash grinned as I met her gaze, the sound of Sean's receding footsteps music to both our ears. "I enjoyed that more than I should admit."

"He deserved worse. Racist pig."

Ash tutted, giving me a disapproving glance. "We can't all help the way we were raised, Kai."

"I can't believe you're taking his side."

"Not taking his side. Just understanding that one's upbringing has the tendency to hone not only one's morals and values, but also one's prejudices. Racism isn't an instinctive or inherent trait. It's a learned behavior."

I folded my arms. "Still doesn't give him the right to disrespect you."

Ash sighed and typed in her own code to reopen the screen. "He just knows what he wants and is not afraid to take it."

"Even when it's not deserved?"

"Especially." She opened her mail and frowned.

I sighed. "You'd think what with all of us being supernatural, he'd be more classist than racist. I certainly know a few people who are that way." The Walker Council for one.

Flipping through screens, she shrugged. "Just because we have powers doesn't mean we lose our humanity."

I conceded with a nod. Ash kept her elemental powers under the radar. Probably a good thing with Sean on her ass, especially since she was a Level 10. Like me.

I listened as she continued, "Racism, sexism, even classicism hasn't gone anywhere because we are inherently a race that wants to be better."

I snorted, wishing I could insist she was wrong. "Some people seem to confuse the desire to be better with being better than others. That's what causes all the shit in this world."

"Not to mention all the other worlds."

We shared a laugh before we both sobered as the screen filled with Ash's report. "I can confirm at least one thing, Kai. The poison is naturally derived, but the origin plant isn't something available in this World – believe me, I've searched hard. We've had the Tree scanned twice, but there are no parasitic organisms either on the surface or inside the trunk that could have transferred the toxin."

Ash sighed and rubbed the back of her neck. "We've documented numerous species from other Worlds, but as of now, our database doesn't contain a match."

"And that same poison can be found in the black substance as well as in the leaves?" I asked, taping a finger on my upper arm.

She nodded. "Different molecular structures, but inherently the same organic substance." She met my eyes, her own dark with worry. "The tree has been poisoned. The toxins seem to have a strange multiplying power, as if the longer it remains within the tree the stronger it becomes. And whoever did this means business."

I stilled. "Meaning?"

"Meaning that if we don't find a way to remove the toxins, the Great Ash will die."

CHAPTER 6

I'd just dropped my satchel on the floor, and was depositing my takeout dinner onto the fake wood laminate kitchen table when a hollow knock sounded at the front door.

I hurried into the shopfront and recognized Mel, her hair haloed by the streetlight from across the street. She wiggle-waved her fingers at me and smiled as I unlocked the door.

I poked my head out, made a show of looking behind her as if expecting someone.

And Mel just rolled eyes. "No, Saleem is not with me," she said dryly.

I raised my eyebrows and waved my hands in defense. "Hey. I didn't say anything."

Mel snorted. "You didn't have to."

She headed into the back room not waiting for an invitation. While I locked up, I smiled. Mel was the only person I knew who could get away with silk peasant blouses and skintight jeans. My attire consisted mainly of turtlenecks, and I wasn't sure I had it in me to wear anything so feminine.

Inside the kitchen, Mel was already digging into my takeout

bag. A cardboard box sat, lid open, and Mel held a pair of chopsticks. She looked at me, already chewing with gusto.

"What?" She raised her eyebrows in mock innocence. "I just got back from a case and I haven't eaten in thirty-six hours."

"Good thing I bought enough for two." I sighed and grabbed the second set of chopsticks, attacking the food with equal enthusiasm.

She looked around the room. "You expecting company?"

I shrugged. "Lily. Usually. But she seemed a bit down today."

She put down the chopsticks and swallowed before saying, "How is she doing?"

Ever since helping bring Anjelo home, Mel had taken a serious interest in Lily and her recovery. She felt responsible in a weird way. Which I had to admit I understood.

"I'm not sure. Some days she seems fine, smiling and happy. Other days, she's someone else entirely. She had a lot on her mind even before losing Anjelo. Now, I'm afraid her load might be too heavy."

"But she isn't alone," said Mel, matter of factly.

"No, she isn't. But Lily isn't known for taking advice, or for accepting help. All I can do is to keep her busy, keep her feeling needed and necessary."

"Well, you know I'm here. You need me to help with Lily? Just yell."

I sighed and nodded before tearing open a second box. We polished off the Chinese food, talking about Saleem and his mother, Logan's condition, the Supreme Elite and how I felt about working for them. Mel had also been asked to join, and at this point she'd accepted on a case-by-case basis. I suspected the only reason she'd accepted was because Saleem and I were both agents already.

Besides, Mel usually had her own plate full. Her search for her little sister continued, and despite numerous queries on my part Mel continued to be reticent. I understood all too well.

As soon as we were done eating, Mel and I cleared away the trash and sat back down.

"So, what can I do?" she asked, curious now that her belly was full.

"I need you to help me track Tara down."

Mel raised her eyebrows. "Sure I can." She spoke slowly. "I'll need something that belongs to her. You know the process."

Mel would need an item of Tara's, preferably something biological to help her track. But Tara had left the place spotlessly clean. When I'd taken over, apart from dust, the place hadn't even contained one stray hair.

I laughed, feeling a little stupid. "I'm not sure what I can give you. Tara didn't leave much behind."

Mel straightened, her face brightening. "I do have an idea but I'm thinking you may not like it."

"Hit me with it. I can take it."

I think.

Mel cleared her throat. "There's a bathroom somewhere here, right?" I nodded, suspecting where she was going with this. "So, point me to the shower. I need the drain."

I made a face. "Tara's going to just love this."

Mel shrugged. "You want to find her?"

"Fine. Let's just keep this between us."

"Let's hope that Tara forgot to clean the drains."

I got to my feet and led Mel down the hall. The building was a large rectangle, the shop making up just a quarter of the space. A central hall led from the store to the back with the kitchen, the bathroom and the little back room on the left, and two small bedrooms on the right.

The bathroom didn't exactly sparkle but it was clean. Lily and I had only made use of the toilet, having never slept here overnight. Though Lily may have been tempted, I knew she returned to the shelter every evening because of Chloe.

Though Storm was gone, the shelter remained open, run by

the Mind Mage Chloe Murdoch who had helped Storm with the kids. She was part mind-melded, part therapist and was well-loved by the kids. She'd taken over the job with a determination that I'd attributed to a deep-seated fury at Storm's betrayal. And Lily had stayed, helping Chloe out in addition to tagging along with me. Her role as sidekick was apparently permanent.

Mel strode to the tub, her heels tapping loudly on the ceramic tiles, and shoved aside the white curtain. I smiled at the gigantic claw-footed tub. Clearly Fae needed their soaking time.

As Mel leaned over I dangled a latex glove in front of her face. She reached for it, slipping it on with a slap and a slight shake of her head as if berating herself for not foreseeing the need. Then she was poking her finger into the drain, wiggling it around and around. I was surprised when she came away with four strands of long black hair.

"That's less than I would have expected," said Mel, frowning.

"That's more than what I would have expected," I replied, more than surprised. "Trust me, Tara is a clean freak. This is unexpected."

Mel grunted as she got to her feet. "Let's hope the hair belongs to Tara or her mother."

"It's Tara's," I said. "Gracie has much shorter hair."

Mel gave a satisfied nod, then rolled the hair into a tiny ball, holding it in her gloved palm as she headed back to the kitchen. She removed the gloves, being careful to keep the hair within the plastic so as not to touch it until she was prepared.

I knew from Mel that sometimes the link to people's minds can render a tracker unconscious. Who knew what an unprotected link to a Fae could do? She placed the glove on the kitchen table. We both sat and I prepared to watch Mel do her tracking thing.

She reached out and removed a single strand from the coil with her bare fingers. I watched as she placed the strand into the palm of her hand and closed her eyes. Mel was an astral projector, but she was also one of the most powerful teleporters in existence.

We were lucky to have her on our side.

She closed her eyes and inhaled, deep and slow. In and out, then in again. She held the second breath longer and I watched closely as her eyes shifted beneath her closed lids, the movement reminding me of Logan.

I pushed him from my mind and concentrated.

The room remained silent except for Mel's slow inhalations. She remained so entirely focused on her tracking that it brought goosebumps to my skin.

At last, what felt like hours later, her eyelids fluttered open. I recognized disappointment.

"What happened? Did it work?" I asked, leaning forward, hoping she'd relieve me of the suspicion that her search had failed.

But Mel shook her head. "No. Her trail feels blocked somehow. The hair is biological and with most species it works even though they are technically dead epithelials, but for Tara I drew a complete blank." Mel's forehead creased with frustration.

"Is it because she's Fae?"

Mel gave a tiny, if unsure, nod. "Most likely it is. Fae are part of nature. It means their existence is one with the earth and all its elements. Fae of the land would be hard to track using earth or plants, and fae of the water would be impossible to track using water."

I nodded, disappointment coloring my emotions. "So we are up the Veil without a paddle."

Mel nodded, her lips curling in a smile. "Unless you have something else that belongs to her that we can use to track her."

"Like what?" I heard the frustration in my voice and gave Mel an apologetic smile.

She just shrugged it off. "She's Earth Fae right?"

I nodded. "Yes. Metal to be specific. She uses her powers to make weapons." I stiffened. "Wait. Can Fae be tracked using their specific essence?"

Mel nodded hesitantly. "I don't have a shit-ton of experience with tracking Fae, Kai. I can only assume that the Fae essence is more or less equivalent to human biological data."

"So if you can track a human using their blood or tears or skin, then you should be able to track a Fae using the traces that they leave behind of themselves. And I know for a fact that Tara leaves a trace of her essence within her weapons. It's something that she worried about often. Very few people know about it though."

"Why did she worry about it? I thought making weapons was her thing?"

"It was. But her Court disapproved of her work here because of her essence remaining within each weapon she made. They were afraid it could be used against her."

"They are probably right." Mel didn't look happy. "If we can track her using her essence, then the Fae Court could be proved correct. But, there aren't many teleporters around with my skill. So it's not as if every tracker would be able to find her just because they looked."

I sighed. "I'm not sure how much she understood of how it worked, but what I do know is she did have a kind of mental link to every weapon she created. I once gave her a tiny sliver of metal and she read it well enough to know that she was the one who'd created the weapon."

"Kai, that could work both ways. It could very well be that as a Metal Fae, Tara was just able to track the life of the metal by tapping into her Fae Ethereal power."

I nodded, a thrill of excitement rippling through me. "I have a couple of knives that Tara made." I leaned over and rummaged inside my satchel, retrieving a wide-bladed, curved knife. I handed it over to Mel, handle out. Safety first.

"Good. This should work." Mel took the knife and turned it

over, studying the finely-honed edge. "Impeccable workmanship. So smooth."

I grinned proudly. Mel knew, like me, that Tara used her fingers. Her body emitted a power which she used to melt metal with a touch of her fingers.

"Incredible," said Mel, her voice soft as she studied the weapon. Then she turned it over, now all business as she prepared to track Tara.

I settled back to wait, but within seconds of closing her eyes, Mel stiffened, her spine going rigid. She took a ragged, shallow breath. "I see her." She paused for a few seconds. "She's alive and well, although she appears to be stressed."

"Where?"

"A house. A brownstone."

"Can you see a street name? A house number?" I was afraid that Mel would shut me up, but I couldn't help throwing my questions at her.

She seemed unaffected. "Outside the window…the house across the street is 1270. I can't see a street name."

"Anything else significant?"

"There's a magnolia tree right outside the window. Nothing in the room that could tell me where she is. And she's alone."

So Mel couldn't overhear anything in a conversation.

"It's ok. I'll project and have a look outside, get us a street name. Be back in a jiffy."

Mel went still and silent, and I scooted forward in my seat, watching her intently.

I knew already that bad things sometimes happened to jumpers. Samuel, Mel's friend and mentor was a perfect example. All he did these days was sit and stare off into space. A man, once the most powerful teleporter in the world, now reduced to a catatonic state, caught in an unknown place while he'd projected to help someone. Until now, Mel had been unable to help him get home.

Said a lot for my chances of being any help if she got herself in trouble.

But my concern was unwarranted. Seconds later, Mel took a shuddering breath and opened her eyes. "You going to fly out to Boston or do you need a ride?"

"Boston?" I laughed. "A ride would be lovely, thanks."

CHAPTER 7

My stomach trembled as we materialized on a Boston street, shielded by the shadows that accompanied Mel when she burst forth from the Veil. I was grateful for them. Appearing suddenly on a residential street would draw suspicious witnesses, or the unwanted attention of the authorities.

But the shadows enveloped us, red smoke that, though it contrasted with our drab fall surroundings, was filled with glamor to make it, and us, invisible. We stood alone on the leaf-strewn sidewalk, hemmed in by the endearingly cobbled street on one side and a row of gorgeous triple-level brownstones on the other. Historical residences that would prove attractive even to the most ardent haters of modern duplex living. Even I would adore such a home, despite knowing I was mere inches from my neighbors at any given moment.

I took a slow step toward the stairs, fingers trailing the wrought iron banister, when I sensed Mel hesitate behind me. Looking over my shoulder, I frowned as she fidgeted, throwing her hair out of her eyes with jittery fingers.

"What's wrong?"

She jerked her head, a ragged excuse for a shake. "Nothing. I just thought that maybe you'd want to be alone with Tara?"

My turn to hesitate. "Maybe. But not for too long." I scanned the street, wary still of curious passers-by. "Is there somewhere you could hide safely and project into the room?"

"You don't need your privacy?" She seemed confused.

I laughed. "Tara is my best friend, not my lover."

After a moment, she shrugged as if having both in the same person wasn't a problem. I accepted that she was just respecting our boundaries and I sighed. "Of course, you may be right about privacy. Tara may not want our discussion overheard, but you and I are here on an important errand. It's not personal and I hardly think she'd mind you listening in."

Mel nodded, although the look in her eyes was uncertain. I ignored it and hurried up the stairs. With one last glance at Mel, I knocked on the door, grimacing at the fist-sized head of a lion, it's giant canines biting onto a brass knocker.

The door opened a few seconds later and a woman, who bore a striking resemblance to Gracie, stared at me. She was wraith-thin, her large glassy blue eyes watery as they reflected light from every angle. Her glamor was ragged, lacking the elegance with which Tara drew hers. And the slim, thorn-riddled branch around her neck confirmed my suspicion.

A Fae slave.

"May I help you?" she asked. Her tone held a hint of annoy-ance that I dared disturb her by knocking. Odd in the demeanor of a slave, but then Fae slaves were known for enjoying their enslavement.

I ignored her tone and nodded, forcing my lips to rise in a smile. Probably looked maniacal, but I couldn't do anything about it. "I'm here to speak with Tara."

The Gracie-doppelganger's eyebrows rose a few inches. Her cheeks flushed and as she swallowed a thorn sank into the curve of her neck, drawing blood. I forced myself not to stare as the blood pooled and dribbled into the neck of her linen shift.

"I'm sure I don't know what you mean." Her eyes scanned me from head to toe and I wondered if she knew she spoke to a shifter, or if she thought I was a human who didn't deserve even a lowly Fae slave's time.

"Look. Let's not waste each other's time. I'm a friend of Tara's." Again the woman flushed, her cheeks reddening as I mentioned my friend's name. Still, she didn't budge. Losing patience, I said, "I'm here on Supreme High Council business and it's of utmost importance that I speak to her immediately."

I didn't usually pull rank but the servant's haughtiness had begun to grate on my nerves.

At the mention of the Supreme High Council the Gracie-duplicate took a step back, gave a hesitant nod. "I can bring Mr Dawson down to have a word with you."

I gritted my teeth, breathing slowly through them. "I'm not here to speak to Mr Dawson." I spoke sharply, annoyed that although she was moved to action, she was still ignoring my request. "I'm here to speak to Tara and I need to waste as little time as possible. Please could you let her know I'm here."

The woman stilled, then straightened, a cool smile on her lips. "And who exactly are you?" Again her tone was dismissive, as if she spoke to a human.

"I'm Kailin Odel. Tara knows me."

One eyebrow rose. *As if.*

I didn't react, just waited on the threshold as the woman turned and disappeared into the front room on the right of the small hall. Footsteps hurried toward me and Tara appeared, flying from the room and enveloping me in a giant hug.

Gracie 2.0 stared from the threshold, shocked and wide-eyed at our physical contact.

I hugged Tara back.

Okay. Hopefully this means I won't be kicked out on my ass.

Then she grabbed me by the upper arms and shook me hard. "What the hell are you doing here?" Her tone was harsh and urgent.

I patted her hand gently, as if tempering a wild animal. "I'm sorry to have to do this, but we need to talk. It's extremely important. Otherwise I would never have intruded on your privacy."

Tara's features softened. Her skin was even paler than normal and as she relaxed her markings surfaced, dark, shimmering and moving lazily on her skin like living things.

The servant gasped as she stared first at the swirling tattoos, then at me. When her gaze returned to Tara's face, the disapproval was clear.

Tara sighed. "Stop being so dramatic, Ani. Kai is a dear friend and she's seen my markings too many times for it to affect her."

"You showed her your markings?" The girl herself seemed horrified, first at Tara's daring, and second that *she'd* had the audacity to question her own princess.

Tara's stern look admonished the girl, the darkness in her eyes deepening to match her ebony hair. Then her expression softened and she sighed. "Yes, Ani. We're best friends. As close as sisters."

The girl sucked in a soft gasp. It seemed everything was shocking to her and I hoped the reaction wasn't a regular occurrence.

Tara looped an arm into mine and drew me into the front room. Over her shoulder she called for something to drink, then said, "You must excuse Ani. She's not used to meeting non-Fae, least of all one that is a confessed, on-hugging-terms bestie of the Queen."

The Queen?

My turn to stifle a gasp. "Crap. Is that why she was so shocked? I didn't bow or scrape or anything."

Tara laughed softly and pulled me onto a white and gold

striped loveseat, its curved legs gleaming with gold leaf. "You are forbidden to ever do such a thing with me."

I shook my head, face serious. "No way. I give kowtowing where it's due." I grinned and then sighed. "I'm sorry again. I never would have disturbed you if it wasn't important."

"How did you find me?" Tara tilted her head and studied my face, genuinely curious, yet the tiniest bit disapproving. I had, after all, broken the rules.

"Mel helped me track you."

Tara nodded, her eyes now shining with amusement. "And it took you this long to come see me?"

Hesitating now, I frowned then shook my head. "Yes, I could have asked Mel to track you weeks ago. And no, I didn't. I respected your privacy, Tara."

"And now you don't anymore?" she asked, her expression neutral.

My heart thudded. Was she angry with the intrusion? "No. I still do. I'll be gone as soon as we've finished speaking. You must know that this is important. It's not personal at all."

Tara made a face. She actually looked disappointed and I wondered if I'd said the wrong thing.

I lifted my hand. "Not that I didn't want to see you. I-"

Tara laughed softly. "Stop it, silly. I'm not upset. And I knew you'd respect my need to be left alone. And I also know that this, whatever it is, has to be important or you wouldn't have come."

She sat back and crossed her legs and only then did I register her dress. Deep green flecked with shimmering lime, it looked like wild moss, only woven into a floor-length dress that would be right at home at a ball or on a runway.

At her neck she wore a string of shimmering crystals, each glittering with every shade of green, which for all I knew were rare gems. Garb fit for a Fae Queen.

I cleared my throat. "The Chicago Ash Tree is dying and we need your help."

Tara's pale skin whitened as the blood drained from her face, bringing her swirling tattoos into stark contrast. "What did you say?" Her voice brimmed over with shock.

Not the kind of shock one experiences on hearing something the first time. No, rather the expression on her face indicated that she'd heard about the dying Ash before.

I leaned closer. "The Ash." She looked upset.

"You know?"

Tara's shoulders drooped. "Yes, and no."

I cleared my throat as the silence dragged on. I seriously didn't have time to waste enjoying deep silences and I had to shrug off the urge to shake her by the shoulders and insist on an answer. But one did not shake royalty, even bestie royalty.

Tara shook her head. It was obvious something weighed her down. "Sorry. Yes, I know about the Ash Tree being sick, and no, I didn't know about your Ash Tree."

"*Our* Ash?" My eyes widened. "Crap. Don't tell me the Boston Ash is sick too?"

Tara nodded. "It's the reason I was called to Boston so suddenly. The Ash is vital to the Fae and signs of its affliction was enough to gather the troops."

"Have you been able to figure out what's wrong with it?"

Tara shook her head. "I've had my people investigating, but they haven't uncovered any definitive reason."

I stiffened, scowling.

"What?" asked Tara, watching my face now. She tilted her head. "What do you know?"

"Something you should know by now if you've been researching the tree's illness."

Before Tara could answer, someone swept into the room, bringing with him a touch of winter.

Tara's gaze shifted to the newcomer then glanced at me giving him a regal introductory wave. "Kai, meet Elan."

He was tall, his body well-muscled despite his slim figure.

He wore an ice-white silk suit, probably something Italian from the looks of it. And his attire contrasted with Tara's gift-of-nature gown. His ice blue hair gleamed, shot with white, and he pulled off the dual tone in a very attractive way.

Attractive probably because of the glamor he wore. The silver of it glittered on his cheekbones, dusting his shoulders and hugging him like a silken shroud. Beneath the glamor, his cheeks were gray, hollow with age, eyes deep and ancient. A dangerous creature to be sure.

He gave a cool smile which seemed to drop the temperature in the room a few more degrees. I considered standing and bowing, but Tara didn't indicate that I should. So I didn't.

"Elan, Prince of the Winter Court, at your service." He gave a small bow. Light glinted off a diamond-carved clasp that held his long white coat on his left shoulder. The cold shimmer of the jewel matched the waves of ice that emanated from him. And despite the nice words I suspected he was very far from at my service. Probably the ice in his eyes. He studied me the way Sean looked at Ash.

Racist Fae.

"Nice to meet you, Elan." I fell silent, finding little to say in the face of his contempt. Probably the wrong move, because he studied me head to toe, his expression dismissive.

"My Queen. If you're done mixing with the rabble, you are needed upstairs. We are about to begin."

"As it happens, Elan, Kai is here about the-"

I touched her arm. "We do have to go Tara. But I promise we won't be gone long."

Tara's eyes shifted away from the snowy-haired fae to me. She frowned as she considered my words and then her eyes cleared, understanding the deeper meaning. She gave Elan a suspicious glance.

Then, to my relief, she gave a firm, regal, don't-try-to-change-my-mind nod. "Tell the council I'll be a bit late. I have an important errand to run."

Elan's pale blue eyes turned paler still, ice-chips now as the air frosted, and ice crept up the sides of the walls behind him. At his feet, frost covered the wool carpet, and crackled against the window beside me.

"My Queen, may I suggest that this is a very bad-"

"Elan." Her voice shut him up. "I will return in a while. The council should be satisfied that what I am attending to is of the utmost importance. I am not known for my frivolity."

Elan gave me a glance. "Very well. But I hope that should this creature be duping you, you will end her swiftly and return to your duties?"

I raised my eyebrows. *End me?*

Tara laughed. "How easy that would be Elan, to end every creature who disrespected me or used me." She paused and watched his face. "Or lied to me."

So it was possible for the ice prince to go even whiter. His blue hair had turned into blade sharp shards and the tips of his collar points both hung lower with icicles.

"As you wish, my Queen." He bowed low, but as he rose he said, "I must assure you though that should you not return within the hour, I will be forced to send out the Royal Guard with orders to eliminate any and all threats to your safety, perceived or real."

He shifted his gaze to me. "Friend or not."

"Is that so?" asked Tara, her expression just as cold as the Fae's.

I hid my smile and watched the Ice Prince cringe as Tara took a step toward him.

When she spoke, her voice shivered with an echo that terrified even me. The powerful, Royal side of her that I'd never seen. "Please inform the Council to await my arrival. I will be back within the hour. Should I not return, then I would suggest you send out a search party for both the Panther Alpha and myself. Only one reason will impede my return, and that is if both our lives are in danger."

The Prince's face turned a few shades grayer, though his eyes darkened with something akin to hatred. "Yes, my lady." He bowed his head. "Please forgive me. My only concern is that of the safety of my future bride." He back-pedaled a few steps, then turned and left the room.

I raised both eyebrows and stared at Tara. "Future bride?" The words echoed around us, my horror impossibly loud. "Please don't tell me you're going to make babies with *him*?"

The future bride snorted, then glared at the empty threshold.

"In his dreams." Then she sighed and met my eyes. "A marriage arranged by my mother when I was born."

I gave a shocked, choke. "Gracie did that? Why would she do such a thing? And where is she anyway?"

Tara opened her mouth to respond, her face bleak, as if drained of all emotion. Then she cleared her throat and her expression transformed, now calm and serene.

"So? What are you waiting for? Take me to the tree." She lifted her chin imperiously but the mischievous smile on her face spoiled the effect.

"I thought you could get there yourself?" I asked, grinning. Fae possessed the enviable ability to move great distances without being seen. Not entirely a jumper's ability, but they still moved with incredible speed and could cloak themselves in invisibility whenever they wished.

"I can, but I think it would be safer if we traveled together."

Before I could ask why, Mel materialized beside us. Tara blinked and smiled. The two women greeted each other, friends too.

Mel held out a hand, one to each of us. "We'd better be going. I'll drop you off at the tree, then I have an errand to run."

We both nodded and Mel jumped us to an alley a block from the Chicago Ash Tree.

We appeared, then used the shadows to scan the street for nosy passers-by. Mel disappeared after giving us a quick wave and a promise to be back in half an hour.

I was about to step into the street and Tara grabbed my arm and pulled me back. "I'm using a glamor to hide us both. I should've said before. I think it's the safest way."

"Good idea. You probably don't want people to see you here."

"Nothing gets by you, does it?"

We exited the safety of the alley, and cloaked by her glamor we crossed the road, passing a small group of college students sprawled on blankets on the grassy knoll beside the tree. Heading across the lawn, we stepped around two couples picnicking before the tree. The Ash towered a few yards away, and you'd have to be blind not to see the condition of it.

"I don't think I would have believed you." Tara shook her head and sighed. "No, I wouldn't have wanted to believe you."

I frowned and looked at her, more because the sight of her was better than the sight of the dying tree. "Why wouldn't you want to believe me?"

"Because this." She nodded at the tree, placing hands on her hips she studied the roots. "*This* is a problem. "

"You don't say," I said dryly, folding my arms

"Shit," Tara said as she stared up into the branches.

"Language much," I said softly, but she wasn't listening.

"This is the reason I was called away all those weeks ago." Her voice echoed in my ears, an effect of the glamor kicking back the sounds we made.

I frowned. "You knew all those weeks ago that the tree was ailing?" What I didn't add was that she'd known and she'd done nothing about it.

"I was called away because *A* tree was dying."

"The Boston Ash?"

"I guess it no longer makes sense to keep this under wraps." Her sigh floated around us.

"You don't say," I said dryly.

Tara gave me a look that confirmed she felt bad about not revealing the truth sooner, but that she didn't regret it. She began to walk around the base of the tree, slowly inspecting each wound, each poisonous excretion. "It's exactly the same. Both trees are afflicted with the exact same disease."

I cleared my throat. "And your people still have no idea what the problem is?"

Tara shook her head. But she studied me with an odd look on her face. "What is it you know?" she asked.

"What I know is something that your people should have

known weeks ago when they initially investigated." I shook my head and stared at her. "I don't understand why you don't know this. Unless of course they're keeping the truth from you. For whatever reason."

"Kai," said Tara, the warning clear in her voice. She was using her regal queen voice. Completely unnecessary.

"We had the black substance analyzed. Pieces of the bark, leaves and even the roots." I took a deep breath, my throat tightening. "The tree is poisoned."

"Poisoned? Poisoned with what?" asked Tara, her voice, volume and tone, a little bit higher, a little bit more frantic.

I pulled my phone from my pocket and swiped through my emails until I found the report. Handing it over to her, I waited while she read.

When at last she returned the phone, the veins in her hand were tight and distended.

"Send me copies of those, please?" she asked softly.

"Consider them sent."

I watched her, staring off into the distance, her mind elsewhere and decided it was time to speak. "I'm a little worried about you, Tara. Why are your people keeping information from you?" My eyes narrowed as I studied her face even as she tilted her head away from me. "Something going on? Why are they keeping you out of the loop? Why don't they want you to know the truth behind the poison?"

Tara looked at me, head on now, as if she'd decided to face it. "The best reason is that someone within my court is guilty of poisoning the tree."

I gasped. "Don't you think that's a bit of a drastic assumption? Maybe they're concerned for your safety. Maybe whoever is killing the tree is after you as well." I was grasping at straws, and I sounded like it too, but for some reason as the words left my mouth I realized that they were a possibility.

Tara's wide eyes said she was on the same wavelength.

She began to pace. "I sent everything out weeks ago to be analyzed. The results came back within a few days. The lab assured me that it was just a phase, that the tree was purging toxins that had built up over the years. I should have understood then what was going on. That it was just a bunch of bullshit."

"You really think they would do this deliberately?" I asked, side-stepping a human couple pushing an adorable gray-eyed baby in a stroller. The baby gurgled as I passed, keeping her eyes on me. If I ever doubted that babies could see through the glamor, then at that moment I was convinced.

"I'm not sure. It's entirely possible especially since . . ." The baby laughed louder as she stared at Tara. I could just imagine what my Fae friend would look like to a human eye, all glowing and gold dust.

"Tara? Maybe it's time to tell me what's going on?" I suggested, mentally crossing my fingers that I didn't have to find creative ways to get the information out of her.

She turned and looked at me, her face filled with worry. "I'm not sure."

"Don't you trust me?" Hurt seared like an iron fresh from the forge.

Beside us, the mother lifted the baby from the stroller, curious what had gotten the kid so excited.

"It's not about trust," Tara said softly as she curled a long lock of hair around her ear. "It's got more to do with protecting the people around me, than with keeping things from you."

"Okay." I spoke with a patient tone, although I didn't have much of it left. "But I can look after myself, as you well know. And if it means protecting *you* from danger then I want to know. I deserve to know."

Tara sighed, and lost the glamor for a brief moment. The baby gurgled. The mother squeaked, her eyes widening at the sight of us. I knew she'd be seeing a shimmering image, almost like a mirage before we solidified.

Thankfully, Tara drew the glamor around us again and we hurried away. A glance backward confirmed the baby's big eyes were still trained on us while the mother stared blindly around her as if demons were about to pounce.

If she only knew.

"Sheesh. That was careless," Tara grumbled as we hurried back to the alley.

"And yet perfectly understandable. With everything going on I have no idea how you're keeping it together." I sent a text to Mel as we walked, and she replied almost immediately. We had fifteen minutes. "So now, tell me what is Elan's problem. Apart from the fact that he likes ending Walkers." I gave a dry smile.

"Elan is . . . complicated."

I pursed my lips. "Not so complicated. He's got the hots for you, that much is obvious. But he's conflicted because he would prefer that *his* ass was on the throne and not yours."

Tara snorted. "Again, you don't miss much do you?" She sighed and leaned against the sun-warmed brick. Now, close to twilight, the warmth was beginning to recede as we stared at the tree in the distance, it's height still making it easily visible above the buildings along the street. A dark pall hung over the Ash, as if the shadows of the underworld were already there to claim it.

I must be upset if my imagination was becoming so melodramatic.

Tara cleared her throat. "We were called back to Allira because the council refused to allow me to choose any longer. They'd been patient with me for long enough apparently, and Gracie's coddling was no longer to be tolerated."

"Where is Gracie, by the way?" I grinned as I asked.

Tara let out a silent breath. "Gracie is dead."

My throat closed as I stared at her, stunned. Unexpected and unwanted news. "What?" The word came out a hiss of air.

After a few moments, I was able to ask, "How?"

Tara watched me, her eyes a green so dark it bled black. "Sometimes bargaining chips end up losing their value."

My ears began to ring. "They killed your mother?" Righteous fury filled me, making me want to go right back to Boston and rip all of their throats out one by one. "I never knew the Fae held their royalty in so little regard as to just kill them off when they wished." My limbs shook with anger.

"Gracie was not my mother."

I wasn't sure what was worse. Gracie's death or this new revelation. "Tara," I said patiently, despite how stunned I felt. "This is called a 'what the fuck' moment. So please can you tell me that you are not messing with me? I'd like to implode for a valid reason." Despite the smart-ass comments I did feel like I was about to collapse in on myself.

Tara curled her fingers around my shoulder, tears glinting in her eyes as she bent to look at me. "She was, for all intents and purposes, my mother. She nursed me, raised me, trained me, protected me. Everything a mother should do. Everything that *my* mother could not be bothered to do."

My mouth dropped open and I had to force it to close again. Overwhelmed was the only word I could apply to the crazy turmoil inside my head.

"My mother is the daughter of the Earth and the Air Fae. She mated with an Aqua Fae and surprising everyone gave birth to me, a Fae with the ability to hone metal. I'm unique."

"I always suspected."

Tara grinned. "Gracie couldn't manipulate metal. We just kept up the show for both our safety, and that of our friends. But someone must have fed the Fae court with information because they forced me to choose; Gracie lives and I become Queen and take on my royal duties. Or Gracie dies."

My voice was granite. "But Gracie did die." As if she was ignorant of the fact.

"Apparently an accident while transporting her from a maximum-security prison to somewhere more comfortable. No-one will tell me how she died but I suspect their reticence is to hide the truth that they'd planned her death."

"What are you going to do?"

"I don't have much of a choice. I have to be Queen, and now with the Ash Trees dying, it's best I remain at the head of the Fae, even if just as a glorified double agent."

"Especially since they seem to want to keep the truth from you." Tara nodded sadly. "So what now? You go back to Boston and keep a keen eye on your underlings?"

"Yes. And you keep me up to date on the forensics. I'll put my own feelers out, see what I can find out. I know someone who has an inexhaustible knowledge of Fae biotoxins."

I took in a breath feeling like I hadn't breathed in days. "While you do that we need to identify possible suspects who may be behind this."

"I'll send you a list from my end."

I chuckled. The sound was mirthless. "At least we know that Storm isn't involved."

"What makes you so sure?" asked Tara.

Her eyes bore the same kind of hurt I saw in my own expression in the days after Storm's betrayal. But Tara's voice was bitter. She was furious at him. Good. Better than wallowing in self-pity.

"I concede to your point. He could have put plans in place before he was caught." I stiffened. "Come to think of it, there was something that one of my contacts mentioned while I was in the Graylands. Something about another attack that was being planned. Why do I feel like I heard the mention of planes?" I shook my head annoyed that I couldn't remember.

"Don't stress yourself. You were injured. Serious blood loss while in the Graylands can affect mental function on many levels."

I stared at her suspiciously. "Have you been keeping tabs on me?"

She shrugged. "Being a queen has its advantages."

I snorted. "Just make sure to be queenly when I visit your palace. I want the gold ticket tour and the penthouse suite." I grinned. "And throw in a sexy bare-chested masseuse too."

"I'll have it all arranged. Just say the word."

CHAPTER 9

As I ran, I reveled in the feeling of the wind against my cheeks. My panther growled, enjoying her freedom. We both needed an outlet of pent-up energy. Tara's news about the Boston tree wasn't what I'd expected, nor was it what I'd wanted.

Add that bad news to Tara's revelation about her true parentage and the death of Gracie and I was a hot mess.

Tears burned my eyes and I felt them hit my cheeks and fly away. It didn't seem fair losing so many people. Anjelo, Logan and now Gracie. Good, loyal, loving people so easily removed from our lives. Sometimes I wondered if anyone realized how tenuous our hold on our loved ones was.

Gracie was loving and cheerful, scolding and cuddly. Not that I'd ever hugged her. I'd thought all along that she was Fae royalty and I'd treated her with the respect she'd deserved. Something deep in my heart twisted knowing I'd been lied to. That all that time I'd known Gracie, all those years of seeing her so often, all those poisons she'd scoured the Faelands to find just for me, all that time she'd been lying to me.

Tara had been lying to me.

But in the face of Storm's betrayal, Tara's omission was

minor. A small hurt that was inflicted because she'd cared for me enough, because she'd wanted my safety above all else. Storm hadn't cared about our safety. All he'd wanted was to ensure he avenged himself for what he'd lost.

I branched off the highway, heading into the trees and up into the hills, my paws slammed into the soil, raising little clouds of dust. The loping movement of running as a cat was calming, everything in sync, fluid, cohesive. Cloaked by leaves and shadows, I pushed myself to move faster, feeling the burn in my muscles, the tightening in my lungs.

So deep was I within my thoughts that only the sound of the gravel beneath my claws brought me back to awareness. I'd run on automatic, heading for my father's house without thinking about direction.

Slowing to a stop, I changed to human form, the rucksack still secure on my back. Naked, I hurried around the house and headed for the old pool house. With us kids all grown and gone, Dad hadn't bothered with the upkeep of the pool, but with our three young guests it looked like he'd finally made an effort.

The water twinkled and the pool house looked almost new with its sparkling lick of white paint. I entered and changed as quickly as I could, before hurrying to the kitchen entrance a few feet away and keying in my code. After the whole Storm debacle Baz, our resident vampire - yes we have a vampire living in our home - had insisted every person have their own codes, and that we all used them when we entered and left the property. It seemed pedantic but with Baz and the goblin twins Alina and Alix Longford still living with my father, it had made a lot of sense.

Technically Baz, or Sebastian Ross, hacker extraordinaire, had been partially turned by a vamp-demon, but the end result after being bitten tends to be the same. For Baz, vamp speed merely made him more dangerous at the keyboard. So we kept him. Or he stayed. I can no longer be sure which.

The keypad beeped and the door clicked open, giving me a chance to get my breath back. I entered the hallway, the empty kitchen offering no warmth or welcome. The living room though was perfect.

Alina lay on her stomach in front of the fire, the firelight making her red hair glow. Mom sat beside her while the two of them discussed the sheer recklessness of Nancy Drew's antics. Mention was made of lockets and a lane called Larkspur, but all was forgotten when Alina looked up and caught sight of me.

The excitement in her eyes brought an answering grin to my face, and although I was eager to visit with Logan, I entered the room and returned her enthusiastic hug. Mom smiled at me from over the child's head.

"So where is your little brother?" I asked softly.

She shrugged. "Doing boy things?"

"Now what in the world could be a 'boy thing'?" I asked, crouching down in front of her.

"Chopping wood. With Baz."

"Ah. I see." I smiled at the disappointment in her eyes. "So . . . did they explain why chopping wood is a boy thing?"

Another shrug. "I think they wanted to be alone."

"Oh." Interesting. "Is Alix troubled by something?"

"Maybe." Alina made a face. "Baz said that Alix needed some manly advice."

I gave an exaggerated sigh. "Well, if Baz thought so then he must be onto something. Has Alix seemed troubled at all?"

"He misses Daddy. He cries at night. And then in the morning he pretends he doesn't because he thinks he should be protecting me and not the other way around."

"Well, there you have it." She frowned. "Baz is helping Alix out with his problems. He's still mourning for your family and maybe it makes him feel weak. I'd guess Baz is just putting him on the right path."

Her eyebrows rose. "Then he shouldn't have called it a boy thing."

I nodded solemnly. "Maybe he shouldn't have. I'll have a word with him."

She nodded and gave a small smile and not for the first time I marveled at the age-old wisdom in her eyes. The poor child was so young and yet had lost so much. What was it like to be the only survivor of a massacre that killed her entire clan? Every single person in her village, everyone she'd loved, dead.

I rose and so did Mom. She whispered something to Alina who nodded and ran out of the room, giving me a little wave.

Again, I received a hug and this time it was me receiving the comfort. "How are you honey?" asked Mom.

I sighed. "How can a girl feel with one guy comatose and another guy trying to sweep her off her feet?"

I hadn't expected to blurt that out, but things like this usually happened to me when Mom was around. There seemed to be some barrier to lies when it came to her. Probably all those years we needed to make up for.

The fire spat and crackled and Mom went over to nudge the logs around with a poker. Her face was bathed in golden light as she said, "Caught between two loves, huh?"

I snorted as I drew closer to the warmth of the flames. "I'm not sure I can describe my feelings toward Justin as love."

Mom smiled. "Kai, from what I gather you were head over heels for Justin Lake from the day you first met. And neither of you ever fell for anyone else until you met Logan in Chicago. You left the Walker lifestyle. I believe the technical term is 'you broke his heart'."

"Mom," I admonished softly. "That's a bit dramatic, don't you think?"

"You did leave without a valid reason."

"I had a valid reason. I felt suffocated. Unable to make a single decision of my own. Even my relationship with Justin seemed to have been orchestrated."

"What the hell is that supposed to mean?"

"Language, Mother." I laughed. "Iain generously informed me that Justin's father and Dad had arranged our marriage when we were both toddlers. He said that neither of us had a real choice in the matter. That joining the clans was of utmost importance."

Mom snorted. "Probably his way of convincing you that you had no choice but to marry his best friend."

"Well that backfired on him, didn't it?" I said, trying to keep a straight face. Had Iain only been trying to help? Had I overreacted and run off for no reason? No. "Besides. Even if you ignored the whole Justin thing, I wasn't in the right place, either to be in a relationship or to be the daughter of an Alpha."

"Kai. You and I both know you had your own demons to fight. And I think Justin knows that too."

I folded my arms. "Even when I'm in love with someone else?"

"It's not as if Justin joined a monastery after you left. You both tried to find love afterward." Mom sighed and moved away from the fire. "One of the biggest problems with Walkers is being long-lived. For each human year, a Walker suffers almost twice as much. I hadn't realized until you were born that a Walker's longevity was so prolonged. I was extremely grateful for my Mage abilities when you were babies. My longer lifespan certainly helped when a year of the terrible twos ended up lasting six months more. My only regret is that I missed your teen years. That must have been something awful."

"It wasn't so bad for me. Greer suffered the most." I hadn't meant it to sound like I was blaming her, but from her expression I knew that's how she took it.

Mom sighed. "It's okay. I know I contributed to Greer's pain. But no, I'm not taking all of the blame. She was troubled from the start, and if I was a human shrink I'd come up with some sort of genetic mental affliction that felled both Niko and Greer."

I snorted. "Are you saying my kid may be mental too?"

Mom smacked my hand. "Don't even joke about such a thing. A paranormal's life is hard enough with extended longevity, and the emotional toll of both our powers and having to hide from the world. Don't go asking for more trouble."

"I know, Mom. I was only joking. So tell me how your investigation has been progressing. I haven't seen Grams in days now."

"Grams has a case in Bali. She'll be back tomorrow. Other than that, I need your help."

"Anything," I said, glad the talk had turned from personal to business.

"I need a ShapeChanger. Ivy said Cassandra would be the best person for the job?" Cassandra Monteith was an agent with Sentinel, rival agency to Omega. She was also a good friend of mine, and as it happens, of Grams too.

I nodded and pulled out my phone. "I'm sure she'd be happy to help. I have it on good authority that she'd do anything for Grams. I'll text her your details and you two can take it from there." I tapped away the message and hit send. "What do you need her for?"

Mom grinned. "The Panther Alpha from Memphis is a concern. We think he's been trading in information."

"And you want Cassandra to take his form and see what she can find out?" I smiled. "Excellent plan. You'd make a good agent yet, Celeste Odel."

Mom laughed and pinched my cheek.

I got to my feet. "Right. Gotta go make my stop. And then I'm outta here."

I entered Logan's room thinking the decor needed a change. Something bright.

Maybe blue.

I'd heard somewhere blue was a good color for hospitals and care centers. Apparently, patients recover faster when they see the color blue more often.

I sighed and walked to the closest window. Gunmetal clouds hung low, promising an impending storm. I shut the heavy drapes and switched on the floor lamp beside the window.

The machines set a background rhythm of low beeps, and Logan seemed oblivious to my presence.

I'd gotten used to that.

My feet felt heavy as I walked to the bed and sat beside him. I was careful not to jostle him but he seemed to have no sense of my presence. He'd gotten paler.

Dad should take him out into the sun a little more. Surely being inside all these weeks would be bad for him. Vitamin D or G or something.

Logan was dreaming again, his lids moving as his eyes shifted frantically beneath them. One of the machines began to beep faster but he didn't seem to be in any physical danger. I took his hand, holding it gently as he began to thrash harder, hoping that my presence would ease his suffering.

With each passing day I wondered how much of a difference I really made to him.

I was studying his hand in mine, tracing my thumb across the back of his wrist when I gasped. A few inches away, just beyond his wrist joint, his skin had begun to glow. So strange, as if a fire burned somewhere deep inside him, his translucent skin revealing the golden embers.

I shivered but didn't let go, stared but didn't call out.

What would my father be able to do anyway? This was Logan's power trying to surface. His fire had been tamped down for so long. Surely that was a danger to both Logan, and those around him.

As I got to my feet, I froze, Logan's voice lifting the hair off the back of my neck. "You must find her. She is the key."

His voice rippled across my skin, guttural and harsh. But when I looked at his face, my heart twisted. His eyes remained closed. He wasn't speaking to me. He'd called out, deep within his dream, and I wondered who he thought needed saving.

Logan moaned and shook his head, saying *no* to someone only he could see. "You must find her. She is real. And you must hurry. The world is in danger. And she is the key."

I held back a desperate sob. Logan was the one *I* needed to save. Not some stranger only he knew. Then his lids opened. Flames danced within his dark eyes as he stared at me. "Kai. Promise me you will find her. She needs me. She needs you. Please. Promise me."

His words tumbled from his lips, as if in that moment of lucidity, he was desperate to get everything out. I grabbed his hand, ignoring the spreading golden glow of his skin. "I'll find her. If that's what you want, Logan. I'll find her."

Logan took a ragged breath. "I don't know what's happening

to me. My mind . . . it's breaking. She's here . . . with me." He tapped a finger at his temple. "But I know she isn't. She's in danger, Kai. You must find my sister."

Before I could respond, Logan's body lifted from the bed, his back arching as if live energy surged through him. He fell to the mattress, then rose again and I shivered with fear.

The machines blared around me and I was relieved that I didn't have to scream for my father. Because at that moment I knew I was incapable of making a sound. Logan's hand was now covered with the pulsing flame, his skin continuing to glow with his fire.

My father rushed into the room, his eyes scanning the machines with practiced calm. Footsteps trailed him and someone else entered. I got to my feet and stood aside, watching my father rush to a small cart beside the bed. He lifted a set of paddles and reached for Logan's shirt, baring his chest.

"Stop." I didn't realize it was me who'd screamed the plea out loud.

Not until my father asked, "Kai? What's the matter with you?" He sounded angry that I'd dared to stop him. But I had to.

"You don't understand, Dad. He *is* living energy." I pointed to Logan's arm. "His fire is inside him, and it wants out. That machine, it's electric energy. We don't know what supercharging him with electricity would do. We could kill him. Or kill all of us."

My father took a step away, placing the paddles onto the cart before rushing around the bed to check Logan's vitals.

"That was good thinking, Kai. Thank you. I never would have thought about it." Dad paused and stared at me. "I could have killed him."

I shook my head. "I think it's only happening because I'm here. He spoke to me . . . to tell me something."

"You think he's awake?"

"Not consciously . . . I think he senses me, some part of him knows I'm here and he's trying to tell me something." I got to my feet. "I think it's time I got Darcy over here."

Dad nodded and came to stand beside me. "Kai. I know you don't want to hear this-"

I cut him off with a raised hand. "I know what you're going say, Dad. He could very well die. I understand that. I even accept that. But whatever it is he wants me to do, I know I have to do it. No matter what it takes. He's tormented. And if I can help lessen that pain even a little then I'll do it. No matter what."

Dad put his arm around my shoulders. "You need to be strong, Kai. But we're all here for you." As I allowed my father to comfort me, my eyes drifted over his shoulder to the door.

And to Lily, sitting on the floor, her face white with shock as she stared at Logan. She didn't even register my attention, her eyes focused entirely on Logan, too terrified to come closer, too terrified to leave.

"How long has she been coming," I whispered into Dad's ear.

"Two weeks now," he said softly. He didn't need to say more.

Now I knew where Lily had been disappearing to all this time.

CHAPTER 11

After a night of tossing and turning, I rose more determined than ever. I had to make a short stop at the Elite HQ.

I smiled bitterly as I thought about Omega. Only a few weeks ago Sentinel and Omega had run our lives. Now, the Supreme High Council had put Omega aside, with the entire agency being investigated on charges ranging from human and paranormal rights violations, illegal experimentation, sedition, to treason. Heads had already begun to fall, but I'd paid little attention.

Inside HQ, I paced the beautiful carpet outside Supreme High Councilman David Horner's office, waiting only minutes before his assistant Barb exited, giving me a pleasant smile and a wave. Inside, I sat in one of his wingback armchairs without being asked, my fatigue over-ruling my manners.

At this point in my day, not to mention my life, I didn't particularly care. Horner didn't seem to care either as he got to his feet and joined me in the chair beside me.

"What did you discover?" His voice was, as always, calm to the point of irritation.

I liked that he'd dispensed with all formality. "I have it on good authority that the Chicago Tree isn't the only one to be affected." I blew out a soft breath.

"Which tree?" Curiosity.

"Boston."

"Any others?"

"That's your department." I wiggled my fingers. "Use your contacts. I suspect you'll find the problem widespread."

"Why do you say that?" Concerned now.

"Because of the toxin."

"I've received a copy of the tox panel." He gave a nod, urging me to go on.

"Because of the nature of the toxins. Firstly, they're not of this earth."

A neutral nod.

"Secondly, I know someone who suspects the toxins have a Faeland origin."

"Which would explain why we don't have a record of the plant." Calm observation.

I shifted in my seat, picking at a loose thread on the arm of the chair. "We still getting nowhere with the Fae High Council on info sharing?"

He shook his head. "Not when it comes to cataloging their flora. They seem to think our awareness of their plant life would endanger their very existence."

"Where there's smoke…"

He huffed and sat back. "You have a point. I'll pursue it with the Elders. In the meantime, what's your next move?"

I hesitated.

He tipped his head to study me, then said, "Speak." Admonition and encouragement in one word. How did he do that?

Clearing my throat, I said, "I've gotten as far as I can go with the Chicago Ash. Until I hear back from my contact there isn't much I can do except twiddle my thumbs." I rubbed the armrest of the sofa. "I need some personal time. Logan needs . . . I . . . there is something I need to do."

He got to his feet. "If it's concerning Westin then I consider that Elite business."

I frowned. "He was never officially made an agent."

"Be that as it may, I'm confident that he would have accepted our offer, and as such I consider him an agent. Any time spent on helping him will be treated as official Elite business. If that helps you at all."

"It does, thank you." I got to my feet too.

"You may report to me whatever you deem necessary. I'm well aware that this is personal, but there may be other factors that you'd prefer to use your discretion with in terms of making it public knowledge."

My turn to watch him carefully. What was he trying to tell me?

I nodded, then cleared my throat. "I'll let you know the moment I hear anything about the tree. Thank you."

He gave a regal nod. "And do keep us updated where Westin is concerned. I trust he is well?"

"As well as can be expected."

I backed away and exited before he asked me any further questions. Horner and Carter, his co-director at the Elite who concentrated more on Forensics, had always given me an odd feeling. My gut said they weren't entirely who they claimed to be. They didn't feel like simple Mages. And they weren't of any other major paranormal species that I recognized.

Immortals? I'd played around with the idea that they were Ancients, like Darian, who'd saved me a few months back.

I'd often gotten the feeling that both men could be just like Darian. But unless they confessed, I had little chance of finding out the truth.

For now, my mind was focused on Logan.

CHAPTER 12

*B*ack in Logan's room I sat on the loveseat by the window, my cup of tea sitting on the sill, long cold as I stared at nothing. I knew I had to call Darcy, but a part of me was hesitant. As if I knew that taking that step would change things forever.

At last I grabbed my phone and made the call. Darcy answered on the second ring and sounded keen on helping, especially if it concerned Logan.

Before I could offer to arrange transport, Darcy assured me that she'd see me in less than an hour. Apparently she was closer than I thought.

I used the time to shower, change and throw a bunch of clothes into the wash. With Logan at my father's house I'd taken to keeping enough clothes in my old closet to be safe. I was glad for the work though.

Chores were calming.

DARCY KNOCKED on the open door. I looked up and knew immediately why she was in Chicago. I'd know the scent of my brother anywhere, and finding the beautiful blonde enveloped in Iain's musk made me want to throw a bunch of inquisitive questions at her.

But I didn't.

I quashed the urge and waved her inside, trying to subdue the grin on my face.

Darcy walked to me, her gaze drifting over Logan's sleeping form, and in her eyes, I recognized sadness and regret. She sat on the loveseat beside me.

"I'm assuming this is to do with Logan's condition?" She glanced at him again, her expression now revealing something I was sure I was misinterpreting.

Guilt.

I had no time to pursue that line of thought. "Yeah. But it's worse than what you can see."

"How do you mean?" Her gaze was still locked on Logan's unmoving form.

"He's got this weird fire under his skin," I said, absently rubbing my forearm and wrist.

The cushion moved as she shifted next to me. "That makes sense considering he's a fire mage."

"But do fire mages have fire living inside their bodies?"

"I'm not sure." I could have sworn I felt her stiffen. Then she let out a sharp breath. "It could be a side effect. Maybe his power is trapped inside him. He's been unconscious for a while. So that would make sense."

My forehead knitted. "I hope it's just that. And I hope it doesn't mean he's going to spontaneously combust or something." I went for the joke, knowing it was something Logan would have found amusing, but for many reasons it fell flat.

Even Darcy didn't reward my effort with a smile.

Instead, she got to her feet and walked to Logan's side. She spent a few moments looking at his face. She seemed about to say something, then hesitated. Instead, she took a few calming breaths, her shoulders rising then falling.

"You okay?" I asked, going to stand beside her. Whatever troubled her was concerning and though we weren't technically friends, I wanted to help.

But she shook her head. "I'm fine. I'm going to need a chair so I don't fall flat on my face, or Logan, while I work." She made a face. "There is a tendency for the MindMelder to faint at inopportune moments."

I smiled and fetched a chair from the hallway. A long time ago, probably a century now, someone had placed a matched pair of spindly-legged chairs on either side of a table topped with a ragged slice of a redwood, felled to make way for the house. The smoothed and varnished surface, bore a giant-sized arrangement of dried flowers, equally ancient.

The chairs with their dainty, soft upholstery with delicate gold-printed cream fabric were astoundingly mismatched, rugged wood set against a chair that looked like a feather would be too much weight for it.

Even Darcy raised an inquiring eyebrow at the chair as I hauled it to her side. "Don't ask."

"Antique?"

I nodded. "In all my years it never once crossed my mind to use it as an actual chair."

"You sure it's not going to fall apart?" she asked, concerned as she studied the chair, her butt hovering a few inches above it.

"I think it's sturdy. You'll know for sure when you sit." I smothered a giggle, watching Darcy perch gingerly onto the chair as she held her breath and waited for it to shatter beneath her weight.

It didn't.

We both sighed, relieved.

Darcy sobered as she studied Logan's face again. I did too. His dark hair, though lacking its usual life, was still thick and tempted me to brush my fingers through it. His lips, once full and firm were much softer now, and paler. How long had it been since I'd last kissed him? This awful sleep kept us excruciatingly apart.

Darcy shifted as she leaned forward and placed her fingertips on either side of Logan's temples. A light dusting of stubble covered his cheeks and I wondered who'd shaved him.

I'd done it that first week or two, but having been away, I'd expected a thicker mat, not this clean-shaven patient. I smiled. Mom or Grams, maybe. I just couldn't imagine Iain or Dad performing that task. My eyes drifted to the open door and a face flashed from my memory.

Lily.

Now it made sense as to who'd been taking care of him while I'd been absent, and where Lily had been in those times when she'd claimed errands or homework.

But now, I pushed her from my mind and concentrated on Darcy as she closed her eyes and fell into a trance not too different from Mel's tracking mode.

Her eyelids fluttered as her fingers tightened against Logan's head and I forced myself to remain as still as possible. With everything going on I was wired and sitting still was incredibly difficult.

Minutes passed and Darcy hadn't moved so much as a muscle. Perspiration beaded her forehead and the skin of her neck, making me aware for the first time how taxing this must be for her, on her body and her mind.

Then she stiffened, her muscles tightening as her head fell back. The veins at her temples flared, rising high and tight; her heart probably speeding like a freight train. A spurt of panic flared within me. Were we endangering Darcy too? Would Logan appreciate lives being sacrificed in order to save his?

Darcy's work felt and looked pretty intense.

Perspiration dripped down the back of her neck and soaked

into the neck of her blouse. I got to my feet as quietly as possible and tiptoed to a stack of clean towels on a cart behind the door. Returning with two, I placed one loosely around her neck and used the other to dab her forehead.

Though I worried I may have disturbed her, when Darcy moved next, two hours had passed and the muscles in both my arms and legs ached. Darcy must have felt worse considering the constant strain she'd shown.

She gave a shuddering sigh, her torso jerking sharply back against the chair. So sharp the fragile seat gave a frightening squeak and I tensed, expecting to have to pick Darcy up from the floor.

Thankfully, she opened her eyes and groaned, leaning forward onto the mattress with the look of a drunk about to hurl a week's worth of dinners. Thankfully, she didn't.

Instead she bent and rested her forehead on Logan's arm. She inhaled slowly and I waited, holding my own breath.

When she finally shifted her head to look at me, I asked, "Are you okay? Do you need anything?"

She shook her head and straightened, wiping a hand over her forehead. She frowned and gave her fingers a strange, confused look. Then her hand went to her neck where it brushed against the coarse weave of the towel.

When she looked at me, a small smile erupted at the corners of her mouth. "Thank you. I'm usually soaked through when I return."

I smirked. "I could hardly allow you to melt all over our good wood floors." She grinned, her eyes sparkling. "Can I get you something? Water? Coffee?"

Darcy nodded. "Water, please. Coffee isn't a good idea."

I was moving toward the door when Darcy touched my arm. She hesitated, then looked back at Logan, her expression filled with guilt.

"Are you okay? Is something wrong with Logan?"

She shook her head then gave a dry, almost heartless laugh. "Something *is* wrong with him."

Then she shifted in the chair to face me. I heard the fabric rustle, watched a stray bead of perspiration drip from the edge of her collarbone and trickle into the hollow at the front of her neck.

Something told me that what she was about to tell me wasn't good.

CHAPTER 13

Odd how things seemed to slow down just when your gut tells you that bad news was about to hit you like a ton of bricks.

"Kai, I haven't been totally honest with you." Then she laughed again, harshly, angrily. "Come to think of it, I haven't been honest with you at all. I owe you the truth, especially since . . ."

"Since what?" I asked, anger burgeoning like a storm cloud. I disliked dishonesty.

Then I tamped down my outrage. Who the heck was I to talk about dishonesty when I'd never told Logan about Justin, his offer or his kiss? That was dishonesty right there.

"I'm not so sure that now is the time for either self-blame or pointing fingers." I sighed, feeling the burden of something bigger weigh down on me. "What did you want to tell me?"

"It was me." Darcy got up and walked to the window, staring out into the black night. The moon was low and curved, a half smile that, like me, didn't appreciate the gravity of Darcy's words.

"What do you mean?" I filled dead air with a question. Darcy seemed to need some impetus.

With her eyes on the moon she said, "In my time inside people's minds, I've seen a million different memories of the moon. Memories are tainted with a person's own state of mind, with the feelings one experiences at the time of the memory."

"So if someone unknowingly says something harsh to you, the memory of that moment is colored with the hurt of it, while the speaker's memory is clear of any negativity." I nodded.

"That's it exactly." She didn't remove her eyes from the moon. "It's so massive, so influential. I've seen benevolent moons, cold unfeeling moons, magical, powerful and powerless moons. There is no end to our interpretation of that ethereal sphere. It's like multiple interpretations of the mind. I'm not sure what human scientists would take away if I had to explain to them how exactly the mind works."

I let her talk.

"The mind is built up of layers and layers of thoughts and experiences and learnings. Everything is coiled together, and it all looks like one big jumble, but it's compartmentalized, organized so well that if you know what you are doing you can go within a person's mind and take from them their most precious memories and they'd never even know they'd had them in the first place."

Darcy was rambling and though I'd heard something similar a while ago she seemed to need to get this off her chest so I let her speak.

"The beauty of our memories is that they each have a tenuous link. Like Logan's memories. The ones that are missing all have a common factor that links them all together. Chocolate cake, an empty swing, and table in a diner where a milkshake stands waiting for its owner.

"All linked together by a thread that a mind-melder can access and use to navigate that mind." She took a breath, a shaky shuddering sound that made it seem like Darcy was going to keel over. "My job with Omega, and Sentinel I might add, was to help them retrieve important pieces of information from the minds of criminals and victims alike. The criminal's mind confirms what they were doing, or going to do or have already done, while victims give confirmation one way or the other. Omega hired me to either remove or mask memories. Most of the time the reasons made sense to me. Make a man forget the face of the person who gave evidence against him; for the safety of the witness. Make a killer-for-hire forget the face of the president in case someone ever pays him to take POTUS out. Make a bomber forget how to create anything bomb-like.

"But then the jobs became stranger. Make this High Council member forget that he was ever wronged by a particular man. Make this mage forget he has a family so he'll stay with Omega forever.

"Make this boy think that he was the one to decimate an entire diner so that he'd think himself saved. Make him forget that he'd been innocent. Make him forget that he'd had a sister. A sister more powerful than him. Make him forget all about her because her safety was at risk. Because she's so powerful that *she* could be used as a pawn if people knew she existed."

My lungs constricted, air escaped my mouth in a soundless gust. I tried to inhale but nothing happened. I stared at Darcy, fury and grief battling for supremacy. And all through it I couldn't say a single word.

She turned to face me. "I couldn't refuse. I knew what Omega was capable of. My grandparents . . . their lives were at risk, my uncle . . . Omega would have taken him out without a single moment's hesitation. It doesn't make what I did right. But I tried to help the best way I knew how."

She stared at me, her eyes wide and glassy. "I broke the rules and helped him. Jess was in the room with me, and she never said a thing. She was meant to be there to watch and ensure I did as was instructed, but she let me do whatever I wanted. To this day I have no idea why."

Her gaze skittered away from my face, guilty and forlorn. My rage simmered, for Logan's pain at her hand. But her own pain shone through and I waited, afraid that if I should open my mouth, if I should ask the wrong questions, that I would break ties that were beginning to bind her to our family, to our lives.

Her mention of Jess had helped temper me too.

I let out a soft breath. "Jess was here to help Logan. She told me on more than one occasion that her sole task on this plane was to ensure his safety."

Darcy's breath shuddered out of her body. "One thing to be thankful for, then." She shook her head, as if the action would erase her own memories. But I couldn't find it in my heart to feel entirely sorry for her. Not until she told me the whole story.

"What did you do?" I asked, doing nothing to soften the harshness in my voice.

"I did the only thing I could do and still escape detection." Darcy left the window and went back to Logan's side. She stared down at him, her expression so sad. "I was instructed to remove all memories of his sister. Going back to his earliest memories."

I came to stand beside her, a part of me feeling like she needed comfort. The hollow tone of her voice was my undoing. So yeah, maybe I was feeling sorry for her now. "I'm still not sure I totally understand the whole process but keep going. Maybe it's best if you get it all out."

Darcy looked at me, doubt filling her eyes along with her tears. "Don't you hate me for what I did?"

I hesitated and then decided honesty was the best option. "I don't know yet how I feel, Darcy. I still don't really know what it is that you did. Why don't you explain it and we'll go from there, okay?"

Although she was a few years older than me, it felt like I was dealing with a child. She seemed so lost. And it made me angry that I could not be angry with her.

CHAPTER 14

I waited while Darcy collected her thoughts.

"I was supposed to do an intensive wipe . . . remove all traces of his sister including every memory that he had which had a connection to her. It's more complicated than the people who give the orders really understand. All they knew was they had a list of things I needed to do and that I had to do it.

"But when I delved into his mind, I discovered what a delightful child he was, so kind and loving. And what he had to go through with his awful beast of a father. Both Logan and his sister were helpless until they began to grow into their powers. From his memories I saw how they cowered under his hand . . . how they'd begun to protect their mother.

"They did it in subtle ways. Small things. Making his plate so hot he burned his fingers. Bath water, iced drinks, even his chair. His father at first suspected evil possession but after calling in people to exorcise the house he inadvertently alerted the paranormal agencies, there was a minor battle between the two agencies. Sentinel should have taken the children into their fold but Omega offered the father money and he agreed.

"But it backfired on him. Pardon the pun. The day he went to take the girl, because Omega decided they wanted her first, she lost control of her power. From Logan's memory, she panicked. She'd always been terrified of her father but Logan had feared her power more. He'd stayed at her side trying to protect her when their father stormed the diner and demanded to take her.

"And she panicked . . . just reacted. Only Logan and his sister survived the inferno. And when Omega arrived, because obviously they were waiting outside, they found both children in shock. They took the opportunity and left with both kids . . . only they wiped Logan's memories, so he'd stay with Omega for two reasons."

"They wanted his power and they didn't want him to go looking for her," I said softly. Logan lay still on the bed, oblivious to Darcy as she recounted his past, a past he had no recollection of.

Darcy nodded. "Only I didn't exactly do what I was asked, and Jess for whatever reason covered for me."

"You left behind the connected memories."

Darcy nodded and smiled pensively. "He was so young, not that much younger than me. I was sixteen to his twelve. I felt like I had to protect him . . . I just didn't have the heart to do such a cruel thing to him.

"His sister though . . . Well she was another story altogether."

"How do you mean?" I stiffened. Had Darcy completely erased his sister's memory?

"Omega separated them immediately. They went to two completely different facilities. Logan was sent to Washington. I never knew where they took the girl."

"So Logan is beginning to remember because you left the connected memories?"

Darcy nodded then tilted her head. "I wasn't allowed to leave whole memories so I planted some. When Logan recalled eating a peach with his sister he'd remember the taste of peanut butter. Small things like that which would make him feel like there was something wrong in his mind. I'd deliberately used a weaker, less permanent technique so that if examined by another mind-melder it would appear that I'd done the job. In reality, it was temporary. But only if and when Logan rediscovered his memories on his own."

"Clever. And, if Omega discovered that his memory had returned, they'd be unable to blame you because they'd certified the job you did in the first place."

"Yes, the only problem for Omega was that very few people know the technique. It's easy to wipe a memory and it's fairly simple to do a temporary wipe. But to find that middle ground that does the least damage and remains undetectable for as long as possible . . . well that isn't easy at all. Even now it's still not a commonly used technique."

"Because it's difficult?"

"That and because it's very taxing on the technician. My nose bled for days and I had a migraine for two weeks. The technician's mind is very much involved in the wipe, no matter what the proponents would have you believe."

I nodded, satisfied now that Darcy had done what she could, within the limitations of her job and the danger to her family.

"What made you think that Omega would target your family if you didn't toe the line?"

"Because it's what they do. For decades if not centuries, it's one of the reasons that I've maintained a freelance contract. Because it gives me more freedom. But back then I didn't know any better. I didn't know how much a freelance contract would protect me. Working for Sentinel meant I was almost untouchable. Omega knew it and I learned slowly."

"And you didn't trust them?"

"Nope."

"Why fix it now?" Did it have anything to do with Iain?

"Because when I linked with him a few weeks ago I saw something that shocked me."

"Which was?"

"Logan is still connected to his sister. As twins-"

"Twins?" I asked, shocked. I shouldn't have been surprised though, considering the strong connection between them.

Darcy replied, "They shared a bond. A mental connection that helped them protect each other. It's very powerful and that link is now fully awakened."

"And you think that his sister is attempting to access that connection."

She nodded. "It's possible, but we can't make assumptions and go chasing after it blindly."

"Because it could be a trap." She nodded. "We need to be careful about tracing the connection back to her. So, how do we access those memories? He isn't exactly able to share."

Darcy sighed. "His mind is in the Graylands."

"You said I couldn't go there," I said accusingly.

"And I was dead serious. I'm sure there is another way for you to talk to his consciousness."

I nodded, annoyed yet relieved because she was right. "Yes, there is."

"You know someone who can help?"

"Yes. And she'll help me with whatever I ask."

"I'm so glad." She sighed. "I am so very sorry. I wish he was awake so that I could apologize." She looked at Logan again.

"Why didn't you just leave him a mental message while you were inside his mind?"

She grinned. "I did."

"So what did you do inside there today?"

"I loosened things up a bit. Weakened the barriers keeping him from accessing his memories fully."

I hesitated. "Will talking to him in the Graylands affect him in any way?"

"No," she said firmly. "He'll be perfectly fine. It's you that I'm more concerned about."

"Don't worry. I won't physically go there. As much as I'd like to be rebellious and go racing off to find my portal key, I know how I felt the last time I made the trip, and how long it took me to get back on my feet. I never want to feel that helpless again, thank you very much."

"I'm glad. At least I don't have to worry about you too." She gave me a tentative smile.

But, as much as I wasn't furious enough with her to rip open her jugular and let her bleed to death, I was still angry that she lied. "Why didn't you tell us when we first brought you to Tukats?"

"Because Logan was Omega." She paused. "Have you ever heard of mental tracking?"

"Like a SoulTracker?" I asked, thinking of Mel

"No. Like a GPS tracker, but with sight and sound capability."

"Damn. That doesn't sound good."

"Damn right it doesn't. I had no idea if he was hooked up. For all I knew, one word from me would have gotten my family killed. But now, with Omega disbanded I'm in the clear."

"Then thank you for helping him. I can't pretend that I'm all fine with your involvement, and I don't know what Logan will say if he sits up and finds out the truth. But for what it's worth, I think you did what you could with his best interests at heart. And right now, our top priority is finding his sister."

Darcy smiled somberly. "Then, let's do this."

CHAPTER 15

After Darcy left, I remained at Logan's side, trying to process her revelation.

I was conflicted. First by Darcy's obvious regret at what she'd had to do. Second, by my anger at what she'd done, and last, by my understanding of why she'd done it.

Logan looked peaceful, but I remembered his dreams. Those nights when he sat up soaked with sweat, terrified for this girl who haunted his dreams. And now I knew who the girl was.

And Logan was still caught within the throes of a nightmare from which he had no idea how to free himself.

My heart tightened and tears burned beneath my lids. I wanted so badly for him to wake up so that I could tell him that it would all be okay, that I was going to find her no matter what.

But he just lay there, still and silent as the dead.

I sighed and traced his cheek with my fingertips. Placing a kiss upon his lips I forced my muscles to comply and move me to my feet.

The hollow sound my heels made on the wood floor matched the echo in my heart. Downstairs, the living room was empty save for the fire, and I went to sit beside it. As I stared at the flames someone moved beside me but when I glanced around all that had appeared was a plate and a glass on the low table beside the sofa.

Food.

A chicken and mushroom pie and a glass of ginger beer. Both brought back remnants of my childhood and I could have sworn the scent of Mom's perfume lingered in the air beside me. I smiled and satiated a hunger I hadn't known I possessed. Minutes later, replete, I dialed Nerina, half expecting her not to answer.

But she did. And she promised to come within a few minutes. I expected she needed to make one last stop with Lady Kira, the High Priestess of the DeathTalkers. Nerina couldn't do much without her Lady's okay, but something told me this visit would be relegated to personal time.

Since our last encounter, finding and apprehending the killer of Lady Kira's estranged daughter, Nerina's attitude had shifted. Away from her high priestess, toward her own personal needs. I meant to ask her how she was handling such a shift, a drastic one – especially for a DeathTalker priestess.

Nerina appeared minutes later, as the warmth of the fire, my fatigue and my full stomach conspired to pull me into slumber. Nerina saved me. There wasn't time for such frivolous things as sleep. Especially not with Logan sleeping enough for the lot of us.

Nerina pushed back the hood of her cloak, the gray fabric dropping softly to her shoulders. Her usually pale gray hair seemed to have taken on some color, a lovely hint of chestnut which I found comforting. It matched the smattering of honey in her usually gray eyes.

"Hi," she said, smiling brightly. "What do you need me for?"

"You seem bubbly," I responded, amused at her enthusiasm despite the gravity of the occasion.

"Whatever you need me to do will surely be a million times

more exciting than communing with the dead and passing messages across the Veil."

I gave her a twisted smile and she returned it with a rueful one.

"I suppose you need me to commune with the dead and pass messages through the Veil."

"Kind of to the former, and yes to the latter."

"Kind of?" She frowned.

"Not communing with the dead." I sighed. "But I guess his condition puts him closer to dead than not." My shoulders bowed and I leaned forward and rested my elbows on my knees.

Nerina pulled a small footstool closer and sat in front of me. "You want me to talk to Logan?"

I nodded. "It's time we did something about his situation. Darcy says he's in the Graylands and that he'll be able to communicate with us but I'm not allowed to go there. Not physically, anyway."

"Damn straight you're not. I know for a fact that those trips to the Graylands have been draining your life force, and I'm not about to allow you to go there again. Not for a long while."

I wanted to bristle. Who was she to order me around? And yet a part of me glowed with the knowledge that she was no longer a colleague. She was a friend. And that also made her dangerous.

I'd learned that friends made a person vulnerable. And even worse, my friends were often in danger, just because of who I was. Clancy – my human mentor and friend had been butchered by a crazed Walker in an attempt to teach me a lesson.

Yes, friends made a person vulnerable.

Nerina wasn't powerful like Tara, nor was she deadly like Lily and Anjelo. But even deadly made little difference, especially when Anjelo ended up very dead despite his capacity to defend himself.

I pulled myself free from the chaos of my regrets. Focusing on Nerina, I said, "Don't worry. I'm not going to cross the Veil anytime soon. Right now, we need to contact Logan. There are things he should know. Things he needs to tell me."

"Okay, then." Nerina stood and dusted her hands. "Let's get this show on the road."

Upstairs, Nerina entered Logan's room and made straight for his bedside. She bent over Logan and my stomach tightened as she lay her hands upon his chest and whispered an incantation, something musical and ominous.

She lowered her mouth until it hovered inches above Logan's. Taking a deep breath, she expelled that air into his mouth, emptying her lungs until her body shuddered.

Leaning back only slightly, she inhaled again and waited.

A few minutes passed before I stiffened. A wispy stream of gray smoke drifted out of Logan's mouth, rising, undulating on the air, like a snake seeking a way into the light. It caressed Nerina's face, then slipped between her lips. She proceeded to inhale the threads of gray through both mouth and nose.

I wondered what that meant, that whether the subject was dead or alive, the method of binding a DeathTalker to them was the very same. I shoved the thought away and concentrated on Nerina.

She lifted her head and stared sightlessly at the ceiling, then exhaled.

The chair I'd given Darcy was still beside the bed and Nerina sank into it. Clearly she didn't have any doubts about it holding her weight, even though she was far more well-endowed than Darcy.

She sat still for a moment then sighed, tilting her head to the side as if encouraging me to speak.

My throat tightened and I had to swallow hard before the first word left my mouth. "Logan?"

My eyes were on his face and I gasped softly as his expression confirmed that he'd heard my voice.

"Logan can you hear me?" I asked, raising my voice from the tentative whisper.

"Kai? How are you in my head?"

Nerina's mouth moved and yet it was Logan's words that left her lips. And as I watched his face, I saw his expression match the tone. Surprised, and glad.

The same way that I felt.

Surprised. And glad.

CHAPTER 16

$\mathcal{I}$t felt strange hearing his words come from Nerina's mouth, and I felt a little uncomfortable, as if my friend was a voyeur, watching something deeply personal between Logan and me.

Not like you have a choice, Odel.

"I've been so worried about you." I leaned closer to him, smiling and blinking back tears.

"I know. But I've been fine. I think." Though his words came from Nerina, a tiny smile lifted the corner of his mouth and just the sight of it lifted my spirits. I'd known he was in there somewhere.

"How does it work? Are you aware of us?"

"Sometimes . . . when the drugs allow me to be." He sighed, his chest rising and falling, air passing through Nerina's lips.

"Do you feel much pain?"

"Not in the normal sense." I was curious but I let him speak. "I feel like my fire is warring inside me. As if it wants out but it also knows there is no place to go."

"I'm worried about you." I hesitated wondering how wise it

was to be telling him this when it could likely make his condition worse.

"What is it Kai?"

"I saw something strange on your body."

"You've been looking at my body?" He gave a mischievous grin.

I shook my head and laughed, giving Nerina a wary glance. "Behave yourself." I steeled my features. Business only. "You glowed, like a fire burned inside of you."

"That would be my power looking for a way out. It's trapped." He hardly seemed troubled.

"How can we help you relieve the strain of it?"

He shook his head, the skin on his forehead creasing. "You can't. The only way is to regain consciousness."

"Dad's doing everything possible, but so far he's failed to find a way past this . . . coma."

"I understand. And Kai. You'll need to come to terms with it if he can't bring me back." He spoke firmly, calmly.

I stiffened and he shook his head again as if he could see me through his closed lids.

"No. I know you're going to be stubborn but you can't blame your father if he can't help me, and neither can you sit around filled with regret. There's more to this than just me."

I sucked in a breath, hoping he wouldn't sense how terrified I was of losing him. "More to this?" I urged, squeezing his fingers between mine. I could feel the pulse of his heartbeat at the base of his palm, the steady throb reassuring, comforting.

"The girl," was all he said.

"Are you still dreaming of her?" I asked, tensing.

"Yes, and I think it's more than we suspected."

"More?" I coaxed him.

"She's in my mind almost all the time."

"Is she telling you anything?" I leaned closer even though Nerina spoke his words from beside me.

"It's not like she's communicating with me."

"More like you're eavesdropping on her thoughts?" I asked.

"Her thoughts and her memories." He sounded so sad.

"And what do they tell you?"

He moved his head sharply, jerking it from left to right as if even entertaining the thought was too much. "I know what it's telling me but I can't quite understand it."

"What is it?"

"It's as if she knew me from when we were little. Knew me so well that we would have had to grow up together or at least be the closest of friends."

"So who do you think she is?" He'd been so lucid when he'd woken up and asked me to find his sister, and now my breath stuttered, fearing he'd been hallucinating.

"My heart is telling me she is my sister, but my brain thinks that's ridiculous and I must be imagining it all."

"You're not."

Logan paused and turned his head, and although his eyes were closed it felt like he was looking right at me. "I'm not?"

I shook my head before realizing that he couldn't see me. "No. It's not a hallucination. She's real and she *is* your sister."

"How do you know this?" he asked, his voice jerky. "What did you find out?"

I cleared my throat. "She was taken from you when the diner blew up."

"You mean when I blew up the diner." Even now, his voice sounded hollow with the pain of the memory.

"Actually, it wasn't you."

"What do you mean?"

"You weren't the one to lose control that day. You *did* have a sister, Logan." I paused and watched the fluttering his lids.

His face held nothing back. Confusion, sorrow, pain. It was all there, laid bare to be witnessed by Nerina and me. I looked at her, finding she was still deep within the trance that connected her to Logan.

My throat was dry as I swallowed before saying, "You are siblings. But she was the one who lost control of the power. She was frightened. But when Omega picked you up-"

"It was her that they wanted and not me?" His voice was bitter. He knew how Omega worked.

I nodded, then supported it with a yes. "They took her away and hid her from you for all this time."

"What did they want with me if they got her?"

"You're powerful in your own right."

"And Omega likes to keep the family of those they want close," he said, his tone dry, hard. Angry. "Like Saleem."

"Like Saleem."

CHAPTER 17

The silence lay heavy, but it only served to make me more impatient.

"How did you find this out?" I knew what he was doing; getting practical, putting aside his feelings to deal with the problem at hand.

"I spoke to the person who took your memories." Logan's face hardened. "I'm surprised you didn't know."

"I'm not always conscious. But I do vaguely remember something strange. Like memories that suddenly became clear after all these years. And feelings that suddenly made sense."

"Yes. She did a mind-meld and tried to ease a few memories out. She said she reset some of what she'd done and wanted to ensure your mind finds the missing memories."

The silence was strong as Logan absorbed my revelation, his face darkening with what I could only assume was anger.

I touched his upper arm. "For what it's worth she really feels bad. But at the time she had very little choice."

He didn't respond.

"She said she put in a few loopholes that would allow you to regain the memories on your own. But it had to look like she did as she was instructed."

"Why are you defending her?" he asked sharply.

"Look, you have every right to be furious with her. But at the time she had little choice. You were both at the mercy of the mechanics of Omega. They wanted your sister so they took her. They wanted you working for them rather than endangering their hold on your sister, so they took your memories."

I was trying to ensure he remembered that Omega was the bad guy in this picture but I couldn't be sure that Logan cared. His cheekbones seemed to stand out sharply as he tightened his jaw.

"Who is she?"

I sighed.

"Darcy?" Clearly he could read me very well.

"Yes." I squeezed his arm. "I'm sorry. I think she'll come by to talk to you when you're awake. Right now, I want you to know that she reversed what she could now that Omega can't stop her."

"How could Omega stop her?"

His expression was odd as he asked the question. As if he knew that answer couldn't possibly be a straight and easy one.

"They threatened her family. She was so young when they recruited, only sixteen when she treated you, and though she tried to remain neutral, she couldn't ignore the threat to her family. So she did what she could, and still ensured your memories would return. Had Storm not done this to you, you'd have regained the memories quite soon."

Logan was deathly still and I glanced at Nerina. I was surprised at how easily I'd forgotten that she was there. That despite the different voice, I still felt like I was talking to Logan.

Nerina remained impassive so I returned my attention to Logan whose chest rose as he took an eerily silent breath.

"What did she do to me? I have more memories . . . images in my head now . . . and they don't all make sense."

"Darcy said she removed more of the blocks and she thinks you should be able to communicate with your sister. With you being twins-"

"How does she know we were twins?"

"From what she heard at her debriefing sessions, and what she saw from your memories. You two were inseparable. You communicated on a more ethereal level than most people. She said that you managed to rein her in just by touching her mind with yours."

"If I kept her out of danger then what would have happened to her without me?" Logan was finally understanding the point of this conversation.

As mercenary as it sounded, we weren't here to help him.

"That's what we're all afraid of. Darcy suspects they may have wiped her mind too, but we need to know what you're seeing through this link with her. Your connection would have gotten stronger now, and you should be able to access her mind. It may not make much sense to you but you need to learn to figure it out." I squeezed his hand again. "Logan, we have to find her. Omega had her hidden somewhere but they've been shut down. I'm guessing their off-the-books agents are still guarding her."

Nerina's voice rose, anger, determination, sorrow. "I'll try, but I can't promise anything. I haven't done this before."

"But you have," I said softly. When he frowned I continued, "All these months that's what you've been doing. Finding your way through to her. Only, it may hurt more now than it ever did."

"I'm not afraid of the pain," he snapped.

"Pain of the mind is a whole different level than the pain of the body." I spoke calmly, ignoring his curt tone.

He didn't answer but he didn't oppose what I'd said. I took that as a good sign.

"Look. Nobody here can even imagine what you're going through. All I can ask is for you to put your feelings aside and think of her safety. We have to find her. And soon. Horner said already that Omega will not go quietly. There are pockets of them still working away beneath the radar. We can't let them continue keeping her."

Logan nodded. "You don't have to convince me, Kai." He smiled gently and I felt it like an embrace. "I'm just not sure if I can reach her. What I've seen so far was purely by chance."

"Maybe it will be different when you actively look for her. This time you have a reason to find her and you know what you're looking for." I rubbed his arm. "You can only do the best you can. If you want, I can stay right here with you."

He nodded and I was grateful. I'd been about to argue with him, expecting him to demand some sort of privacy while looking for her, but maybe he'd forgotten that it was Nerina who linked us together.

I didn't plan on reminding him.

I sat on the bed beside him, not letting go of his hand, watching as his lids fluttered, as he concentrated deep inside himself. Nerina too sat very still beside me and I hoped she was okay.

"Sienna," he whispered. "Her name is Sienna."

It was a beautiful name and I wondered if I should respond but I was a little afraid of disturbing him.

He smiled sadly. "She's grown so much." And, as if in response to the question I wanted to ask, he said, "She seems unhurt. And she doesn't seem to sense me. I think this is what's been confusing me these past few weeks. She's thinking about the past so that's what must have brought the memories up for me. Every time she accesses the past she stirs something inside me."

I listened in awe, filled with a deep sense of sadness for what Logan and Sienna had lost, what Omega had taken from them.

"She's walking along a beach. Barefoot." Logan paused as if looking around. "White sand, gulls, blue sky. The sun is hot. There's a lighthouse on a rocky point in the distance. There is something sparkling in the sand. Like glass or some kind of crystal."

Logan frowned, the vision strange enough to confuse him.

"Nothing on the horizon to tell me where she is." His voice softened. "She's sad. Lost."

I cleared my throat softly so as to not shock him with my voice disturbing his thoughts. "Can she sense you?"

He started to shake his head. Just one jerk and then he stopped. "She's standing, looking around . . . as if she heard someone call her."

"Try to talk to her. Mention your name, maybe your Mom?"

Logan nodded, and then fell silent for a while. After a long while he took a deep breath. "She's afraid. I don't think she knows it's me."

He sounded so hurt that tears burned my eyes.

"Omega would have tampered with her memory too."

He nodded. "I'll need to take it slow. For now, you can start searching for beaches with lighthouses on rocky points."

I smiled. "I'll get on it."

I shifted away but he tightened his grip. "Kai." I paused. "Thank you for doing this for me."

I laughed softly. "You're so silly. You know by now that I'd do anything for you."

His smiled thinned. "And Lake?"

A chill skittered down my spine. "You heard."

"Some."

"It's not what you think."

"My ears work fine. When they are working."

"What I meant was Justin is the past. You are my present."

"And who will be your future?" he asked softly.

I opened my mouth to say that of course it was him. He was the light of my life, the person I wanted to spend my years with, but his face lost the liveliness that he'd had while talking to me and I sensed movement from Nerina.

When I glanced back at her she was lifting her face to the ceiling, readying herself to expel his spirit. I stepped away, allowing her to complete the process, watching in fascination as the gray smoke looped and curled, sinuous. Ominous.

When every last dreg of smoke had returned to its owner, Nerina shuddered, sucking in a long ragged breath.

Her shoulders drooped forward, and I touched her arm. "You okay?"

"Fine. Need a minute." She got the words out one by one and I let her have her space. Getting to my feet, I used my phone to search the Net.

Beaches with lighthouses on rocky points. To my disappointment there were dozens around the country, but I refused to allow myself to be defeated.

We had a certain hacker in our midst.

$\mathcal{N}$erina got to her feet and I shoved my phone back into my pocket before righting Logan's sheets.

"You okay?" I asked, giving her a quick glance.

She nodded. "It was a longer session than I'd anticipated. But given that he wasn't dead, a much less taxing experience on the body."

I patted the mattress and smiled, although there was no cheer in the expression. More manic than cheery. "Any thoughts on what you heard?"

A blush of pink polished her cheeks. "Unfortunately, eavesdropping is part of the process. I didn't wish to intrude."

I waved away the apology. "Don't worry about it. I knew you'd be privy to private information. And I was fine with that. If not, I would have looked for someone else." I smiled but it didn't reach my eyes.

"Now what?" she asked as we exited the room.

"Now we research the location, then we go and find Sienna Westin."

We descended the stairs and came face to face with my parents.

"Hey you guys." I smiled. "We've made progress with Logan."

Both looked curious. So I pointed at Nerina.

"Nerina helped me talk to him. He's tried to communicate with her. We have to locate her before Omega realizes we're onto them."

Dad made a face. "Looks like every time I leave that boy's side something happens."

"Then next time don't leave him alone," admonished Mom with a wink. Then she turned to me. "Any idea where she is?"

"Logan said the seaside somewhere. Nothing significant to use to locate it." Something was bugging me. Something that Logan said that I'd missed. And I couldn't put a finger on it.

"That's disappointing. You must have gotten something to go on."

"Yeah. Sun, sea, sand, rocks and a lighthouse."

Dad laughed. "Well, that is something."

I nodded then shook my head. "Too many somethings. We have to weed out the right ones. Where's Baz?"

Mom pointed a thumb at the back of the house. "Library. He lives there. Your poor father is now second in command."

I laughed.

"What's so funny," asked Dad, looking affronted

"You giving someone else reign over your domain."

He made a face. "The boy is too damned good to deny."

"Oh. I see." I raised both eyebrows and folded my arms.

Mom laughed. "Don't even start. Go see what Baz can find and I'll get dinner on. I'm not here for much longer. Knowing you, you'll be flying out of here as soon as Baz has something."

"Food is overrated, Mom," I said over my shoulder as Nerina and I headed to the back of the house to find Baz.

"What about success? Overrated too?"

I groaned. "What about nagging, Mom?"

Dad burst out laughing as they disappeared into the kitchen.

"Hey," said Baz, looking up as Nerina and I entered the den.

He was seated at Dad's ancient executive desk, the dark skin of his face glowing green and blue from the light of the laptop.

"Hey yourself," I replied, stopping at his side.

Nerina went to the window, her shyness with others seemed to extend to Baz and I made a mental note to dig further into her hesitation to become friends with him.

"Need help with something?" That's Baz for you. Straight to the heart of the matter, he lived for the opportunity to tackle the next big problem.

"Sun, sea, sand, a white lighthouse sitting on a rocky point."

"Huh?"

I grinned. "I need you to scan the coastlines and find me a place that matches that description."

"Okay." Baz nodded, his eyes sparking with curiosity. "Something to do with Logan?"

At his expression, I frowned. "You developing vamp hearing now too?"

He looked guilty.

"Good grief, Baz. You need to tell us these things." I met Nerina's gaze over his head and raised an eyebrow.

He shrugged. "It's not important."

"Of course it is. We could be talking about all kinds of things not a few feet from you. State secrets, love stuff. Not to mention that time of the month. Or even what a total creep you are." I poked him in the side and we both laughed.

Then he got serious. "Okay. Let's see what we have." He glanced at the screen. "You two want to get something to eat in the meantime?"

I nodded and strode to the door, my stomach now churning into painful knots at the thought of food. Nerina offered him another soft smile as she followed me out.

"Oh. Hang on." Baz called out. "What time of day was it?"

Brilliant question Baz.

"It was definitely daylight. The sun was bright. Hot."

Without a response he was back staring at the screen concentrating on his task.

AFTER A QUICK DINNER of lamb stew and dumplings, Nerina and I returned to the study.

Baz looked frustrated.

"No progress?"

"There are a few options but none that seem likely." He glared at the screen as if it was the cause of his frustrations. Then he looked up at me. "Are you sure you haven't forgotten something?"

I scrunched up my forehead.

"A particular tree, color of the sand, the grass on the shore."

"Baz, I didn't see what he was seeing. He was merely telling me."

"But I saw." A soft voice.

"You did?" we both asked, heads snapping to stare at Nerina.

I slapped my forehead. "Yes, you did. You were in his thoughts."

Baz cupped his hand and wriggled his fingers at her. "Gimme."

"Everything is as Kai said. Just the crystals in the sand."

Now, I wanted to smack my head even harder. "Shit. That's what I forgot. I kept trying to put my finger on it." I snapped my finger and pointed at Baz. "Where are the beaches where lightning strikes create crystals?"

"All around the world. Not only beaches but deserts have them too. But let me see what people are saying online."

"Yeah. There's a message board for everything right?"

He didn't answer. Baz just sat there, head poked out at the strangest angle, like a turtle who didn't get out much.

He stamped the enter key and said, "They're called fulgurites.

Root-shaped crystal formations created when lightning strikes sand."

We nodded, happy to be educated, yet still impatient.

After a few moments he said, "So we have Sand Beach, Maine, showing a huge increase in incidences. Apparently it's quite unusual."

I knocked on the surface of Dad's mahogany desk. "Right. Sand Beach."

"How will you get there?" he asked.

I grabbed my phone. "Mel," I said, mentally crossing my fingers.

A couple of texts later I looked up, disappointed.

"What happened?"

I sighed. "That was Drake. Mel's busy. She's not even in this world." I laughed, disappointed, upset, frustrated.

Baz's chortle drew me from my reverie. "Not as if you can't run fast," said Baz, grinning.

Living in Tukats, the only vamp-demon among a population of panther walkers, Baz had seen more panther shifters than some people would see in their lifetimes.

I pushed to my feet. "Right. I'd better get moving."

CHAPTER 19

"Baz, can you keep me updated if you find any other locations. This visit is merely a scouting mission. If she's not there, we have to keep looking."

Baz nodded. "Couple more look likely. A beach in Florida and one out in Hawaii. I'll keep you posted."

I gave him a grateful wave then left Nerina to take her leave on her own. Dad strode into the hall before I reached the front door, rubbing his chin, his forehead scrunched with worry.

"What's wrong? Is it Logan?" I stepped toward him.

"No. But I do need to talk to you."

"Okay," I said slowly.

Dad was already heading out into the living room and I followed quickly. He began to poke at the dying fire. I knelt beside him and handed him fresh wood and the fire lighter. We worked in silence getting the fire going again.

At last, he got to his feet and sat in one of the armchairs that flanked the fireplace. I stayed where I was, cross-legged on the thick wool rug, my shoulders and cheeks warming from the flames.

He rested his elbows on his knees, then leaned forward to rub his forehead.

"What's up, Dad? Take it this is bad news?"

"No. I wouldn't say it's bad news. Just something I'm worried how you'll take."

I snorted. "How bad can it be? Look at everything that's happened in my life. I'm not sure anything could make it worse."

He cleared his throat and stared at the fire for a few moments. His eyes reflected the dancing flames, shifting from dark green to a bright emerald, his panther stirring, uneasy.

Something was definitely up.

I waited until he cleared his throat again. "I think I found a way that I could help Lily."

Now that, I hadn't expected.

"Oh?" I leaned forward, curious now.

"I've been looking over Niko's research."

My ears began to ring, muscles stiffening at the mention of my uncle.

I scrambled to my feet so fast that I felt lightheaded. "No. No way." My voice had risen. A little too high to be respectful to one's Alpha, but Dad remained unconcerned.

"You have to try and understand what I want to achieve here, Kai." He used his calm voice.

"And what is that? More manipulation of a girl that's already been through hell and back?" I shook my head in disbelief.

"Of course not. All I want is to help Lily. She deserves it. Being unable to shift is an awful burden. And Lily . . . she's been through so much. I see her struggling . . . and I want to help her. How can I ignore the possibility that I could help her heal both mentally and physically?"

"But Dad. You don't understand."

"What don't I understand, Kai?" he asked softly.

I could see he meant it. He cared about Lily, wanted the best for her. He probably wanted to help her in a way that he'd been unable to help his own daughter. And I understood that. But he didn't know.

"Who you are. You're his brother, Dad. Do you not know how similar the two of you look?" I asked. Then smiled. "Apart from the crazed, maniacal gleam in your eye, of course."

Dad only stared into the fire. "I know, honey. I know. That's why I've been so worried." He paused, rubbing his chin again. "I want to help her, but if she doesn't want *me* to administer the treatment, then I'll get someone else to do it. And if she doesn't want to do it at all, then I'll support her decision."

I took a step away, feeling the heat of the fire at my back. "You would do that?"

"Of course, I would." He frowned. "Lily means a lot to us. Your mother and I, we see her as our child. You've taken her under your wing, and so have we. We want what's best for her and from the point of view of a family who has had to deal with Pariah for two generations, I think I can speak for all of us. We want Lily to get better. And maybe she will also want a chance at a better life."

My stomach turned. "I know what you're saying, but you weren't there. You didn't see how she suffered. And drugs? She's a recovering addict. How will she handle Synthe again? That horrible drug was at the core of Uncle Niko's research and Brand got her addicted to it. How will she survive a relapse, Dad?"

I was terrified, and horrified and my father could see it. He got to his feet and came to stand in front of me. Lifting his hands, he placed them on either side of my face.

"Kailin Odel, I am so very proud of you. Your love and loyalty are a sight to behold." He laid his forehead on mine, his nose touching mine, shifting slowly to a panther's nose. The kiss of the Alpha. Nose to nose, granting power from one to the other.

I stiffened and wanted to spring away but he held me firmly. "I don't mean anything official by it, Daughter. I'm just showing you respect," he said, his words soft against my face.

His tone made me aware of my father's bearing, and his voice.

The respect it held, the emotion too. I realized then that Lily's situation affected more people than just me.

A few months ago, when it was just Lily, Anjelo and me, things had been different. My family hadn't even been in the picture, and Lily... well Lily had been hooked on Synthe. A drug created by my own uncle whose obsession with his inability to shift had led to years of research. Research that had led to the creation of a drug that could halt the shifting process. But Uncle Niko was never known for his street smarts.

Before he knew it, he was under the control of two very awful people; Brand, a shifter who believed in humans as his dinner, and Widd'en, a wraith from Wrytthin, a demon realm beyond the Veil. At their behest, the man I'd called Uncle had committed awful, painful acts on innocent shifters.

Lily had been one of his victims.

And he'd used her to get to me.

So there was history where Lily and Niko and Synthe were concerned. Not the least being her inability to shift. Anjelo had soothed her pain while he'd been around, but without him she was left to lean on us. And Lily and her pride didn't allow herself to be seen as weak.

Even with me, she was the badass sidekick, ready to face any and all danger beside me. It took every ounce of willpower to say no every time she demanded to join me on my Elite cases.

And I knew Lily felt sidelined.

I would too if I were her. But I couldn't help it. Horner wouldn't be too accepting if I hauled Lily in every time I had a case. I'd considered putting in a request for the Elite to recruit Lily but the very thought of her in danger made me ill.

Yes, I'd trained her and yes, she'd come with me on a few missions but that had been a long time ago, before people close to us had died.

I wasn't afraid to admit that I didn't want to lose Lily. But something told me she wouldn't see it that way. She'd want her own choices no matter the circumstances.

I accepted my father's respect and took a deep breath as he stepped away. I'd waited a long time to meet this version of my father. Corin Odel had for years been distant, cool. Unemotional. But the loss of my mother had changed him, and not everyone is able to do the right thing when grief darkened their heart.

"I'll speak to Lily before I leave. I'll tell her to contact you either way."

Dad nodded then reached out and held my arm. Giving it a squeeze he said, "Be careful, okay?"

I nodded and was about to turn to leave when he said, "Wait. One more thing."

I spun on my heel in time to see him press one of the rocks on the mantlepiece. The whole thing was designed to look like a stack of rocks had fallen into place, albeit vertically.

When the rock shifted aside I wasn't surprised. I'd seen hidey holes like this before. The burial caves up in the mountains had just such an entrance.

I moved closer as Dad retrieved a slim box which he handed to me. "Take this. Let it protect you."

Peering into the box my eyes widened. "The Glyhs?" I said, my voice breathy, filled with awe.

"Yes. The Glyhs was entrusted to our family after a terrible battle, one so terrible that the earth was soaked with blood for decades after. Only a chosen few have wielded this weapon. If she works for you consider yourself deserving."

The slim dagger, encrusted with diamond mined from the heart of Drakys, the land of the Dragons. It had always amazed me that diamonds so clear and so bright could come from a land filled with fire and lava. I wasn't sure what to say, too busy wondering what would happen if the Glyhs decided I wasn't worthy.

Instead I said, "I'll keep a backup just in case."

Dad laughed softly, his low timbre rolling over me like a comforter. "I expected you'd say that."

I smiled, happy that he finally knew me so well, but my attention remained on the gleaming dagger. It was said to have survived five centuries of protecting the supernatural world. How it ended up in my father's possession I didn't know, but I was grateful that I could have it with me even if it was just for the mental support.

Of course, I was afraid that the dagger would fail me in a fight. I still didn't know if it would answer to me as it's bearer. Apparently, the Glyhs tended to be fussy about who wielded it. The weapon would defeat one's enemy in entirety. But I knew one thing - if it's power failed me, its blade certainly wouldn't.

Or at least I hoped it wouldn't.

I left not much later, with the dagger in a sheath at my hip, as close as I could possibly keep it. The weapon was said to glow when an enemy of the bearer was near. And I had a lot of enemies.

I took a breath and patted the sheath.

Glyhs or not, I was prepared for whatever they had in store for me.

Bring it on.

CHAPTER 20

I headed home, pushing the motorbike harder than it deserved. I regretted having taken it, especially now when all I wanted was the feel of the wind on my fur, the feel of the soil beneath my paws as I ran.

Not today.

The streets were quiet this late at night and in the distance the dull lights of the Aon Building and the Willis Tower glowed like glow-bugs. The tree was somewhere out there, invisible without its own lights to reveal it from this distance, and yet just the thought of its sickness weakened me.

I drove into the rain-soaked alley behind our apartment, rolling to a stop beside the wide metal door that led to the back of our building.

The hairs on the back of my neck stood on end and my nose twitched, my panther sensing something was wrong.

Key in the lock, I turned and scanned the alley. Everything glinted silver, the gray moon shedding its light on street and doors, windows and garbage cans, all wet from the dusting of rain.

The narrow street was empty, nothing stirring except for a

tomcat - a real cat from the scent of it - lurking in the furthest end. A light breeze blew through the alley, lifting the hair on my head, disturbing the surface of a puddle a few feet from me.

The silvery surface shuddered and I swallowed a gasp. Something moved within the puddle.

A reflection.

The pool had reflected the passing of something. Something in the alley with me, but what I couldn't see. Not with my human eyes.

I shifted partially, bringing my panther sight to the fore while maintaining my human face. No sense letting whatever it was know I was onto it. The feline sight caught movement to my right, just beyond the puddle, moving out of the alley toward the street.

A shadow, dark and wispy, taller and wider than I was, hovered along the street. It didn't touch the ground, it had no descriptive markings. Just smoke, thick and black.

And I didn't like it one bit.

People - paranormal or not - I could handle. Shadows were a little harder to fight, or to contain. The dark blotch floated around the corner and the hairs on my neck subsided, as if my instinct was finally calm in the absence of the shadow.

I left the lock alone and ran after it, skidding to a stop at the sidewalk. The street was empty. Not a hint of the shadow remained. But I knew as well as any supernatural that just because I couldn't see something didn't mean it wasn't there.

I gritted my teeth. I could call Horner for backup, but I was heading out of the city anyway. There wasn't a point. Not until I returned.

A tiny part of me was fully aware that the shadow could probably move as fast as I did in shifter mode, but I also knew that the timing of this shadow's appearance could be linked to any number of possibilities.

It could be someone sent by Elan, the Ice Prince, or someone else from the Fae Council. It could even be Sean taking his envy one step further.

Or, just maybe, we were onto something regarding the toxins killing the Ash Tree. The appearance of the shadow meant we'd shaken something up, and now all I needed to do was keep an eye on my *shadow* shadow.

I kept my guard up as I returned to the door, one eye on the alley as I unlocked it and rolled the bike inside. After locking the door and securing the bike to the railing at the bottom of the stairs, I hurried up to my apartment.

I tugged my phone from my jeans pocket and tapped out a message to Lily.

Need to talk. Urgent. Meet me at my apartment.

I was about to shut off the screen when I paused.

After a moment I texted *Please*.

Like Lily, I didn't enjoy being ordered around. I smiled as I pulled a change of clothes from my closet and headed into the shower. Lily had a key, so I enjoyed the heat of the water on my skin in peace, however hurried the shower may be.

I escaped the shower before I became too relaxed, then dragged on black jeans, and a black long-sleeved turtleneck. The weather had changed, nights bordering on icy, and Christmas was around the corner.

I was buckling the holster for the dagger around my waist when I heard my room door open.

"You here?" her voice came through the closed door.

"Yeah."

I pulled the bathroom door open, then scraped my fingers through my long hair. I was looking around the room, frowning when a brush came sailing through the air.

Catching it with a grateful smile. "Hey," I said, as I dragged the brush through my hair.

Lily sank onto the bed and crossed her legs, swinging it back and forth. "So what's up?" she asked, watching as I drew my hair into a high ponytail and secured it tightly.

I refused to hesitate on this. Best to get it over and done with. I cleared my throat and set my hands on my hips. "Dad took me aside today. Just before I left the house."

"Sounds ominous." The swinging leg stilled.

I straightened then turned on my heel and headed to the closet. "He came across some research while he was working on a treatment for Logan," I said as I pushed the clothing aside and opened the secret panel on the back wall.

It opened with a whoosh as Lily asked, "So what was so important about this research?"

I slipped on a holster for the gun over my shoulders, and another around my thigh for a knife. "He found something that he thinks can help walkers who can't shift."

A glance over my shoulder confirmed the leg was swinging again. While she digested that, I took a handgun off its hook, popped the chamber and filled it with bullets, before sliding it into the holster. My movements were practiced, sure and quick. Nothing I haven't done a million times before.

Lily was too silent.

When I turned to face her, her eyes narrowed. "Where are you going?"

I shrugged. "Sand Beach, Maine. I need to check something out."

More swinging. "At this time of night?"

I raised my eyebrows. "When has the time of day ever been a problem?"

She avoided my gaze.

"Lily?" I didn't need to threaten her. She and Anjelo had long ago declared me their Alpha, and ever since Lily usually did what I asked her.

Usually.

She sighed. "I have it on good authority that you need to be more concerned about your safety."

"Whose good authority is that?"

Her back stiffened as she folded her arms.

"Lily?"

I took a step closer and she threw her arms in the air. "Okay. Okay. If he ever asks I'm going to swear you forced me to tell."

"Lily." More warning now than question.

She boosted to her feet then walked around the bed to the window. "Anjelo." Facing the street, I couldn't see her expression and I suspected she needed the privacy.

"What about Anjelo, and what about my safety?" She could have her privacy but she still needed to answer my questions.

Without turning she said, "I've been talking to Anjelo."

The room vibrated with silence.

"How?" I was stunned.

"He's in the Graylands. Apparently some people," I noticed she didn't say ghosts, "have the ability to travel to this world. Anjelo's been coming to see me ever since he died. It took me a while to realize he wasn't a figment of my imagination."

I sighed. "I should have told you more about the way it works."

"It's okay. Anjelo explained."

"How is he?" I wanted to cry. Just the thought of Anjelo made me want to scream and throw things.

"He's … adjusting." She laughed softly. "I think he's frustrated at not being able to do anything."

"He *is* talking to you, isn't he?" I said, understanding how unsettling it was to not be in control, to be at the mercy of someone else entirely. With Anjelo caught within the bounds of death and undeath, Lily would forever be in limbo.

It was something that I needed to fix.

Lily nodded, her hair dropping forward to frame her face like a curtain ready to hide from the world as soon as she felt threatened.

"When did he first make contact?" I asked, moving slowly, afraid she'd stop being so forthcoming.

She sighed. "From the beginning." She looked up at me, guilt flickering across her honey eyes. "I knew before he was dead because he came to me. It's not ... I mean I didn't know at the time that he'd died. I just began to see him, to hear his voice. At first I couldn't make out what he was trying to say but maybe he got stronger? I dunno. Eventually he became clearer, and he was able to explain what happened."

I stiffened, sure that the pain in my eyes reflected her own. "What did he say?" My voice was hushed and outside a soft rain began to fall.

"He fought back. They beat him up pretty badly. Something must have been wrong with him because when he went to the lab, he suffered convulsions. They were confused but they couldn't help him. Whatever was wrong with him . . . he said they never spoke about it."

"Could have been a broken rib or pierced lung or arteries. Something during the fight." I was talking to myself because one glance at Lily confirmed her thoughts were elsewhere.

"He said that I need to take care of you. That something terrible was coming and that you need to be prepared for it. And that your life was at risk."

I frowned. "I'm always in danger. Surely he knows that?"

"But that's what he was trying to say. This is way more than your normal danger. He couldn't be specific because he wasn't able to find out details. But what he did say was don't trust Agent Chou. Anjelo thinks he's only there to safeguard the interests of Omega and the people who run it."

I raised my eyebrows. "Maybe Anjelo and I need to have a chat." Agent Chou had proven his loyalty with the help he'd given me but I wasn't naive enough to think he'd never double-cross me.

Still. A talk with Anjelo would help.

"He said you'd say that." Lily grinned.

"He knows me too well." I sank to the mattress and rubbed my forehead, mimicking my father's actions. Did he feel this way too? Like the weight of the world lay on his shoulders.

Not that I was arrogant enough to assume I was so important, but sometimes it all just felt too much. The Ash was dying, Tara was in trouble, Logan was adrift in the sea of his own memories, and now Anjelo was implying there was danger on the horizon.

I groaned and pushed to my feet. "Okay. Tell Anjelo I need to see him as soon as he can arrange it."

Then I frowned wondering how he'd arrange it. Would he appear beside me, or visit my dreams? Let's hope he wasn't about to pop into my bedroom to discuss world-ending stuff.

"So, about what Dad said," I said, facing Lily. I'd given her enough time to digest the line of thought. Now, I had to be straight with her. "Dad suggested that he could try with you."

She didn't reply.

"I told him I thought it was a lot for you to consider. I said I'd tell you, but that it would be your decision entirely."

When Lily finally raised her eyes to me they were filled with tears. "He'd do that for me?" My father's intentions were clear enough to her, and I was relieved it hit her deeply.

I nodded. "I was afraid you wouldn't want to consider it."

With a tilt of her head she asked, "Why not?"

"Because of Niko. His brother..." Shame filled me. I'd never been able to erase the shame of my relationship with the man who'd hurt her so badly.

Lily sighed and came to stand in front of me. "You're the smartest, most stupidest person I know."

I scowled. "Eh?"

"How could you ever think that I'd hold you all responsible

for what your uncle did?" She was shaking her head, looking at me with disappointment in her eyes.

Sighing, I said, "Guess it's what family does. We all feel responsible. And it's not as if he's been properly punished either, languishing in some Sentinel prison awaiting some sham of a trial." I drew a breath. "Even now I'm so afraid that having Dad be the one to help you, to administer the drugs and be there while you shift–"

"You're afraid they look too much alike?"

I nodded.

"They don't. And they aren't the same person. Even *I* can see that, silly."

I smiled weakly.

"Kai. You have to stop worrying about everyone else. It really is time to let me make my own decisions."

Pursing my lips, I said, "Okay, Lynx. I promise to try. But right now, I have somewhere I need to be."

Lily gave a firm nod. "And I'm coming with. Logan is my friend too."

"No–"

Lily raised a palm. "Don't even bother."

I narrowed my eyes at her, but I didn't fight her. I had the power to stop her, all that was required was a flick of an Alpha eyebrow, but our family needed help. Did I have the right to stop anybody from helping?

"Fine." I stood stiffly and pulled on a suede leather jacket. It crackled as it settled against my body. "But you'd better keep up."

Lily snorted. "I'm Pariah, but I can still run, you know."

We headed into the living room and I smiled as Lily threw her backpack over her shoulder.

"What? Did you bring every single piece of weaponry that you own?"

Certainly not the first time.

"Never hurts to be prepared."

"Always hurts to have too much choice." I raised an eyebrow. "Use what works for you so it comes naturally in a fight. You don't want to be reaching for a gun, then have to struggle to find what you need. Or grab a dagger and waste time remembering what to do. Your muscle memory is still a little too young."

Lily shook her head, a little impatient as she rolled her eyes. "Geez, Kai. The bag is just backup. In case we run out, or need more."

I smiled and said, "Let's hope you don't stab yourself in the back while running."

"Way ahead of you, sister." She opened the backpack to reveal a thick leather lining.

"Smart thinking." I gave the bag a nod then asked. "You have enough ammo?" I gave the two pistols and three revolvers a pointed look.

"Yup. And I'll grab more if you think we may need it."

I nodded absently as she hurried back into the bedroom. She was back in less than a minute.

We locked up, then fell into shifter speed, racing out of the apartment and down the street so fast that only Superman, and demons, would be faster.

Or maybe the Fae?

CHAPTER 21

*L*ily ran beside me, her shifter speed much slower than mine. But I didn't mind compensating for her. She was so strong now, since Anjelo's death, so determined. I didn't have the right to tamp that part of her down.

We reached Bar Harbor after sunrise, using country roads and national forest routes, stopping every hour or so to catch our breaths. The advantage of being a shifter meant that even traveling at supernatural speeds, we recovered pretty fast.

Unless of course we were injured.

The coast was beautiful, the sand and ocean drenched in the dull morning glare. Gulls rode gusts of wind and salt coated my lips as we stood on the rise above the nearest beach. It wasn't Sand Beach, but it wouldn't take long to find the place. I checked my phone for the coordinates Baz had sent, then plugged them into the GPS.

"We're about a mile from Sand Beach so let's move."

Lily stayed a little behind me, following my lead as we ran.

And when we did stop on the hillside above the beach, the view caught my breath. The curved sandy shore was a narrow golden strip, bracketed by a verge of grass and tall fir trees, and the blue waters of the North Atlantic. The shore opposite us was a disorganized pile of rocks. All in all, it was a stunningly gorgeous beach - the perfect place to hide out.

Not that Sienna would know to hide out.

Logan hadn't mentioned trees or grass. But if Sienna had been looking out at the sea the entire time, he would have missed it.

I shook my head and stared down at the empty beach. Hidden by the firs along the rise we watched the shore. "You think she'll come here this early in the morning?"

I shrugged. "It's a Saturday. Who knows?"

"Doesn't she have a job or something?"

"We don't know. And besides she's only twenty. She may be studying somewhere and Logan just caught her in one place on a road trip somewhere." I sighed. "This could just be a wild goose chase."

Or worse. Sienna could very well be studying abroad and that beach could be Mykonos or Ireland or Durban for all we knew.

"But we have to chase it." Lily nodded then glanced back at the sand. A gust of wind threw sand in the air and I heard the rustling of the grains as they landed. "You want to get closer?" Lily asked.

I studied the shoreline all the way until the rocks. "I'm not sure we should reveal ourselves so soon. Or at all."

"Nobody knows we're here, Kai. Only Baz, and you swore him to secrecy."

I grunted, then headed down the hillside and out of the trees.

"So what's our cover story?" asked Lily, tramping behind me.

"Sisters? Taking a road trip?"

"How do I explain not being in school?"

"You're not as young as you look?" I said, raising my eyebrows. At her smirk I said, "Sorry, you're the one who wanted to tag along."

She stuck out her tongue and we continued to pick our way

toward the narrow strip of grass. "Anyway, sisters on a road trip is probably a better cover than a loner."

"Yeah, especially considering you look a little too badass to be safe." I raised my eyebrows, amused.

"Probably the BO." Lily snorted then evaded a loose punch that I aimed at her shoulder. We were laughing as we got to the sand, and the timing couldn't have been more perfect.

A girl approached from the other side of the beach, her eyes narrowed against the harsh morning light.

"You think that's her?"

Her dark clothes were more goth than even Lily could hope to be. From her shitkickers which she hadn't bothered to remove on the sand, to the chains on her purple and white checked skirt, to the spiderwebbed fingerless gloves and the dark eyeliner, she was the quintessentially goth girl. And beautiful.

Even the streaks of indigo and mauve and teal in her hair only helped to make her look just perfect.

"Could go either way. Although how many people lurk around on the beach, alone at sunrise."

For a twin of Logan, her hair was dark, but a more than cursory glance at her roots confirmed it as a wig.

Not hiding out?

"Be careful okay?" I said to Lily from the side of my mouth. "If it's her then she's more powerful than Logan."

"And more dangerous," said Lily dryly before she gave Sienna a shy wave, accompanying it with a shy smile. "Hi."

Lily's breathy, hesitant greeting put a smile on the girl's face, and she drew to a stop.

"Hi." She glanced at me, then back at Lily. "You guys not from around here?"

Lily shook her head. "Nope. We're from Nebraska. We saw this photograph on this site online - you know the one people post photos on from their travels?"

Goth girl nodded, a little smile turning up her mouth. Lily

must have taken an acting class somewhere along the line because I could have sworn her accent was taking on a little bit of a country lilt. "Saw the photo and had to see it for ourselves. And boy are we glad."

"It is a beautiful place," she said softly. "Are you here for a while?"

I shook my head. "Just a few days." Sticking my hand out I said, "I'm Kai O'Neil. She's my sister Lily."

I wasn't sure why I used our real first names, from the widening of Lily's eyes I could tell she was more than amused at my made-up last name. She could hardly blame me. I'd totally forgotten about names and had to come up with something on the fly. So much for smart and experienced super-agent.

"Sienna Blake." So it was her. "You guys came at the wrong time of the year if you wanted to work on your tans." She grinned, allowing a cheeky smile to come through. She sounded relaxed, but I caught an edge of tension.

I waved my hands. "Are you kidding. I like my butt unfrozen, thanks."

Sienna laughed. "You and me both," she said with a sigh as she turned to gaze back at the water. "It makes me sad that I can't go in. The water is so calming. So peaceful."

She spoke wistfully, her voice so filled with yearning that I wondered what it was she longed for so deeply.

"So where's a good place around here to grab some breakfast?" asked Lily, making me laugh.

"Is that all you think of?"

Lily glared at me. "Food is the most important thing in the world. Besides, we haven't had breakfast yet. I'm starved."

I made a face. "Ugh. I can't think of anything worse than eating this early in the morning."

"You can have a coffee then," said Lily as if she'd decided on the whole thing.

Sienna smiled and pointed south. "There's a small strip mall a few minutes that way. I'll give you a ride there if you like."

I nodded then stared out at the lighthouse. From a distance it appeared perfect, but now that we'd gotten closer, or maybe it was the shifting of the sun, I could see the broken walls, the toppled bricks and crumbling mortar.

"What happened to the lighthouse?"

Sienna's smile faded. "It's tragic local lore." She turned and headed up the sand, slow enough that we could hear her continue with her tale. "Five decades ago, a local fisherman's wife would come here to watch for her husband's return. One morning it was storming, waves six feet high and deadly. She battled the spray and the rain to get to the lighthouse, even lit the flame to warn her husband of the danger. But it was too dark, or she was too late, or fate had other plans, and his boat crashed onto the shore as she watched. He drowned before her eyes."

"What did she do?" whispered Lily.

"She jumped," Sienna said simply, before walking off.

At the top of the hill, Lily followed Sienna while I paused to study the lighthouse. Waves smashed against the shores, sending fine spray reaching up to coat the rocks above. I could imagine the place, draped in the darkness of the storm, angry waves lashing out at the rocks. Claiming the boat and the man. And then the woman too.

Maybe it was the darkness of the tale or the fear within me of losing Logan, but as I stared out at the water I felt a deep, unequivocal sense of loss. I blinked away the hot rush of tears and clutched the strap of my rucksack so tight I could feel the imprint of the nylon on my palms.

Get it together Kai.

I took a breath and followed the girls.

CHAPTER 22

We sat in a small ice-cream shop that had probably once sold milkshakes for a dime and soda for much the same. The place was small, the walls painted a pale pink, furniture mostly chrome and pink, a very feminine version of the Hard Rock Cafe.

I stared at the customers as they streamed in, as if the day was sweltering and they were in desperate need of something cool to soothe their parched throats.

Sienna had claimed a small errand, leaving us to order, and was now weaving back through the morning rush to our table, her expression slightly strained.

Lily had decided that waffles were a suitable breakfast and oddly enough I agreed with her and had ordered my own. Maybe the run from Chicago had taken my strength. I ate quietly, listening to Lily maneuver answers from Sienna with such ease that I was beginning to realize I'd underestimated my sidekick.

"I've always wanted to see the world. What's it like out there?" She tilted her head, her eyes gleaming. She seemed different, harder somehow.

I frowned. "You make it sound like it's another world."

She laughed and spooned strawberry ice-cream into her mouth. "Sometimes it truly feels that way." She waved a hand at the shop and then pointed at the street through the glass window. "We're just a small town. And sometimes it all seems so … claustrophobic. And yet to others it feels so filled with freedom. Probably just depends on one's personal outlook I guess." Her tone was forced and I frowned as I studied her face.

"Would you want to leave? See the world?" I asked, sharing a quick glance with Lily.

Sienna lifted a shoulder. "Maybe. I guess if I knew there was something worth seeing." She sighed so deeply that is sounded like she too had the weight of the world on her shoulders. Her purple strands lifted on a gust of wind brought in as a new customer entered. "Sometimes I feel like there's something waiting for me out there, you know. Like I have a purpose that's more than just life here."

Her sigh seemed to bring me down a notch or two. The girl had been ripped from her only family, spirited away to this tiny little town so far away. It wasn't surprising that her spirit yearned for him.

I reached over and held her hand.

"Sometimes all we can do is follow our dreams." I smiled, but I had to force my lips to hold the gentle curve. Force my eyes to reveal only pleasant grace.

While inside, my mind and gut were in turmoil. Something was so very, very wrong.

My throat began to close, cutting off my air supply and I took a discreet breath, maintaining my composure.

I kept my smile bright and gaze neutral even though I knew that this woman, whoever she was, was not Sienna Westin. Not anymore.

She was a ShapeChanger, using her mage power to veil herself with Sienna's face and body. She had no idea who we were, but she was testing us.

We had to be very careful.

But I also had to ensure that she had no idea that I was onto her.

So I relaxed against the back of the booth and played with my ice-cream, spooning and talking, as the room grew warmer.

Finally, I couldn't take it anymore. "Hey Lil's. We need to find a place to stay. Bryan will send out a search party if we don't make that Skype session."

Without a blink my trusty sidekick nodded. "Oh, yeah. I could so do without him nagging me today."

"Who's Bryan?"

I paused, praying that we both didn't answer at the same time. But Lily pretended to be searching for something in her backpack.

"Bryan's my husband. He didn't even want us to take this trip. Two girls on their own, seeing the sights. So that means he's super worried." I rolled my eyes. "Makes us Skype every night. Swears he'll call the cops if we're so much as one minute late."

"Men," said Lily, giving an inelegant snort.

Faux-Sienna snorted too. "Yeah. Can't live with them . . ."

"Can't live without them." Lily and I laughed loudly and Faux-Sienna joined in. Her mirth was fake and she failed to hide her annoyance.

She scooted along the seat and pouted. "I'm really sorry, but my brother will be waiting for me back at the house. I promised to go sailing with him." She paused as if she expected us to look back at her, aghast at the mention of a brother.

When neither of us even registered a raised eyebrow or a suggestion of a blink, she got to her feet. And that's when I saw it. The strange shimmer around her body. Invisible in the bright sunlight, but to a trained eye, a dead giveaway.

We waved her off, bright smiles blooming even as she left the shop and headed outside to a waiting limo.

As the car disappeared down the street, Lily opened her mouth. But I lifted a finger and she clamped her jaws shut slowly.

"I'm pooped," I said leaning against the back of the seat.

"But we just got here," whined Lily, raising her voice for good measure.

"We can find a place to crash, then we can go exploring okay?"

"You're so boring," Lily said, rolling her eyes as she slouched and slurped on her milkshake.

"We can always go back home," I suggested airily.

"No way. We just got here." Whining again.

"So behave. Let's walk this junk food off then find an information center to see what's interesting around here." I used a bossy, overbearing tone that made the people at the table beside us hide their grins.

"I knew I should have gone to Lake Tahoe with Bree and the girls," Lily grumbled, getting to her feet and grabbing her rucksack a little too hard. The guns clinked together as the bag bounced against the seat.

I curbed the instinctive urge to give the bag a concerned look, and Lily a much more annoyed one. Instead, I gathered my things and headed outside.

Lily was right behind me, scanning the streets with curious touristy looks. We maintained the cover of two sisters on a tour of the little town.

At the end of the street, Lily glanced down at her phone, a strange look on her face.

"What?" I whispered.

"You know how the intelligence people can clone phones and shit."

"Yeah?"

"What if they did that to ours?"

"If they did, what would they find out?"

She looked up at me, wary, worried. Scared.

"Geez Lil's did you rob a bank or something? You're getting

all jumpy about nothing." I grabbed her sleeve and tugged. "Let's go find a place to stay. I want to soak in a tub for a while."

We headed off the main strip, turning right into a stunning road that was the epitome of fall perfection. Leaves of every color from brown to russet to gold covered the sidewalk and much of the streets.

"Doesn't look like people sweep their streets around here," said Lily as she looked around.

"It's gorgeous," I said, a threatening note to my words. There was something strange about the street, and the edge to Lily's voice told me that she was not oblivious.

"Of course it is. But it looks like home, Kai. I wanted to go somewhere different."

"Like where," I played along, a little distracted.

"Bali maybe?"

"What's in Bali that's so fascinating?"

Lily just shook her head. We were both tiring of this game. The run had drained us and the shock of feeling the energy of the mage had taken its toll on me too. We needed a place to lay low, and I wasn't sure we'd find it here in the town. I was beginning to feel like we were caught in some kind of time-warp.

"Okay." We paused at a wooden bench and wiped off a layer of leaves. "See if you can find a place to stay," I said as I slid the dagger a fraction of an inch from its sheath. It didn't indicate any danger and as I held my phone to it, I could see no paranormal interference. I knew the dagger wasn't a glorified paranormal detector but I'd hoped it would sense any form of danger.

With no luck I figured I'd call Baz.

He answered on the second ring. "Hey, honey," I said, laying on the sweet, hoping he'd play along. My tone was pitched higher than normal so I hoped he'd sense something was up.

"Hey you," he said. I could almost see his dark brows rise in confusion.

"Bryan, I know we said we'd Skype tonight but we need to find a place to stay first."

"Nothing yet?" he asked.

"Nope. We almost found something but we were wrong. Reception here is sketchy."

"Want me to look for something for you?"

"Yeah. A bed and breakfast place would be nice. Something without bugs please."

"Oh, yeah. Sure." I almost heaved a sigh of relief when he got what I meant.

I heard him tapping away. Then he said, "You're clean. And in case you weren't, I set a rerouter on your phone. They can't tap it but they'll be able to follow it. Only they'll be looking in Timbuktu and Shenzhen first."

"Thanks. Did you find anything else?" No time to waste.

Lily was still sitting beside me on the park bench, fiddling with her phone. I listened to Baz, pulling my panther senses to the surface, scanned our surroundings. As far as I could tell there was no one on the street or close enough to leave a scent. Unless of course they had had the presence of mind to stay downwind.

That would mean that they knew who we were. What we were.

Baz grunted. "There is a good possibility that you're in the wrong place." When I said nothing, he responded. "I'm sorry."

"Don't be sorry. We knew that there was a good chance that this was a wild goose chase. You can only do so much."

I caught myself quickly as I realized we'd forgotten exactly what type of conversation we were meant to be having. "Look, we'll come straight back home. But there's one thing that I need to do before we leave."

"What's that?" asked Baz, worried now, probably imagining some hare-brained scheme. The guy had no faith.

"Nothing much. I just saw something . . . interesting." Lily and I shared a worried glance.

He promised to send us any further information, and I rang off, sliding the phone back into my pocket as I got to my feet. "Lil's, we need to make tracks."

Her agreement glowed in her eyes. We both knew it was time to call timeout.

CHAPTER 23

We both got up and began to walk away from the strip to the edge of town. Once there we'd drop into shifter speed and get out of there.

A few feet ahead was an old house, and as we drew closer I noticed the garden. The roses drooped, heads, dried and dark. A tulip-type plant that glowed with a strange purple luster seemed to dominate the entire garden.

The flower distracted me, so the woman seemed to appear out of nowhere, her glamor draped over her like a gown. "Can I help you ladies?" she asked, smiling widely. Wide enough that I made out the strangely smooth teeth, the too unblemished skin, the reed slim form to her body.

I glanced at Lily, wondering if she noticed but she seemed oblivious.

"Yes, we're looking for a place to get a room. Could you direct us please?" I had to come up with a response out of the blue. First the ShapeChanger and now a Fae? Something was up in Sand Beach.

"Not from around here I take it?" she asked. I shook my head, refusing to say more. "There's one down the road, about two blocks on the left. That's Mari Santiago. She'll make you comfortable."

"Thanks," I said, herding Lily out of the small garden and down the road. "What's wrong with you?" I hissed in her ear once we were well away from the garden. The Fae still stood at the open gate, staring at us.

"Nothing. I was just too shocked to say anything. Besides Tara and Gracie, I've never seen a Fae before."

"That wasn't her real form."

"You can see her too?"

I frowned. "See her too? What do you mean?"

Lily shrugged. "I thought you could see what she truly looked like."

"I can see past glamor yes, but her magic was strong. It's not common to have sight that strong, even in a Walker."

Lily shrugged. "Well, I could see her anyway."

"Wow."

"What's *wow* about it?"

I pinched her arm. "You have the Sight. Wait until I get back home. Mom and Grams will faint when I tell them."

"What's so special about it?" Her curiosity seemed to wane.

"Walkers with true Sight are rare. Just about as rare as humans with Sight."

Lily's lashes dropped and she shrugged, still keeping pace with me. "A power like that isn't worth all that much. Not as if I can throw fire, see the future."

"It's still a rare gift, Lily. Nothing to sniff at." I couldn't help my admonishing tone, and even when I realized that Lily would no doubt give up that Sight just to get her Lynx to come to the fore, I was irritated.

People never got to choose what they wanted in life. It's given to them, handed over like a gift. And what else can we do with those prizes than to make use of them, enjoy them?

Lily didn't seem to see that, but there wasn't time to discuss it.

We were about to cross the street when a gust of wind caught my ponytail and slapped it against my face, ends dragging almost harshly against my cheek.

I blinked.

Touched my cheek in surprise at the vehemence of the air.

My fingers came away streaked with blood.

Lily gasped, her eyes wide, staring first at my fingers then my face.

Around us, a dark wind gusted, lifting leaves and sand from the sidewalk, drawing them into a swirling tornado of debris. Before I could warn Lily, the tornado sped to us, exploding in a shower of dirt. I'd shaded my eyes in time but it did little to protect my skin. The already shredded skin burned as dust skimmed the surface, taking a second layer of flesh with it.

Lily cried out, a grating, pained sound that pulled at my panic. I reached for her, feeling her fingers grab hold of mine, clutching as the wind gusted harder, thrusting against our bodies so that we were bent over trying not to fall, or worse, be blown off down the street like tumbleweed.

My face bled, but I ignored it as I drew on my panther senses, trying to get a better sense of what was around us. My guess was an Air Mage or an Ethereal Fae, someone filled with righteous anger from the feel of it.

Another gust had us pinned against the fence, head and torso bent back over the low wall. And as I stared into the whirling dust, a shape began to take form. And a man stepped from its depths.

Not any kind of man I'd ever seen.

Lily let out a soft gasp.

His skin was shadow, dark and silky, undulating as he walked as if he wore the darkness like a suit. Only his eyes gleamed, like twin moons in a face as dark as night. He raised his hands, and each contained a fat black tornado of shadows. Within them spun pieces of glass, metal spikes and an assortment of other sharp objects I'd prefer to remain ignorant of.

At my hip, something vibrated. A low steady hum that confused me. Then I stiffened.

The Glyhs.

I fought the pressure of the wind, shifting my hand across my body to grab hold of the dagger. It glowed, edged in a faint blue light.

The shadow man paused, his pale eyes shifting to stare at the Glyhs. Good. At least he knew what he was up against.

Not that it stopped him. He seemed wary of the weapon, but determined to complete his mission. I gripped the handle of the dagger tightly and waited as he drew closer.

The shadow man lifted a hand and Lily and I were tossed into the air. We flew a dozen yards down the street, smacking hard against stone walls and wood fences alike. I heard something crack as we hit the sidewalk and I wanted to laugh, purely because I had no idea if it was me or Lily who'd just broke.

Lily groaned and mumbled something about being grateful for leather linings. At first, I was confused. Then I grinned. The dangerous contents of her bag. None of which could help us out of this particular jam.

A loud crack sounded ahead of us as the Shadowman continued his assault. A splintered tree limb hit the ground and shattered into dozens of deadly spikes. The shadows tossed them at us and though I held out the dagger, I still felt the wood piercing into my flesh. Still heard Lily's sharp scream as she too was hit.

Impaled by two of the splinters I felt a wave of fury wash over me. I refused to go down like this. I'd defeated Wraiths and demons and more. No way was I going to let a puny shadow mage cut me down.

I shifted forward, pushing myself to my feet, barely registering the fat splinter that sat deep within my upper thigh, and the second stake that had plunged straight through my arm.

Wood piercings could come back into fashion, Odel.

Standing, barely, I straightened and threw the dagger at the shadow figure. I hadn't expected anything to happen. Even though I'd thrown the Glyhs as a last resort, sending a prayer to Ailuros, I hadn't really believed it would save us.

But the creature screamed, the sound piercing my eardrums. The dagger slammed into him as if he were a solid being, then passed through, hitting the sidewalk with a clatter.

The metal no longer glowed, but when I looked back at our assailant I could see where the blue light had entered and exited. It had struck the wound in his abdomen, spreading through his darkness like a poisonous wave. The shadows began to recede, giving way to pale blue light, destroying the darkness until it exploded into a shower of wispy blackness and sparks of blue light.

And the Glyhs saved us.

I stumbled forward and fell to my knees, grasping for the dagger. The street spun around me as I turned to check on Lily. She lay on the cracked sidewalk, taking harsh breaths that sounded like sandpaper on wood.

I scrambled closer, shaking with terror - or maybe it was shock considering my twin set of impalements- to inspect her for wounds. I sighed with relief. Lily had escaped with a flesh wound on her neck and half inch splinter in her upper arm. Maybe being so protective of Lily was a bad idea. Maybe she needed to toughen up a little.

Judging by the shock on her face, and her rapid breathing, I suspected I was right.

I was shocked that nothing more vital had been hit. With all those flying splinters there were jugulars and major arteries that could have suffered. Instead we both got to our feet, grabbed our bags and hobbled across the street as fast as we could.

A glance behind us revealed an eerily empty street.

"What the hell just happened?"

I shook my head, staring back at the town. "I think we got made."

"And Sienna."

"If that was really her, then she's long gone."

I didn't care to remain, either for apprehension or vengeance. Both Lily and I needed medical attention because unlike bullets and small flying objects, a panther was unable to eject wooden objects from the body without outside assistance.

So, though injured and slow, we made our way toward the nearest stand of trees.

Leaning against a tree trunk, I took a deep breath and dialed Cassandra, and put a call in for speedy transportation.

She sounded concerned and promised to arrange something immediately.

Larsson, Cassie's red-headed teleporter friend arrived within minutes, his easy grin having a calming effect on both Lily and myself. His eyes widened as he took in our various impalements, but I shook my head. No time to debrief him.

He seemed to understand, and just offered an arm to each of us. We held on tightly as he jumped us back to my father's house.

Funny.

I didn't recall telling him where I wanted to go.

CHAPTER 24

The jump took a lot of energy out of me, my injuries contributing to my weakness. I'd passed out for a few minutes after arriving, only to be brought back to blazing consciousness by a wild stab of pain searing my thigh.

I cracked open my eyes, one lid at a time, and found my pant leg torn off at the top of my thigh, my pale skin bare as Dad tried to work the ragged piece of wood free from my bleeding flesh.

Blood soaked my pants, my body, and stained my father's hands. Beneath my leg I felt the soft squelch of blood-soaked fabric.

Perspiration sprang on my forehead, not even bothering to elegantly dot my skin. Instead it fell in rivulets as I bit back a scream when Dad cracked off another thin piece of wood. He had no other way to work. He had to remove the wood, but its edges were jagged, catching easily against the raw flesh in which it was embedded.

Add to that the copious amounts of blood I seemed to be shedding and it didn't make for a simple procedure. Dad however seemed unfazed, and untainted by such normal things as perspiration. The man didn't have the decency to stress.

His eyes remained focused on my thigh, his hands moving confidently as he plucked at the wood in my wound with a pair of medical tweezers.

I winced as he broke off a particularly large piece.

"Maybe you should knock her out." Darcy's suggestion.

Now where had she come from?

"I don't think I have enough for the both of them." Dad's voice was tight with fear. I'd never seen him this way before and I reached out to touch his arm.

"I'll be fine, Dad. If I pass out don't wake me up until it's over." There was a note of amusement in my voice that didn't match the pain I was in.

Dad saw right through me.

He patted my hand and glanced up at Darcy who moved slowly to my side. I was on a bed somewhere in the house. The room, also unidentifiable, seemed to spin despite the fact that I was lying flat on my back.

I closed my eyes and breathed slowly, wincing as the movement made the splinter in my arm sting. I flicked a glance at it, noticed it still stuck out from both sides of my arm, and wondered when Dad would get around to removing it.

"As soon as we remove this one," said Dad pointing at the remains of the splinter in my thigh.

Apparently I'd spoken aloud.

I turned to face Darcy. "Can you make sure he doesn't leave a scar?"

She laughed. "Is that all you're worried about?"

I cleared my throat and shifted so that I was no longer looking her in the eye. "Of course. How am I supposed to land a great guy with legs that look like ground meat?"

She shook her head, but reached for my hand. One of the biggest problems with being a walker and getting injured is that the lack of painkillers was a killer.

You couldn't even pretend to be badass if the pain was awful because you felt every second of it. Horse tranquilizers worked best in high doses and I understood my father's reluctance to obtain more just for this surgery. It would take time, and it would knock me out for more than a day.

The last time I used the tranquilizer, the Ancient, Darian, had attended to my wounds – under Logan's watchful eye, of course. I recalled how foggy I'd been after taking the drugs and right now we were all too vulnerable for me to be unconscious.

"What happened?" asked Darcy.

"I know what you're doing," I said softly.

"And what is that?" Her voice was amused.

"You want to distract me while Dad butchers my leg."

"Pretty much."

I laughed.

"Okay." May as well debrief someone. "Baz sent us to Sand Beach, and ironically the beach is more rocks than sand. Beautiful though." I swallowed, wincing as the movement tore open the dry skin on my cracked lips. I licked off the blood. "We thought we found her. She came up to us and introduced herself as Sienna. She seemed legit until the diner. I should have known something was up but I was too focused on finding her, helping Logan." I tried to subdue a cry of pain as Dad snapped more of the stake off.

I failed.

Panting, I closed my eyes, feeling the tears fall out of the sides of my eyes and run into my hairline. I ignored the moisture and cleared my throat. "She offered to show us where to have breakfast, asked a few questions. She said she had some errands to do. So she joined us after a few minutes. I'm beginning to wonder if that's when the real Sienna was switched out. Maybe they saw us as a threat and took her to 'safety'. We did maintain our cover, though. Or so I thought. Not sure how they made us."

"How did you figure out something was going on?"

Another snap and another cry of pain. Darcy gripped my

hand tight, as if the pressure would help ease my pain. Funny enough, it did.

So debriefing her was a relief.

"I sensed it when I touched her. I tried not to show it, but maybe I gave it away. I don't know. When the ShapeChanger left it didn't seem like she was aware that I was onto her. But maybe she's a better actor than I thought."

I was about to lick my lips again when I stopped in time.

"Hold on," said Darcy. She reached into her pocket and I smelled vanilla and strawberry. Lip balm. The woman was an angel of mercy. "There," she said. "All done."

"Thanks." I managed to croak the word out. I coughed again and then continued. "So, after she left in her limo we pretended to look for a place to stay but they must have been watching us. ShapeChangers, Fae, and then a Shadow Mage?" I shook my head.

"Certainly not a coincidence."

"Exactly what I was thinking."

"How did they know?" I croaked.

"It's probably just a case of them watching the agents they feel are the most risk to their op. You being with Logan makes you a prime question mark. They've probably always been worried that Logan would suddenly regain his memory and look for her."

The shadows outside my apartment.

I stiffened, wondering if they were linked to the shadow Mage I'd killed in Maine, or if someone was just using the shadows to watch me.

My gut said two sets of shadows a few hours apart, were far from coincidental.

I was about to fill them in on my shadow stalker when I was cut off by a blinding stab of pain as Dad freed the spike from my leg.

"Honey, I have to pick out the splinters. It's not going to be easy but it will be less painful than removing these things."

Dad bent over my leg, and I stared a little lightheaded at the growing silver in his hair. Then I focused on Darcy and my story.

"The Fae woman. She looked like she'd either been waiting for me, or for someone like me. But what was the purpose of the whole charade? Frighten us off? Were they afraid Sienna had made a connection with us? And if it's just a ruse, then where have they hidden her?"

Darcy nodded. "I suspect you're right. They are probably just watching the perimeter, so to speak. She's well hidden. We just need to find out where."

Dad looked up as he reached for the bandages. "What if she is there, but she isn't."

"Speak in riddles why don't you," I grumbled.

His response was an amused smile. "What if they have her right there, but in a different dimension?"

I nodded. "Okay. That's an option to consider. But if Logan is able to maintain a link with her, then wouldn't that mean she's in this plane? I haven't heard of cross-veil communication even with powerful Mage twins."

Dad frowned. "You have a good point. Scratch what I said."

"I won't scratch it entirely. Maybe they do have the power, but she may be protected. What if there is a glamor or a protective spell either around her or around the area she lives in? That would keep her safe from detection, or at least provide a barrier in order for them to move her if they feel her safety is threatened."

"Right. So what you're suggesting is I go back there and look again." I nodded. "But this time take reinforcements."

"Isn't that dangerous? They know what you look like." Lily stood at the threshold, arms folded, eyes dull as she leaned against the door. She sported torn sleeves, and a bandage on each arm. She gave Darcy a wary, but accepting smile.

"Yes, it is dangerous, but I can go undercover. Change my look."

"Didn't you touch one of them?" she asked dryly.

"I'll make sure I don't touch anyone again." I rolled my eyes.

"You think it's going to be that easy?"

I narrowed my eyes. "What's this about, Lily?"

She tightened her jaw. "It bugs me that you won't acknowledge the danger you'll face. You would have died if it hadn't been for that dagger-with-a-kickass-mojo."

"But, I didn't die."

"And that's supposed to mean what?"

I sighed, paying little attention as Dad began attending to the splinter that ran through my upper arm. I could already feel the flesh in my thigh knitting together. Heat spiked through the wound, regenerating the cells and repairing the damage.

"Look, Lily. I know you're worried."

"Worried? I'm not worried. I'm terrified that you'll end up getting yourself hurt and this time worse. I was there and I couldn't protect you."

I let out a pained laugh. "You weren't there to protect me, Lily."

"Then why did you let me come?" Demand in her posture.

"So that you could be part of this mission to save Sienna. Not for *my* personal protection."

Lily paused, her gaze drifting from my face to my Dad's.

"It's not as if I don't need protection. Ailuros knows I get myself into all sorts of dangerous shit. But you came along *with* me. We were a team so we were responsible for each other, yes. But we were both injured. In case you've forgotten."

Lily smiled wearily, shrugging her shoulder the tiniest bit in response to my words.

"I'm not negating your help, Lily. But you should know that in a situation like that everything is up to chance. We just fight back and hope for the best. We could have both died there today. But that's the risk we took." I paused. "It's the risk we both took."

Lily stepped closer and pretended to be inspecting the wound in my arm. She needed time to absorb my words. Lily was complicated where I was concerned. Declaring a different Alpha is a dangerous thing, and both Lily and Anjelo had done it. Yet she was still welcomed into my father's home, the home of *my* Alpha and she didn't suffer for it.

My father had given her a concession that he wouldn't have granted to any other member of our clan. I looked up at him and his tender expression as he flicked a glance at her, made my heart swell. He was looking out for her too. I only hoped she knew how important she was.

Lily cleared her throat and looked at my father. "Sir." She paused, hesitated. "Um, Kai told me about what you wanted to try and I . . . I think I'll do it. But only if you're the one to look after me."

My ears rang at her words and had I been able to stand I would have thrown my arms around her and given her a giant hug. For all her abrasiveness, Lily could be the sweetest, kindest person I knew. To think she'd once thought of me as the bitch who was trying to take Anjelo away from her.

I suppressed a laugh at the memory as Dad tilted his head, his expression serious. "I understand how much courage it would have taken to agree to this, Lily. And I promise I'll take good care of you. No less than if you were my own child." His tone lowered and her eyelashes fluttered as she looked up at him.

She nodded, either too terrified, or too emotional to respond.

Dad proceeded to administer to my shoulder wound and Lily ended up stepping over to help Darcy mop up the blood. For some reason the arm wound hurt more, and bled more, but I didn't get too much time to think about it. Dad moved something within the wound that sent searing agony through me and before I could gasp or cry or scream, I passed out.

Thank Ailuros.

CHAPTER 25

When I came to, Lily was nowhere to be found, and my visitor was the last person I expected to see.

Tara sat beside the window, eyes on a dusty old novel. The room was silent, apart from the rustle of the pages as she turned them, and my irregular breathing of course.

I blinked, feeling the lashes crinkle painfully on my lids. Strange how you feel everything on a microscopic level when injured. Tara shifted, laying the book down on the table beside her, the soft silk of her rose gold cowl-necked gown whispering against her skin.

As she walked to the bed, my heart warmed as I scanned the room.

Greer's old bedroom. What would she have thought about her bed being used as a hospital gurney? The Greer I'd met before she'd died would have approved.

"Hey," said Tara, the curve of her lips soft and benevolent. She moved to sit on the bed, curling up next to me, paying no attention to the possible creasing of her regal robes. "I leave you alone for five minutes and you go and get yourself killed?"

I snorted, then inhaled hard from the ache it caused. "I'd say you should see the other guy, but there's nothing left of him."

She laughed and I joined in, and ended up coughing like I had lung disease.

"Hey, calm down. I don't want to be the one who finally flips your switch."

"Just try. I won't go down without a fight."

A wary glance at the door.

"Any news?" I asked.

She nodded. "This time our lab has similar results to yours. And we found the origin of the poison. I sent the reports to your phone, but essentially the toxin has a Fae origin." She frowned. "Or rather it has had Fae influence during its extraction process."

I touched her hand. "That doesn't mean that the perpetrator is Fae, Tara. And even if it is, they may have a good reason." I'd learned as much from Darcy. "Don't go around mistrusting everyone. But also, don't go trusting everyone around you."

She offered a regal wave. "Don't worry. I haven't been that trusting in a while."

"And Elan?" Just the thought of the frosty Fae made my jaw harden.

Tara pursed her lips. "Not a thing. He's off doing something in the Winterlands, so I'm not sure what he's up to exactly." She sighed, an air of defeat enveloping her. "He's either clean and honest as the rain, or he's too damned good to give anything away."

"Not all rain is honest."

"Huh?" she asked, clearly confused.

"Some rain is poisonous. Acid rain?"

"Ugh, Kai." She rolled her eyes. "Sometimes I have to wonder if you have all your marbles in there." She poked a finger against my forehead.

We both laughed.

"So any ideas on who could have poisoned the Tree and why?" I got back to business.

"I've been talking to a few people. There was a small uprising a few years back when I was still in Chicago. An outlying faction, mostly Winter Court, wanted to reassert their control over the other planes. They felt their old ways were better for the earth, and that most of the worlds would do well by returning to the Fae-controlled past."

I shuddered even though it hurt. "Who would want that?"

Tara looked guilty.

"Don't tell me you agree with them?" I asked, shocked. I had to force myself to breathe because believing Tara could be behind this was too much to handle. I was certain my brain or my heart would explode.

Or both.

Tara laughed, shaking her head. "A long time ago I did. I was young and naive. I'd been taught the old ways from birth and that's a long damned time to be brainwashed. It's why the Fae court demanded my return. They thought I'd be a proponent for the cause, but I think I disappointed them." She fell silent as her eyes stared off somewhere distant. Then she shook the thoughts off. "They'd expected a different type of leader. They didn't get it."

"I should hope not," I mumbled, remembering too late that I was talking to royalty. I snuck a guilty glance at her. "Sorry."

She snorted, staring at me down her slim nose. "You've never been sorry in your life. Now stop treating me like a fragile queen and talk to me like a friend. What can I do?"

My Tara was back.

I shifted against the pillows. "Do you know of any Fae living in Sand Beach, Maine? Not too far from Bar Harbor."

Tara pursed her lips, her eyes again taking on a faraway look. "I'm not sure. I'll have to check." Something she wasn't telling me? Then she gave a nod. "Yes, let me get back to you on that. Text me the address if you have it."

"I'm not sure that the address will help. I highly doubt that they were living in that house. If I were them I wouldn't. Or am I over-estimating their smarts?"

Tara sighed. "You're right. But our records are precise. Even if a Fae doesn't report his location we have scryers who find them within seconds. So we'll find them."

"Okay, can you also see what you have on any ShapeChangers and shadow mages who have a connection with Fae, or have a rep for causing trouble?"

"Consider it done. This all sounds rather mysterious, Kai. What have you been up to?"

I gave Tara the rundown on Logan, his sister, our trip to Maine and our inevitable mauling at the hands of the elusive shadow man despite the special dagger.

"You have the Glyhs?" was all she said, her eyes wide with surprise.

I scowled. "Out of everything that I just told you, that's your takeaway?"

Tara rolled her eyes. "Okay . . . Oh-dear-what-a-terrible-ordeal-I'm-so-glad-you're-alive-and-well-hope-you-recover-soon." She lifted her hands. "Happy? Now, how did you get a hold of the dagger?"

I shook my head and tried to smother my laughter. Tara cracked me up.

"The dagger has been in our family for decades. Dad said something about it being entrusted to us for safekeeping after a particularly brutal battle."

Tara nodded, "The battle of Ghila. It was a gruesome thing. I remember looking at the dead and thinking it was like a sea of bloodied corpses. Such needless death."

My eyes widened. "I keep forgetting you've lived so long." I watched her as she shrugged, as if living for eight hundred years was nothing. Walkers are long-lived but we have nothing on the Fae.

"I was alive to witness the massacre." She didn't look like she was happy she'd been there. "I'm just glad the Glyhs is safe. The Fae didn't deserve to possess such a weapon. I remember my mother . . . so furious when she couldn't find it."

"The dagger belonged to your mother?"

Tara snorted. "Only after she stole it from an Ancient." Tara sighed. "The Glyhs has a long history of destruction. Not the dagger causing it but people who want it. I suggest you keep your possession of the weapon a secret."

"Too late. The Prince of Shadows must have seen it. He did explode in front of my eyes, so I'm hoping the dagger terminated him for good. But, if he was working with someone, or channeling a master, then someone will know about the dagger. Although . . . That is a big fat load of assumptions."

"Assumptions are dangerous, so you be careful. There's no telling what would happen should the location of the Glyhs become public knowledge."

I shifted, tired despite my rest.

"I should go," said Tara giving me a worried glance.

"Before you do. One thing I meant to talk to you about for a while now."

"Shoot," she said, smiling.

I cleared my throat. "So I've been given a piece of information that's very important."

"And?" She tilted her head. "Can I help you with it?"

"Maybe." I inhaled, then recited the words.

In the DarkWorld, when the night is black,
When darkness looms, to swallow you whole,
A quintet of courage will bring forth hope,
And reach across the planes to save heart and soul

She who shreds the Veils and she who hunts the Demons,
She who mend Minds and she who speaks beyond the Grave
And she who bears the face of all - these five shall be as one.
For they are the saviors of the DarkWorld, they are the Ni'amh...

"OH," she said sitting back. "I see."

I scowled. "You knew."

She sighed and leaned closer. "The Fae are long-lived, near immortal. Sometimes we are privy to things that should remain out of our control. In this instance, intervention is not acceptable."

"Because you're part of it?"

She inclined her head. "That and because people I care for are part of this Fate."

"Then why the long face."

"Because where the Prophecy goes, death follows."

"Oh. I see."

She looked at me sadly. "I'm here if you need me. If any of you need me. But all I can do is my part. Nothing more."

"I understand."

We sat there for a few minutes, absorbing the ramifications of our shared fate.

Then Tara got to her feet, smoothing the front of her dress, making the gold thread blink against the light. "I'll send those reports to our forensics people. See what they can come up with. Right now I think we are left with *leg* work rather than forensic work to make any sense of this case."

"We'll figure this out. You, however, need to get yourself better and find this girl. Whoever they are, they think she's important. To me that means she needs our help. They want her for something, and with this much maneuvering, they don't want to play double dutch in the sunshine."

I nodded. As much as I agreed with her, I was beginning to fade.

Tara patted my shoulder gently, taking care not to jostle my injured arm, then moved soundlessly to her feet.

I was asleep before she stepped through the Veil.

a few hours later I awoke fresh, though still in a good amount of pain. Enough to remind me that despite my walker DNA, I was still very much breakable.

A pinching in my arm caused me to raise both eyebrows. While unconscious, my father had inserted an IV drip. I knew I should be grateful that he'd thought of my health when I couldn't, but right now I needed so badly to pee that I groaned loudly as I sat up and fumbled with the needle.

"Are you okay?" a voice asked, the sudden sound making me yelp and almost lose control of my bladder.

"Shit! What the hell is wrong with you? You almost made me wet my pants," I yelled, furious that Justin had found that particular moment to come visit. Furious, too, that the shock had caused me to pull the needle out from my hand with more force than wise. Blood streamed across the back of my hand and I grabbed the edge of my t-shirt and used it to staunch the flow.

My bladder throbbed, and I pushed to my feet as Justin moved away from the window and into the light from the hallway that cut a path across the room.

The room was dark, which is why I'd had no idea he was

there. Not to mention he had Alpha mojo working for him too. That made me feel more than uncomfortable and I wondered what that said about my feelings.

I left him chuckling as I entered the en-suite. I used the toilet, then washed up and studied my reflection. Although I was grateful that I was wearing clothes, they were much too minimal for me to be comfortable with my visitor.

A navy singlet, bra-less naturally, and a pair of black boyleg shorts, courtesy of the spare set of nightclothes I'd left in my old room. The attire left my arms and legs bare, revealing purple and yellow bruises near both bandaged injuries.

Someone had removed the high ponytail and brushed my hair so that it lay straight and flat against my head. Probably Lily.

There were dark circles under my eyes, and even the deep emerald had faded to a lackluster green. I tucked my hair behind my ears and headed back to the room, taking each step slowly and carefully.

Perching on the edge of the mattress, I scowled at Justin who now sat cross-legged on the other side of the bed. As if he belonged there.

"Can you make yourself useful and help me?" I snapped.

I heard the ice in my voice and knew I sounded like a bitch but I ignored it. And strangely so did Justin.

He got to his knees and crawled over to my side.

"What do you need?" His lip curled suggestively.

"Keep your dirty thoughts to yourself please, or I'll call someone else to help."

He raised his hands in defense. "Okay. What can I help with?"

I pointed at my bandaged arm. "Help me get it off."

"You think that's wise?"

"I don't particularly care about wisdom. I want to see how it's healing. Now."

"Fine. But I will tell your father I helped under duress."

I snorted. "Big strong Alpha afraid of one little female?"

He shook his head slowly as his hands made deft work of unwinding the bandage. "Kai, you have no idea how frightening you can be. Add Alpha to the mix and you're a bomb waiting to explode."

"You make me sound volatile." I flinched as his fingers touched the bare skin of my arms.

Justin snatched his hands away. "Did I hurt you?"

"No. I'm okay. It's not your fault. The wound isn't fully healed." I didn't tell him that it was his touch that had made me flinch. Now, I wanted to stay as far away from him as possible.

He was my past, Logan my present and future.

But that didn't mean that just because a relationship was over the two parties stopped having feelings for each other. I wished that I'd never come to that realization.

Ever.

I didn't want permission to feel anything for him. I didn't want a reason for it to be okay that I thought of him as special. It should be wrong.

It *was* wrong.

I shook my head as he lifted the edge of the bandage to reveal the wound. Dad had coated it with a layer of BioHeal, a thin silicone/water blend that was infused with nutrients, minerals and Vitamin E.

Through the transparent layer, I could see the raw wound, moist and healing but still horrific proof of what had happened. Not often a girl got impaled with a stake.

Thank Ailuros I wasn't a vamp.

"Want me to help with that?" Justin pointed at my thigh and I gave him a withering glare. He checked and repositioned himself, lying back on the pillows beside mine. He rested his head on his hands and stared up at the ceiling.

"What do you think you're doing?"

"I'm keeping an eye on the patient."

"I hardly think that's necessary. I'm healing fine, thank you."

He managed a shrug, even while lying down, and I had to admit the man was a magnificent specimen. Any girl would be proud to have him as a life mate.

A trickle of unease filtered down my spine. "I'm not going to fall asleep with you lying next to me."

He spoke with a smile that bordered on sinful. "Why not? Do I make you uncomfortable?" We both knew what he meant but I didn't bite.

"No. You snore. I won't be able to get any rest."

"I do not snore." He looked appalled at the suggestion, as if I'd called him a serial killer or worse, a poacher.

"You do. Even Sara admitted it, so go away. I need my rest. I don't have time to lose sleep because of you."

I flicked my fingers, shooing him away, hoping he'd leave fast. My eyes were already drooping and if he delayed any longer I really would end up falling asleep with him next to me.

And that was not going happen.

Thankfully, he relented and scooted to the end of the bed, standing and arching into a lazy stretch. "You get better, Kai. I don't like seeing you hurt."

"It's my job, Justin. Getting hurt is part of the deal."

"Well sue me if I dislike seeing you in pain." He headed to the door, turning on the threshold to flash me a toothy smile. "Sweet dreams."

And then he was gone, leaving me shaking my head, unable to decide whether the sadness I felt was because he'd left or just due to fatigue.

I chose to believe it was fatigue.

CHAPTER 27

When I woke up later, I felt a whole lot better. And so did my wounds.

Someone had come while I'd slept, and stuck a light plaster onto my arm and I smiled. No matter how hard I try to rebel, someone always tried to keep me in line.

I sat up slowly, testing the reaction of both my head and body. Both seemed agreeable to movement. The IV was gone, needle and all, and I was free to get out of the bed and move around.

After washing up and combing my fingers through my hair, I rummaged in Greer's drawers and found a pair of ancient tights and an oversized cable knit sweater which made me shake my head and smile.

Now I knew where my favorite old sweater had gotten to. Greer had been known for sneaking off with my stuff, the reason for many of our spats when we were little.

Much warmer and far more decent, despite being unable to locate shoes, I headed for Logan's room.

The door hung open, and the room lay shrouded in darkness. Logan still slept, his condition unchanged. Despite talking to him, despite his connection with his sister, he remained the same.

I swallowed the rising tide of despair that threatened to overwhelm me, and forced myself to head downstairs. And was surprised to find Darcy pacing in the living room, her forehead a blur of lines.

"What's up?" I asked, moving closer to the fire.

She glanced up at me, winding a long lock of her blonde hair around her finger. "I'm worried about Logan's condition."

"What's changed?" I hadn't seen any difference.

"Nothing. That's the problem." Darcy sighed, her eyes darkening as she turned from the fire and began to pace. "Even after talking to him there's been no change. I expected some kind of reaction . . . Even a little."

"I know how you feel. And all we can do is try." I shifted to face her, feeling her emotions wash over me. I hesitated, then said, "What is this about?"

She lifted her lashes. "I . . . *I* did this to him." She stabbed a stiff finger into her chest twice, her ragged voice broadcasting her inner turmoil. I had to admire that she didn't hide the truth of her feelings. "I put him in this place. He wouldn't be suffering if it wasn't for me."

I shook my head and touched her arm. "Darcy. You know better than that. Had it not been for you, Logan would never have known he had a sister. He'd have never known that he wasn't alone in this world. He has *you* to thank for that."

I tried to meet her eyes but she shrugged my hand off and took two steps away as if she wanted to run. Then she took a breath and turned. "You don't understand."

Her voice shuddered as she shook her head, as if she knew I totally didn't get it. Her tone hardened as she continued, "If it wasn't for me, he'd be at peace. He'd never have regained any of his memories if I'd only done what I was told." Darcy's voice, her expression was bitter and angry.

I laughed softly. "That's the stupidest thing I've heard to date, and let me assure you that in recent months I've heard some pretty stupid things." I stepped closer to her, face-to-face, but she didn't flinch, just stared at me, confusion making her eyebrows wiggle.

"You don't know what you're saying. I was given a set of instructions and I took it upon myself to ignore them. I let my personal feelings cloud my judgment and now a man's last moments on this earth will be spoiled, ruined because I couldn't obey the goddamned rules." Her voice had risen to a pained cry.

I laid a hand on her shoulder. "No. If he were able to, he'd thank you. You've given him, even if it is for a brief time, the joy of knowing that he isn't alone, that he still has a family. He would thank you." I shook her shoulder. "You hear me?"

She gave a tiny smile but I could see she wasn't convinced.

"Darcy, by allowing Logan to regain some of his memories you've given him a chance to find her. And us a chance to rescue her. Someone is determined to keep her hidden. She's important, so important that they'd ruin lives, even kill to keep her away from us. From him. Anybody would be grateful for what you did. You risked your life to allow Logan the joy of one day finding out the truth. He will thank you when he recovers."

"If he recovers."

"Even if he doesn't recover, don't you think he'll leave this life happy he found her, and grateful to you for helping him do that?" I shook her shoulder again, this time a little harder. "At least allow yourself to see that some good came from your actions."

"Okay." She looked away, the fire drawing her gaze. And as she stared at it, flames danced in her eyes and she let out a sigh. I felt a little weight lift from my heart. In trying to convince her of why her actions had been for the best, I'd allowed myself to see it too.

I sighed as well. "I was so angry with you."

That got her attention and her eyes snapped to my face.

"I was furious that you wiped his mind, furious that you allowed him to be tormented by returning memories, furious that you didn't tell him the truth earlier." Her eyes shuttered and her shoulders dropped the tiniest fraction. "And then I saw Logan's face when he made contact with her, the joy he experienced when his mind first touched his sister's. That's something nobody can put a price on. And you did that for him."

Silence fell around us and the crackling of the fire was a gentle interruption, as if it too understood the gravity of the moment.

Darcy looked hopeful and I smiled, only a small one because that was all I could manage, but I could tell it was enough.

"I've forgiven you, but the hurt hasn't gone." I sighed and gave her an encouraging smile. "But that's for me to deal with. You just need to know that I am so very grateful that you helped him find her. And now, for everything you're doing to help him."

She shook her head, looking so lost. "But I can't promise that I can help him fully recover. That is what I'm terrified of."

"You realize we can't expect you to do that?" She looked confused. "How can we ask you to wave your hands and magically make him better? We use what we can and take it one step at a time."

Finally, she nodded jerkily, then gave a tight smile. "Yes, and the next step is to see what progress he's made."

I turned on my heel and strode to the door. At the threshold I glanced back at her, studying her face, profile backlit in fiery gold. "You coming?"

She started then stared at me. "Yes. I'm coming. But not until you get something to eat."

"Dear Ailuros, is every person in my life out to baby me?"

"If we don't, who will?" she asked, grinning.

I failed to come up with an appropriate response.

CHAPTER 28

I sat beside Darcy as she hunched over, and concentrated on Logan's mind. Her eyes were closed and her fingers pressed gently at his temples.

When Darcy stiffened I leaned closer. Her eyes opened eerily, and she stared at me. Blind.

"He's touched her mind a few times although she was frightened at first." She smiled tenderly. "He was very sweet. Tried to ease her into the joining of their minds, careful not to frighten her."

I waited, holding my breath as she spoke.

"He's seen the place through her eyes. He was confused at first because it wasn't the beach he'd sent you to, although he somehow knew that he hadn't been wrong on that end. She'd been there." She paused and swallowed, tilting her head to one side. "This time he saw a barren land, all craggy dark mountains and red skies. The rivers are red, and their sun hangs low and bloody on the horizon, as if about to explode."

I worried what that meant for Sienna but Darcy said, "The girl is ignorant of everything around her. She's living in the palace, a human servant of the queen. She's quiet, and unassuming. Unless it comes to her knowledge of weapons technology. She believes she is without power. Humans are mere chattels in this land, and have no freedom beyond their master's needs. But it has been known to happen that outlanders – as they are called – sometimes achieve high standing in the community."

All the more reason to find the place and restore the people's freedom, I thought.

"Funny thing, and this is something even Logan finds odd, though they believe her to be human and powerless, she is guarded at all times when she leaves the palace.

"She's privy to much that goes on at the court, attends the queen almost constantly, has minimal contact with others. She's intelligent, and very learned. And from what he saw she's a master tactician and the queen takes her opinion on board. Apparently she's proven herself in past battles and skirmishes. She's still treated as a servant, though." Darcy let out a soft laugh. "Logan is worried that she's in danger. He's happy that she can take care of herself but she doesn't use her power."

"Odd, considering she was so devastatingly powerful not too long ago." I hadn't realized I'd said that aloud.

"Logan thought so too," said Darcy. "Seems her memory was also tampered with. She can't recall anything about her past with him and their parents."

"I'm beginning to wonder if his parents were their real ones."

"The thought had crossed his mind but it's not something he wants to consider seriously. His feelings for his mother are too strong. But if that is the case, he'll have to address it at some point."

"Any distinguishable features of this world? Buildings, land formations, people?" I asked.

Darcy frowned as if trying to grasp at an elusive thought. "He was trying to be as observant as possible. The mountains are obsidian black, and dangerously sharp. Unscalable to his eye, but he can't be sure."

"Doesn't sound very hospitable."

"No. But the palace is stunning. Sienna and Logan both think it's a thing of beauty. Everything is made of obsidian, walls, roofs, parapets, towers, all obsidian, gleaming like black glass. Only the streets are paved with black stone mined from the mountains."

Darcy seemed lost in the details of the world and I had to admit I was fascinated too. What I pictured in my mind was a city of beauty and danger, that is both home and prison to Logan's sister.

"There are strange outcroppings on the mountaintops, and around the city."

Darcy paused her forehead creasing as her blank eyes suddenly cleared and I found her staring at me shocked.

"Holy crap I think I know where she is."

"Where?" I urged her to answer.

Though she seemed disconnected from Logan's mind, she wasn't listening to me. "I can't believe I didn't realize it. I've seen it before in the mind of a Drakyr. The statues were the giveaway." She waved her hands above her head. "Gigantic statues of women with towering crowns and even taller wings. "Dragons, Kai. Sienna is being held in the great city of Dyr."

"Dear Ailuros," I whispered.

Dyr, the mother city of the Dragonlands, the home of the great Queen of the Drakyr.

"But isn't-"

Darcy cut me off. "The Drakyr currently have no queen. To be queen, the dragon female has to be a very powerful alpha. The most powerful of all. And queens are always born paired with a twin brother. Powerful twins are born, the female becoming the queen, the male her General. The twins feed off each other's powers and it is said that the male is often just as powerful as the female hence the whole leading the armies thing. The last queen of Drakys was Shrya. She was killed two decades ago - her newborn babies too."

"Twins?" I asked, already knowing the answer.

Darcy nodded. "Right now, Sienna is attending Shrya's sister Lyra. The substitute queen has no alpha power but she remains ruling the land until a new queen is found. What's worse is that Drakys needs a new queen and fast."

"Why?" I asked, a little distracted with the thought of twins. Sienna and Logan were twins.

Twins born two decades ago.

"Because the red sun of Drakys is directly connected to the power of the dragon queen. She is its keeper and protector. It's said that the power of their sun lives within the queen and since Drakys has no queen the sun is doomed."

"Talk about a buzz kill. This story was going well until now. Dead queens and dying suns?" The story was so bizarre that I actually believed it. The truth was usually the craziest version of the story.

"There's some kind of ritual held in the largest volcano of Drakys where the queen imbues all her power into a giant egg. And when the power is returned to her, the sun glows brighter."

"And without a queen to complete the ritual, the land is doomed." I said the words unable to comprehend how devastating that reality must be for the people. "And they haven't found a new queen in all this time?"

Darcy shook her head. "There is only one queen at any point in time. If the twins are out there somewhere and are not found, a new set of children will be born only when the living ones cease to exist."

"And while they're out there do they know their destiny?"

"Not if they're undiscovered. But if they did exist, they'd have been found by now. The Drakyr armies have a dedicated squad that works solely on finding the next queen. They have the ability to detect the power. No matter how far they have to go, they will eventually find the twins."

"So the sixty-four-thousand-dollar question is 'What do

Sienna and Logan have to do with this?" Darcy and I stared at each other. "Could they be the undiscovered twins?"

Darcy hesitated then began to shake her head.

And I nodded in agreement. "And of course, if Sienna was the one they would have discovered it by now. She's been right there all this while. No way she's the future queen right under their noses."

"Unless—"

"Unless her memory has been tampered with and her powers bound."

Darcy's mouth hung open and I got to my feet. I paced three steps then turned and went three steps back. Then I looked over at Logan.

"He can sometimes hear us, you know."

"Then hopefully he heard what we said and does what he needs to find out more about Sienna and the palace." I thought I saw Logan's eyelids twitch but I couldn't be certain.

Then Darcy straightened and looked at me. "So what's the plan?"

"The plan is to find out more about Drakys and the situation there, then find a way to get in."

Darcy nodded then clapped her hands together lightly. "Then Sienna can help Logan recover. I truly believe they are linked in some inexplicable way, and that without her help he may not regain consciousness." I swallowed hard.

We had to find her.

"And if she is the real queen, which is highly unlikely and pure speculation on our part, then she can hone her skills and return to retake her kingdom with the support of the Elders."

"Come what may, we bring Sienna home."

I appreciated her positivity.

It made up for my complete lack.

CHAPTER 29

Pacing the patterned carpet of Horner's office, I scowled and said, "How long does it take to get clearance?"

He shook his grayed head as if I was an errant child impatient for a reward. "It takes as long as it takes. We have to wait for the Elders to decide. But don't worry, Kai. I believe it's merely a formality. They will grant you the clearance."

There was a cadence to his speech that I hadn't yet identified, and it bugged me. But his certainty was reassuring and I stopped pacing and faced him, folding my arms tightly.

"Sure, it's just a formality. But I can't afford the time it's taking."

I was grumbling but I didn't care. Horner had wanted me on his Elite team, even made me a senior agent, so he had to put up with me.

I'd arrived forty minutes ago and considering I'd been waiting for clearance for thirty minutes, my mind kept entertaining every possible scenario that involved me turning up late for something.

Late to save Sienna, late to save Logan.

Somewhere in the pit of my stomach a sense of anxiety

bubbled, filling my gut and making me sick enough that bile rose in my throat.

The phone rang, the sound shrill and sharp enough to cut ice. And eardrums.

I jumped, unable to control my response. I glanced up quickly at Horner, hoping he hadn't seen my reaction.

Horner's attention was on his tablet, and he'd already lifted his phone from its ancient cradle. The man insisted on using a telephone that harked back to a time when telegraphs had only just gone out of fashion.

He spoke a few words - a language that was foreign to me, yet offered me a strange comfort. His tone was respectful, his expression so neutral that I had no idea whether the council had approved or not.

I was antsy, wanted to demand the result, but I forced myself to wait.

Horner thanked the caller, then slowly placed the phone back onto the cradle with a soft click. He leaned back in the chair and rested his elbows on the armrest, pyramiding his fingers.

"They have approved," he said, a small smile on his lips. I guess he had the right to be self-satisfied.

I took a couple steps forward and sat in one of the chairs in front of him. It suited the décor of the place, one of two wing-back chairs, in a striped cream and brown fabric, another throw-back to an era long passed. To say it was comfortable, was a bit of a stretch, but I wasn't here to get comfortable.

"So?" I raised an eyebrow. My arms were folded and the finger of one hand tapped steadily against my arm. Horner's eyes settled on the moving finger, then shifted to watch my face.

Then he cleared his throat. "Access to Drakys has always been limited. Free travel across the Veil into the lands has never been allowed, not by the Drakyr and not by the Supreme High Council. As of now, there are only three entrances to Drakys. One of those locations is within the lighthouse on the shore of Sand Beach."

I stiffened and stared at Horner, openmouthed. "We were so close and we had no idea." Then I paused, eyes narrowed. "They were protecting the access to Drakys. But were they also protecting the girl? Or was that only a coincidence?" The questions flowed and I suspected that most of the answers would be mere conjecture.

Horner shrugged but he didn't change his contemplative position. "It could be either one of those. But for security purposes you need to assume the worst."

Sounds ominous.

"So you're going to give me access to that portal?" I asked, questioning the wisdom of accessing Drakys from a location in which I'd almost been killed.

He was shaking his head. "The Elders don't believe it is in anyone's interest to have you risk your life accessing that particular portal." He got to his feet, sending the armchair swiveling behind him.

Horner walked to the floor-to-ceiling bookshelves on the left wall. The shelving was ornate, mahogany with a glossy veneer that made it look more ancient than his telephone.

He opened one of the drawers and retrieved a small black box. Returning, he placed it carefully in front of me.

I reached for it, opening the box just as carefully. Inside, lay a carved bronze disk. A portal key not much different to the one I'd had fashioned for me by the High Priestess of the Death-Talkers to give me access to the Graylands.

I frowned, lifting the key from the silk-lined box. "Doesn't this need blood to allow the bearer to move through the Veil?"

I knew because Lady Kira had bled me to give life to the portal key. Keys were created specific to one person only.

Horner looked at the key as I weighed it in the palm of my

hand. "Most keys are fashioned that way. But there was a time, centuries ago, when the keys were more flexible."

Flexible? "You mean the bearers could change?"

Horner nodded then lifted the silk fabric that covered the base of the box. Beneath lay a silver knife, its blade deadly sharp, and I knew. "The keys could be recoded with the blood of the new bearer?"

Horner lifted the knife and stared at its point. "There are very few of these universal keys left. The DeathTalkers hunted them down and destroyed them. I doubt they know about the existence of this one."

"But why did they destroy them?" I'd never heard this particular story before.

"Across the planes, people were taking advantage of the flexibility of the keys. Agents of the different races were moving from plane to plane wreaking havoc. Portal keys that are so flexible they allow thieves to cross the veil unchecked."

"But demons move through the veil as they please."

Even I knew that.

He nodded. "They are *of* the Veil. In a sense the in-Between *is* their plane. Hard to stop them from residing within it. Besides, demons leave a trace of themselves behind. If they commit crimes then they are tracked, found and punished."

"Including ghosts?"

Horner laughed. "You and I both know that ghosts are particularly hard to punish. Beyond exorcism."

I smiled. Even the big bad Supremes couldn't punish an evil spirit without ending their existence in totality. I didn't feel bad though. Beyond the Graylands, lay the land of light. An existence of the soul that is said to be beyond happiness and joy. But the dead who commit the worst, the most unforgivable crimes, once exorcised, move to a plane of nothingness. An existence feared by all paranormals. An existence that humans cannot comprehend.

My boss shifted, his stiff coat rustling, then handed me the knife. He pointed to the seal.

"Okay then. I guess it's time."

He cleared his throat as I held my hand over the seal. "Of the other two portals, only one is accessible from this plane." He watched as I sliced the heel of my hand open with the barely visible blade of the knife

"So where exactly is this access point?" I fisted my hand, forcing the flow to increase.

Blood dripped onto the seal, pooling along the crevices and carvings until every valley and hollow was filled with blood. A searing heat began to rise from the metal and a red smoke rose as the blood began to boil, then burned off the surface slowly.

Oddly enough no odor of burnt blood emanated from the boiling portal key. At last, every last vestige of my blood was gone, absorbed by the metal itself.

The ritual complete, Horner sighed and walked around the table, taking a seat in his chair and sliding it back into place.

"The Mendenhall Glacier."

CHAPTER 30

My eyes widened.

I huffed. "Guess I'm going to have to dress warmly?"

He nodded. "The third entrance is top-secret. Need to know only. Right now, the glacier access is all I can give you. Use the portal key. And you enter Drakys as an official envoy of the Elders."

I stared at him, shocked, sliding forward on my seat. "Why did the Elders think that was necessary?"

It seemed unprecedented for them to support me in this. Could the whole search-and-rescue be of more importance than I knew?

Horner averted his gaze, concentrating on the screen of his tablet. The irony of the modern device sitting right beside his ancient telephone did not escape me.

He said, "I requested the envoy position to sweeten the deal . . . so to say. But from what I've been told, the Elders believe it really would be the most advantageous route for both you and them. Our treaty with Drakys is on dangerous ground. It has been for the last two decades, considering there is no residing monarch on the throne. There is much danger within the land, and we cannot trust that the current Queen will continue to uphold the treaty."

"So despite the treaty, I will still be in danger?"

Horner nodded. "I wish I could ensure your safety, but unfortunately I can't. We haven't had an envoy enter Drakys in at least five years."

"Why is that?"

The air between us simmered with tension.

"Because the last envoy was killed under suspicious circumstances." Horner's eyes were hooded with shadows, regret, fear. "We could never be entirely certain how he died. If he was assassinated, if it was an accident, or if he brought his death onto himself."

I cleared my throat.

"But we can't sit here wondering about something that happened in the past. The only hope for saving the girl is to enter Drakys and find her. If you're telling me that an envoy will gain easier access to the palace, then I will take that, no questions asked, despite the danger."

He stared at me for a moment then reached for the tablet beside his hand. He swiped the app open then handed it to me. "This is a copy of the letter from the Elders, declaring you as our official envoy to Drakys. I will have the jumper give you the original when he takes you to the portal. The Elders also require that you act on their behalf, both officially and unofficially. Officially, you will attempt to regain the Queen's trust, and put forward a proposition that will allow us to provide them with an income again. And to provide us with access to their lands. A situation of mutual benefit if you will."

Interesting turn of events. "So how are we giving them an income?"

Horner sat back again, rocking in his chair. "The mining industry on Drakys has been stagnant over the last five years.

The envoy that we had placed with them was responsible for overseeing mining of Erulite. It's a rare mineral that we have used for centuries to support the effectiveness of our ammunition."

"It's a poison?"

"No. It acts as a carrier, ensuring the effectiveness of the ammunition. In the old days we used to dip our arrows in a muscle relaxant, then in the Erulite. It helped us to avoid the use of deadly force. And allowed us to use less poison with greater result."

I nodded. "So, a small amount of poison goes a long way. Less pillaging of our flora. Less damage to the suspect." I could see the benefits. I knew that Tara had always used an enhancer that amplified the toxins she put in my bullets. Could that have been Erulite?

"After our envoy's death, the Drakyr refused to have any other representatives of the Supreme High Council on their land. The mines were shut down, and of course their income ceased. We know they suffer for it, but the queen refused to budge."

"So I'm supposed to convince them that it's a good idea to begin the mining again?"

Horner nodded although he still looked troubled. "You will need to do your very best to convince them."

"But why not just send a second envoy and plead our case?" I asked.

"The body of the envoy was sent back to us in pieces." Horner sighed. The look he gave me was one of regret, as if he suspected that he was sending me to my death. "The Supreme High Council was very afraid that sending anyone to Drakys would needlessly endanger their lives."

I nodded, fully aware of what was going on. "And now, considering I have no choice but to go, the Elders can't ignore the opportunity."

Horner looked guilty on behalf of the Elders.

"I understand, and really it's no problem. I'll do what I can to help."

"There is one other thing."

I raised an eyebrow.

"Part of the mission is to find out what, if anything, the queen is doing for income. The Drakyr had always depended on us to help sustain their people. Their lands have never been bountiful and they'd always depended on mining and trade to boost their coffers. Since the death of the last Queen, Drakys had pulled away from all their trading connections. The Elders believe they are still trading with someone, but we have been unable to ascertain who."

"Who stands the most to gain?" I asked, curious now.

"Anyone who needs the power of the DragonFyr." Horner's smile was cold, unfeeling. "The power of the average dragon is an asset to anyone who wants to manipulate it. But the power of the queen is incomparable."

"And the power of the twins?" I asked, beginning to understand as Horner's expression hardened at my words.

He didn't need to answer.

CHAPTER 31

*B*ack at the house in Tukats, I sat at Logan's side, hoping he could hear me.

"I'm going to Drakys to find her, Logan. Darcy and Nerina will be here with you."

I smiled at him, and my heart ached when he didn't open his eyes.

"What we need for you to do is keep in contact with Sienna. Keep talking to her. Make her understand that the two of you deserve to know each other. And while you do that keep trying to find out more about where she is. I spoke to Horner today, and he said the queen may be in contact with other paranormal councils. The Elders are hoping she's not up to something nefarious and since Sienna is close to her maybe what she sees could be important."

I sighed and traced his cheek. "But most importantly you need to help her remember. I'm going to try and get her out but you need to convince her that I'm safe. That when I come for her she should join me. I'm entering as an envoy of the Elders and I'll get access to the castle and to the queen herself so I should encounter Sienna fairly quickly. She needs to trust me, Logan. Please make sure she knows I'm there to help her."

I leaned over and kissed his forehead.

Dear Ailuros, please keep him safe. Please bring him back to me.

I sent up the prayer, putting every iota of my emotions into the words. I wasn't the bargaining type. The goddess aided us out of love, not in exchange for trifles we may offer her or any bargains she would see fit to enter into.

She was an eternal goddess, who watched over us, gave us the strength to pass through each of the trials that life brought. I could only hope that she would hear my plea and send Logan the strength that he needed.

With a deep sigh I pushed to my feet and stared at his sleeping face. His eyelids flickered and I stiffened, holding my breath.

Had I just imagined the movement?

When his lids shivered again, I was certain he was trying to tell me something. I hoped he was saying that he'd heard me, that he'd do as I asked as best he could.

I left the room and walked slowly downstairs, my heart aching. I hated that I was so helpless, so unable to save him from this nightmare.

In the kitchen, I found Darcy, Lily and Nerina, gathered at the table, their expressions expectant. Each had a mug of something in front of them, and all had failed to finish their drinks.

"You ready?" asked Darcy, spotting me first. The others looked up.

I didn't miss Lily's accusing glare.

I nodded, pasting a smile on my face. "Ready as I'll ever be."

Nerina scowled, her pale features tightening. "I have to be honest with you. I think this is way too dangerous. I completely understand why you need to be the one to go, but why do you have to go alone?" She gave Darcy an accusing glance from which I understood that the two had disagreed on the necessity for me to travel without company.

I sighed and sank into the nearest empty chair. On each side of the table sat a friend, and they were all waiting for my answer. "Because that's the only way I'm allowed. And because even jumpers can't travel into the Dragonlands. The Veil around their plane is much denser than the other realms. Only the strongest jumpers can get through, but the trip weakens them too much. I won't put Mel in danger."

Darcy nodded. "And if Kai took someone else with her, they'd have to go in secret because neither the Elders nor the Queen and her court can know. And that would increase the danger. Besides, what difference would one more person make?"

"The difference would be in awareness. Someone to watch her back." Nerina's spine was stiff, and I could see that this discussion had been raging since before I entered the kitchen. Before I could comment Nerina said, "Besides, I can enter the Dragonlands."

"You can?" Lily and I asked in unison.

"Yes. With you as a host, the same way I contacted you in the Graylands."

"Right." I nodded. This was definitely a possibility. "Okay, you can also dial in to let me know if Logan found anything."

"I can do more than that."

"How so?" Darcy leaned closer, intrigued.

"I can piggyback on your awareness in such a way that I can be in the same room as you. I can essentially watch your back from here."

"Sounds like a plan to me," I said with far more cheer than I felt. Again, I was leaving to cross the Veil and enter a strange land where I'd encounter people who didn't want me there. Why did I always end up in this situation?

A glance at Darcy confirmed that though she approved of the plan, she was still concerned about something. "What's wrong? I need us all to be on the same page here."

She shook her head, her golden hair swinging. She'd let the severe ponytail down and her hair framed her face nicely.

Iain must like her hair down.

Darcy cleared her throat and leaned toward me. "It's not doubt. I'm just worried about you being in danger. You don't have any backup other than one ethereal presence." She pointed a thumb at Nerina, "And an ancient dagger."

I glared at her. "How do you know about that?"

She shrugged, completely unapologetic as she said, "I had to access your mind while you were unconscious." At my angry glare she raised her hands. "Your father's orders. Sorry."

"Why did he do that?" Although annoyed at the invasion, I knew that my father would never have suggested such a thing unless he felt it was completely necessary.

"He wanted to be sure that you didn't forget any crucial information. You were out of it for hours, and he couldn't be sure that you weren't magically injured as well as physically. And since I was here, I offered to help."

A tiny part of me hoped she hadn't messed with any of my memories and then I blushed.

As I opened my mouth she raised a hand to stop me. "Don't worry. Whatever I saw in your head will remain in your head." There was a mischievous smile on her face that I didn't like.

I raised an eyebrow. "And what happens if some other Mind Mage accesses *your* mind?"

She shrugged. "Then they get nothing. I've erected shields around my thoughts that'd fry the mind of any Mind Mage who wanted in."

I laughed. "Harsh."

"Necessary, to protect the people I care about." She grinned as I got to my feet, coming around the corner of the table to take my hands in hers. "You be careful, okay?"

I smiled. "I'll do what I have to."

"I know," she said sadly.

Nerina was up too. "I'll check in every few hours. If I have something to report I will, otherwise I'll just take a quick peek. I won't have the energy to stay too long. I want to preserve my power for when you need me the most."

She was less emotional than Darcy but her pale eyes told me how worried she was. She did have a reason since the last time I'd gone off-world I almost died.

She took a step back and Lily left the table. "I'm going with you, at least as far as headquarters."

"You don't have to, kid. It's a long trip."

She pursed her lips. "I don't care. I'm coming with so you better tell your private Teleporter that I'm on the passenger list."

"No, Lil's. I'll be fine. I promise." Time to put my foot down.

Lily sighed, giving in at last. She raised an eyebrow.

I snorted in response.

Lily cleared her throat. "I'll be starting the first of my sessions with your dad while you're away."

Her soft voice was calm and even, and I was relieved to see that the decision wasn't stressing her out. That meant she was happy with her choices.

I drew her into a hug. "Good luck, okay. You take care of yourself. And don't push yourself too fast. You'll know when you're ready." She nodded calmly. "Be strong, kid. I need you to be okay when I get back."

"I will." Then she sighed. "I only wish I was coming with you."

I nodded, understanding her longing to be there for me and her regret that she couldn't.

CHAPTER 32

After a quick stop at my apartment to pack a small overnight bag, paste on some goth-girl makeup – an attempt to hide my identity in case those who protected Sienna in Sand Beach were around - and to load up on ammo, I headed to Elite HQ. Just outside the house, I received a message from Tara.

The suspicions that the Winter Queen was connected to the poisoned trees was now stronger. Tara had found compelling evidence in the form of two witnesses. She wasn't happy to go on hearsay so she planned to put someone on the inside.

I texted my thanks for the update, then sent off messages to my parents and Grams.

I'm off, take care. See you when I get back.

I shut off the phone before I could get any responses. I didn't have time for soppy farewells or well-meaning probes for details.

In addition, I'd have no reception in Drakys, so there was little point to keeping the device on. Larsson entered the room, his stride confident and sure. He wasn't much of a talker but he'd always seemed genial enough.

Now his familiar smile was comforting and he handed me a

leather folder without saying a word. The brown folder weighed my hand down and I rifled through it quickly. The paper was thick and expensive, and inside I found official documentation confirming me as the envoy of the Elders of the Supreme High Council. Along with them was a map of Drakys. I appreciated Horner's forethought, since I had no idea where the portal would deposit me.

There were other papers, but I didn't want to waste time going through them. I shoved the file into my satchel before depositing the whole bag into my rucksack. I'd packed light for a good reason. I didn't plan on being in the Dragonlands for very long.

He held out his hand and transported me in one stomach-churning ride straight to the Mendenhall Glacier.

We arrived in a swirling blizzard, snow blowing in every direction. Thankfully I'd come prepared. Thermal underwear and socks, wool-lined waterproof boots, an insulated jacket that even a K2 climber would appreciate, and a fur hat that made me look ridiculous but was satisfyingly warm.

Once there I hardly registered the crunch of the snow beneath my feet, or the bite of the icy wind.

Larsson leaned closer and yelled in my ear, "I'll return for you every eight hours for the next five days. If you're not here, then I will go back. If you miss me, wait."

If he hadn't been screaming, I would never have heard a word he said.

And then he was gone, leaving me to make my way across the bank of the wide river.

To my left the tongue of the glacier seeped into the edge of the river. I focused on putting one foot in front of the other, my shoes sinking deep into the snow, the biting wind scraping the still tender skin on my cheeks.

I was glad for the goggles, glad for the fur-lined parka. Horner had said that the portal was located, like all other portals, deep in dark water. The only problem was how to access a frozen river.

A small boat sat on the ice lake, frozen in place. It was tied to a short, narrow jetty, and I trudged toward it, taking care not to step too hard on the wooden planks. I had little idea of what icy weather did to wood, and I tried not to think about it cracking beneath my weight and sending me plunging into the ice-cold water.

I focused on the jetty and struggled forward, bent over, fighting the wind, taking one step after the other. It took longer than I'd expected to reach the iced-over mooring line, intending to use my panther strength to lift it off the ice and reveal the water below.

When I looked down I knew that plan wouldn't work.

But I was determined to try. It was better than having to walk on that unpredictable ice.

I set my rucksack onto the deck, and grabbed hold of the boat's mooring line. I tugged hard but all I heard was the straining of the fiber of the rope. The boat didn't budge.

Frustrated, I decided to tackle the problem head-on. I headed to the rickety stairs nailed to the side of the jetty and stepped into the little boat, testing its solidity. It held me, so I jumped. Once, lightly and when that didn't work, again, using my full weight. The sound of ice cracking all around the edges of the board was welcome. My weight had done the trick.

I leaned over and prodded the ice beyond the boat, comforted to see that it was thick and solid. I stepped out carefully, holding still as an ominous crack sounded.

My heart raced.

Perhaps I wouldn't need to move the boat at all if I ended up plunging headfirst into the freezing waters.

Or maybe not.

I reached into my pocket and retrieved the portal key. I threw the key up into the air and it came falling back down onto the ice with a loud crack. So much for that.

I retrieved the portal key and stepped closer to the boat. Pulling at my panther strength, I gripped it by its stern and tugged, glad that it was only a small fishing vessel.

The boat moved, wood groaning as I tugged.

Then, all around me, ice began to crack.

Terrified I pulled more of my panther strength into my limbs, lifted and swung the boat far away. It landed a dozen yards off, but I barely paid any attention. The piece of ice that I was standing on let out a loud crack.

The section, only about five feet wide, tilted beneath my weight and I was almost tossed into the freezing water. How the hell was I going to come back?

I stiffened. I wasn't about to let that stop me now.

With the water revealed, I tossed the portal key into the air, and thankfully this time it hovered above the inky surface.

The key spun for a few seconds then slowed, turning horizontally. I blinked and a column of white light soared from the heavens, then plunged straight into the center of the key. The light exited the metal disk and pierced the water below.

No time to think.

The ice began to wobble beneath my feet. Gathering my strength, I jumped.

CHAPTER 33

The push sent me soaring through the air, straight to the key. The column of white light grabbed hold of my body, a powerful gravity field that sent me spinning around like a leaf in a hurricane.

The magic of the seal and its light possessed me, changing my body, my shape, allowing me to pass through the very center of the metal. I closed my eyes.

My feet hit solid ground, my ankle spasmed, and the key clattered as it struck stone. When I opened my eyes, I blinked against the near pitch darkness. To my left, a few yards around a short corner, a soft light glowed.

I'd arrived a few feet inside the mouth of a dark cave, and it took me a moment to get my bearings. I leaned over and grabbed the portal key, sliding it into my jacket pocket for safekeeping.

I hurried toward the mouth of the cave and peered out into the distance. The cave sat high on a mountaintop, and the view was astounding.

Barren as the land was, with all its dark soil and trees that looked perpetually in fall, it was also breathtakingly beautiful. The mountain range snaked out, carving this way and that, as if reaching toward the distant sun which hung low and threatening, throwing a red glow on the landscape.

The journey was not going to be easy. Not that I'd expected it to be. I'd been to Wrythiin after all. And that was a dark, cold and forbidding place, that was a contrast to this blood and stone landscape.

The cave opened onto a small ledge. From it I had a clear view of the narrow ravine below, and the river that ran in a sinuous red line, as ominous as the sun.

To my left a narrow ledge led away, hugging the side of the mountain, likely my only route down the mountainside. Only the further it went the narrower it got.

I dropped my rucksack on the floor, and knelt beside it, rummaging inside to withdraw the files from my satchel. Removing the map, I studied it in the pink sunlight.

The map was an aerial, hand-drawn sketch of the city. Naturally it gave no indication of how I was supposed to descend from the mountain. I had to get across the range, and move northeast toward the city.

I folded the map and carefully slid it into my jacket pocket with the portal key. Throwing my rucksack onto my shoulders, I followed the path along the side of the mountain.

Logan had not lied when he said that the mountains were black. They looked like they were made of smoky crystal, which glistened pink in the sunshine. Despite the strange beauty, it was so sharp that I kept grazing my hands when I looked for handholds or tried to steady myself.

The ledge narrowed further, now only two feet wide. Below me, another shallow outcropping beckoned, this one wide enough to stand on. I sighed, accepting that I had little choice but to use my panther from here on out.

Thankfully my rucksack was special. Made in such a way that I could carry it on my back while in panther form. After placing my satchel inside the rucksack, I removed my clothes, wondering when a fabric would be invented that would mold to the skin of a walker in human form, and adjust naturally to the body of the panther after shifting into the animal.

I shook my head, annoyed and amused at myself. Right now, I had to work with what I had available to me. Unbuttoning my jeans, I slid them down my legs, and tried not to be amused at the sight of my pale thighs.

A clear bandage still covered the wound there, but thankfully it had healed enough that I barely felt a twinge, even in this cool mountain air.

Everything went into the rucksack, which had two more additional straps that I buckled as tightly as possible around my waist. All the straps were elasticated, and held so tightly that I would have been afraid of stopping my circulation if I was going to remain in human form. But the straps were made to be comfortable on a panther.

As the wind blew in, icy and cold, and as the red sun began to sink lower on the horizon, I shifted from human form into a panther. Ears lifted, lengthened, fur covered the skin. The bones in my face shifted, mouth forward, jaw narrowing, eyes growing deeper and wider, teeth becoming sharper and more dangerous. My limbs filled with fire and my muscles felt like liquid, forming again into the slim and elegant legs of the Cat.

In feline form, I shook myself, allowing the muscles, sinew, and bones to settle around me. The rucksack straps loosened, and were now much more comfortable. I moved to the edge, aimed at the ledge below, and sprang. Landing softly, I scanned the outcropping. Below me to the left was another ledge wide enough to support my panther. And I jumped.

On and on I went, until I reached the bottom of the canyon, a few yards from the Blood River.

The map had said to follow the river, which snaked out in the opposite direction of the sunrise. Here, in Drakys, the sun set in the East, which felt odd until I got my bearings.

Judging from the distances on the map, I knew the trip to the city would take at least four hours in panther form.

The river continued east, staying at the base of the rocky mountain range, and narrowed at one point where it sank underground leaving me with no choice but to climb the mountainside again.

The wind began to let up, the cold no longer biting, and at least there was no snow. Hours later the height of the mountain range began to decline, and at last I stood on a rocky outcropping, studying a flat plain that reached out for almost five miles before it ended at the walls of the great city.

Even from this distance the walls and the guardian statues were imposingly tall.

I'd walked all night, and lost track of time. Also, because I suspected that the sun rose earlier in this part of the universe than it did back home. The sun was behind me now, still the same red threatening and ominous, but this time it was much higher in the sky.

And where last night the sky was a blend of grays and red, this morning it was every shade of red imaginable. Blood red streaked the sky, blending with the pale pink and a dusky rose. If I stopped to enjoy it, I would have to admit that it was an incredible sight. So far this land was impressing me greatly with its beauty.

I couldn't go any further in panther form in case I was seen from the battlements or from the palace that sat high on the mountain. I transformed, and changed, then set out at a brisk pace.

The road, which ran beside the river, was compacted dirt more than anything. Wheel-tracks marked the soil in deep gouges. And little puddles of red gleamed.

Red water, red rain. Of course.

I'd seen the statues from afar and they only looked more

imposing up close. They guarded the entrance of the city, a pair of sentinels that were both frightening and majestic.

They towered above me, wing-tips reaching at least three hundred feet into the air. They'd carved the form of a woman, slim waist, impressive bust. From the back of her shoulders, a pair of wings grew, spreading above her in height equal to her own. Her face was regal, nose patrician, lips full. She looked human, except for the scaly skin.

The twin to this gigantic statue stood on the other side of the entrance, two female dragons warning travelers to beware. It was enough to frighten the most sturdy-hearted man, the artist having captured a terrifying expression in the faces of the pair.

Guarding the city were walls at least a hundred feet high, and ten feet wide, with battlements on the outer edge to guard the city. Though the creation of such a majestic wall would be easy enough for a battalion of flying creatures, it was still an amazing sight.

Back home the Great Wall of China could not compare.

The gates to the city of Dyr were guarded by a pair of soldiers, they wore armor that resembled the scales of a dragon, their bodies molded in a skin-tight sheath, as red as the bloody sun. Swords at their waists, and daggers at their thighs, they looked like any human soldier, but I had no doubt that they were capable of unfurling great and powerful wings.

Their faces were hidden by masks that were made in the form of a dragon's head. Narrow slits in the eyes allowed the soldiers to watch me. The taller of the two took a step forward, a movement designed to be threatening.

I wasn't intimidated.

I'd been up against worse. Although, if he did decide to go all scales and teeth on me, I would probably turn and run.

"What business do you have in the city," he asked, his voice loud and ringing in my ears.

Talk about border control.

"I am an emissary for the Elders of the Supreme High Council, and I come in peace." I spoke loudly too. Letting him know I wasn't quivering in my boots.

It wasn't as if we had an audience, as behind me the road was empty. But I also had to remind myself to be nice to the man. He could easily not allow me entry into the city.

I handed him the sheet of paper that Horner had given me, and prayed that it would be enough. The soldier stared at the writing, his dark eyes hidden by the shadows of his mask.

CHAPTER 34

From the expression that I could make out through the slit in his helmet, the soldier looked undecided. He pointed at his partner and said, "Take the emissary to the guardhouse. I'll notify the general."

The second guard nodded and waved me over. As I followed, I watched the first guard stare up at the top of the wall, and wave, making an oddly familiar circular motion.

A loud rumble echoed within the wall, and the gigantic doors began to open. It was obvious that heavy machinery would be required to move them.

I followed the second guard to a small building just inside the wall. I remained polite and didn't make a fuss. The guard did not inspect my bags, nor did he examine me for weapons. So the emissary of the Elders did enjoy a diplomatic immunity of sorts.

Once inside the office, he waved me to a seat by the window and returned to his post. He didn't seem worried about security either, leaving me without a guard.

I could be a Trojan horse assassin for all they knew.

Not much good being Trojan or otherwise when you could end up barbecued alive.

The room was spartan, stone walls and floor, and not much else except for my roughly-hewn chair. I was beginning to get bored when the first guard returned, filling the doorway and blocking the light.

I grabbed my bags and got to my feet, then faced him, wondering if he would have the decency to remove his helmet. As I stared, waiting for the general's answer, he fidgeted as if disliking the scrutiny.

Instead of removing the helmet, he said, "The general will receive you in his quarters. His page will take you to him." He glanced at a figure, standing outside the door just beyond my line of vision.

Outside I came face-to-face with a portly young man. With his flushed cheeks, he looked like a cherub.

He gave a small bow and said, "If you will come with me please the general will see you now." Then, unsmiling, he turned and began to waddle off without a backward glance.

I hurried after him, taking in the details of the city as I went. Slate-paved roads, walls made of gleaming obsidian stone. None of the streets here were parallel, or even straight. Everything curved, snaking this way and that. A slight incline lay ahead and when I looked up, the castle commanded my attention.

The page stopped so suddenly that I almost walked right into him. Thankfully, I sidestepped at the last minute. He waved at a small building; a house made of black obsidian instead of simple stone.

Double doors guarded the interior, and the page knocked before entering. Inside, the room was spartan again, everything from shelves to tables to chairs merely serving its purpose, as opposed to providing any sort of decorative purpose. Only a single set of armor stood in the corner, black as night.

A large table occupied most of the left side of the room, and seated behind it was an old man, so thin and feeble that it looked like his armor was about to swallow him whole.

I was surprised the new queen hadn't seen fit to appoint a man who would instill fear in his men, rather than one who broadcasted his weakness the first time a person set eyes on him. Maybe I was wrong, and maybe he was a strong man, hiding behind a sheepish facade. For the sake of the city, I hoped the latter was true.

The general rubbed his chin, and stared at the piece of paper on his desk. The official verification letter from the Elders seemed to trouble him.

"Is there a problem?" I asked, ensuring that I kept any impatience out of my voice. Seems I had the hidden talent of a diplomat.

He gave a small shake of his head then looked up at me. His eyes shifted left and right, and I wondered if he had a problem meeting my gaze. It occurred to me at that moment that perhaps the Dragons were an old-fashioned race, one that subjugated their woman. From the way he avoided looking at me, I assumed he felt I had no right to gain the position of the emissary of the Elite.

I straightened my spine and ignored the look, focusing on the job at hand. When he still didn't answer, I said, "I would like to see the Queen. If I may. The Elders wish me to convey their good wishes, and there is a lot to be discussed. Is there any reason why you wish to delay me?"

The general shook his head. "I fear you are mistaken. I do not wish you to be delayed. I have sent word to Her Majesty, and I am awaiting her response."

Just as he exhaled, another page rushed into the room with a small envelope. The general ripped it open and got to his feet. He gave me a short bow. "Please come with me."

I hitched my bags back onto my shoulders and followed him. He led me outside and up the hill, and I noticed the weather had warmed a little. Twenty minutes later, most of which comprised of walking up a slight incline along serpentine roads that led up the side of the mountain, we arrived at the palace gates.

The view from here was breathtaking. One could see across the planes, all the way to the nearest end of the Black Mountains. The rustling of the guard's armor brought my attention back to the iron gates, constructed with metal shaped into scales and layered to look like dragonskin, and to the palace beyond. Up close the building was incredible. Midnight towers rose above us, black obsidian glass and obsidian molded together to create something out of a fairytale, complete with towers and turrets and parapets.

At every corner, I was further impressed at the beauty of this realm. It was such a pity that so few people knew it existed, and even fewer people had the opportunity to visit here.

Travel across the planes was not common.

But if we were able to police the travelers, perhaps visiting other planes would become commonplace. It would certainly boost the economies of many planes. It worked in the Earth World, and I didn't see why it couldn't do the same for worlds across the Veil.

The great doors opened with a similar mechanical creaking as the doors to the city, and the general waved me into a large entry hall. The black and white marble tiles shimmered in the yellow light cast by dozens of torches dotting the walls.

The hall was straight out of an old English castle, complete with rich wall-hangings and tapestries, hand-carved furniture that looked like it belonged in an antique shop, all heavy hardwood legs.

The general strode up the stairs without a word, leaving me to pace. Not that pacing in such a room could be deemed a mediocre task.

Right now, despite the generosity of the elders, all I wanted to do was race around the castle, find Sienna and take her back to her brother.

I paced more.

A few minutes later the general returned, gave me a stiff nod, then walked past me and straight out the door. I scowled.

What was I expected to do now?

Footsteps echoed along the corridor to the left, and a woman hurried into the reception hall, shadowed twenty feet off by a pair of guards.

She stopped in front of me and extended a hand. "Hello. I'm Sienna."

CHAPTER 35

Sienna Westin strode toward me, her eyes bright and welcoming as she grasped my hand.

Gone were the purple hair and goth attire. Instead she wore a beautiful dress. Pieces of black kid-leather, in the shape of dragon scales were sewn together to create a dress that began as a corset, molded to her body and hips, then fell to the ground.

The corset was tight and hugged her waist, making her bust appear more impressive than it really was. Beneath, she wore a silk blouse, the sleeves of which were flared like a tulip, and were at least four feet long. They trailed the floor as she clasped her arms in front of her.

The hem of each sleeve was embroidered with hundreds of little black beads. Clothing like that made me rethink my love for pants and serviceable shirts. I couldn't deny that I was quite partial to her corset and blouse.

"Welcome to Dyr," Sienna said, her voice ringing around the hall. Although her eyes were shining and her lips were smiling, there was an edge of wariness in her expression. And, recognition.

She opened her mouth, her expression implying that she was

going to confirm meeting me on Sand Beach but I shook my head. Just the tiniest movement but it was enough. She stiffened, taking a small step back.

She didn't trust me. Not yet.

Not that I expected her to, so soon. "I will be attending you while you conduct your business within the city. Her Majesty, Queen Lyra will receive you in due course. If you will please follow me."

I was shocked beyond words. The last thing I had expected was to be gifted with the very person that I come here to rescue. It seemed too good to be true.

My wariness levels just hit the roof.

"I'm Kailin Odel. Good to meet you." We shook hands, and I noticed the firmness of hers. She was confident and sure of herself. Certainly no mousy handmaiden.

Odd that Darcy had reported otherwise.

Is this her public persona? Quite likely, considering what Logan, and Darcy, would see was how she *really* thought and felt. Not what she showed the outside world.

But, it was good to see that she was well. My only concern was where her loyalties would lie.

"Do you know anything about the city?" she asked as she began to walk toward a grand marble staircase. The fabric of her gown whispered as she walked.

I gave a mental shake of my head, and tried to focus on her words. "No. Unfortunately, I was only given the most recent history of the country. And a cursory version at that."

She smiled. "Then we will have to ensure that we correct that. We'd like to know that the emissary of the Elders will return with information to satisfy the Supreme High Council."

I frowned as she led me up the left side of a gigantic double stairwell, complete with marble balustrades and carpeted risers.

"What do you mean?" I didn't lower my voice despite the guards that followed.

"All it means, is that it has been five years since the last envoy passed into the Light. The rift between the Drakyr and the Elders has not been easy to endure."

I wondered what that meant, considering five years ago she would have only been a teenager. But perhaps she'd been privy to royal politics from a young age.

"It's why I've been sent. To attempt to repair it."

"You are not here to find out what happened to the last envoy?" She was asking another question altogether.

I shook my head and gave her an encouraging smile. "That's not part of my role. At least, not at this time. All I was requested to do was to open discussions with the queen in order to facilitate a boost to your economy."

I wondered whether I should be discussing such things with Sienna, but I wanted her to see that I was on her side. That I wasn't the enemy.

When I glanced over at her she was looking at me, admiration and something else in her expression.

At the top she strode straight down the central corridor and I marveled at the stonework, the carvings along the floor and around the doors. Intricate and convoluted, probably harking to the history of Drakys, the continuous pattern reminding me of Viking tree designs. We stopped at the very end, at another pair of giant double doors watched over by twin guards. Everything within the palace was huge, wide enough to accommodate ten people abreast, tall enough that even a giant would pass through without stooping.

The construction of the palace was more in keeping with the size of the builders, in dragon form.

Would the Queen welcome me in her dragon form?

There was no time to wonder, as Sienna neared the door and the guards automatically turned and opened them. She led me into another enormous room. Three walls were covered in some type of brocade fabric, and the one to our left was a single floor-to-ceiling window.

Despite the incredible view, the room was imposing and serious, if ostentatious, likely a meeting room or one in which royal dinner parties were held. The center of the room was dominated by a gigantic table that would seat at least forty people.

At the head of the table sat a small woman, her hair honey-blonde, eyes a pale gold. Queen Lyra didn't rise as I walked toward her. The part of me that wanted to believe that Sienna was the rightful queen bristled at the Queen Regent, feeling she didn't have the right to such airs and graces if she was sitting on a throne that didn't belong to her.

But then, wouldn't she need to appear strong and imposing so she wouldn't end up being someone else's puppet?

She regarded me with a tilt of her head, the arrogance clear, scanning me from head to toe.

I hadn't arrived to meet her in full Alpha Walker formal dress, and the worst part was I had a set that I could have brought with me had I had the presence of mind to.

Then again I didn't think that she would be too impressed with the long white Roman gown and the gold-plated body armor. It paled in comparison to hers.

Queen Lyra was dressed as a queen, similar to Sienna, but more elaborate. Her blouse was made of blood-red fabric and adorned with gold beading. She wore a black crystal crown, flecked with gems.

The queen sure knew how to enjoy the privileges of being Regent.

She waved me to a chair, I took it obediently. No sense in pissing off the person that I'd come to a treaty with. Lyra held a piece of paper in her hand; my confirmation from the Elders.

I dropped the rucksack and satchel on the floor beside me and crossed my legs daintily. I didn't look all that impressive bundled up for a mountain climb, and wished that I'd been given time to change.

I stiffened my spine and met the Queen's eyes. "Thank you very much for agreeing to hear me."

Queen Lyra smiled, her mouth moving into a thin line. "It does not appear that I have much choice."

"Why is that?" I genuinely wanted to know and she could tell.

"Because it is not something to ignore . . . this request from the Elders." Her voice was bitter, edged with anger.

"I don't see why not," I said, giving a slight frown. "You have the upper hand."

"How do you assume that?"

I leaned forward slightly. "Our last envoy died on your lands. Five years later, we still have no idea how he died, or who the perpetrators were. What we know is he came home in pieces." The blood drained from her face.

Now why would she be affected so deeply? Curious.

I continued. "All communication ended from your side, and it was clear to the Elders that you refused to help in the investigation. It wouldn't be so different right now if you refused to listen to what I have to say."

The room was silent as she sat there staring at me. Had I managed to stump her with my big mouth?

"On the other hand, the Elders were also open to considering another possibility."

"And what is that?" The color was slowly returning to her cheeks now that the subject had changed.

"The possibility that you and your people had no part in the envoy's murder. That perhaps it was just an accident. Or he'd been involved in something nefarious and gotten himself killed. They are well aware that there are a number of possibilities around his death. The only negative thing in the investigation is that we received no information from your side. If you'd been more open and accommodating to the investigation, things would have been cleared up a long time ago."

Her jaw tightened, a look of desperation flickering in her eyes. This woman was a bundle of contradictions.

Sienna shifted to the queen's side. "What happened five years ago was regretful. The court and Queen Lyra have decided it is time things were put to rights."

The queen gave a tight nod, although the expression in her eyes did not change. She looked like a woman who had suffered a great loss. But surely she'd have recovered from the death of her sister and her family so long ago?

Sienna said, "We are happy to accept you as the envoy, and hear what you have to say. But we're unable to provide further information regarding the death of your predecessor, as our own investigation has not been fruitful."

I shook my head, unsure if I'd heard right. "The reason why you didn't comply, and help with the investigation, was your people had no idea how he died or why?"

Sienna nodded. The queen inclined her head the tiniest fraction.

"Then why didn't you just tell the Elders that? Surely you would have known the Elders wouldn't assume you were complicit in his death?" I asked, shaking my head. "They would have understood. Sent their own team to investigate."

The queen shrugged, but her eyes were moist now. Sienna said, "We regret the decision that was made at the time. The council felt that the safety of the kingdom had been threatened. That the actions of the army and the queen would have been questioned. We understand how such a standpoint would have been seen as being defensive, even appearing as guilty. Which is why we want to comply, and help you in every way that you may require."

I nodded and sent them both a reassuring smile. "As I said, I'm not here to clarify what happened to my predecessor. In fact, I'm not here in the same capacity at all. My role here is to meet, and discuss mining opportunities, and methods in which to boost your economy. Helping you will help us," I said with what I hoped was a friendly smile. "Those are, of course, the words and sentiments of our Elders."

Sienna smiled, and glanced over at Her Majesty. The Queen's wintry expression gave away little. The woman was hard, and emanated a low throb of anger and resentment, and pain. She was about to say something when the inner door of the great room opened and a man strolled in.

The dark-haired man wore an ice-white knee-length coat that glowed with a blue tinge even in the pink light that drifted in from the window. The garment was fashioned with the dragon scales pieces, and remained open, diamond buttons glinting beneath. A diamond clasp glittered on his right lapel, adding to the glamor.

Under the coat he wore slim black pants that molded to his well-muscled thighs, and a generously cut white shirt that resembled Sienna's silk blouse. I wondered whether he too had gemstones on the sleeves.

I wouldn't be surprised.

Inching forward, Sienna waved a hand at him. "This is Commander Andyr Dar-ys, Royal Solicitor. In your land I assume he would be considered a lawyer of sorts."

Andyr's eyes narrowed at Sienna's words, and I didn't miss the coldness in her tone. It didn't take a genius to figure out that she didn't like him.

He gave her a seductive yet indulgent smile, which felt wrong on so many levels, then walked over to me, holding out his hand. The closer he got to me, the more uncomfortable I became. The hair on the back of my neck stood on end. But I forced myself to remain still and take his hand.

I had to be civil, perform every action as it was expected, within keeping of the expectations of the people of this court.

When his skin touched mine, goosebumps rippled across my arms. There was something very wrong about this man. I frowned, studying the beautiful lines of his face, the hooded eyes so gray they almost appeared white. Then I quickly smoothed my features. There was something so familiar about him.

But it wouldn't make sense to alert him to my awareness, or my suspicions. I plastered a genial smile on my face and hoped it appeared genuine and I shook his hand firmly, but not too firmly.

"Truly good to meet you. I believe legal representation would be very helpful in these negotiations." That was going to be as close to flattery as I would ever get with him.

This man brushed me up the wrong way, my gut told me he represented some form of danger. I drew my panther sense of smell to the surface and scented him.

He did smell familiar, as if I'd been around him before. But I couldn't put my finger on it.

Familiar. And dangerous.

CHAPTER 36

He let go of my hand and then walked to the opposite chair. A guard scurried forward and pulled it out for him. The flustered man hurried back to his post against the wall beside the closed door.

Once seated, Andyr pulled his chair closer and rested his elbows on the table, performing the same steepled finger motion that Horner had in his office not too long ago.

"So what is it the Elders wish to propose?" he asked, the smile on his face neutral as he watched me.

There was an arrogance in his expression, his bearing conveyed that he thought he knew more than I did, and that he had the upper hand.

I smiled pleasantly, ever the diplomat. "The Elders wish to reinstate the mining agreement, and renew trading for Erulite."

"I wondered how long it would take for them to demand this again," said the Queen bitterly.

I couldn't help the frown that appeared on my forehead. "Do you not want to boost your economy with the mining trade?" I asked, watching her expression.

She gave a tiny shake of her head and took a breath. "That's not what I mean."

Andyr leaned closer. "You must excuse our Queen. The murder, and the accusations involving the death of your predecessor, affected her greatly." They exchanged looks, the queen's slightly embarrassed, Andyr's slightly arrogant.

What in Ailuros' name is going on here?

"But I do hope that we can move past that," he said, giving her a cynical look.

"Move past it?" she asked, leaning forward until her ribs touched the table. Her cheeks blazed red, her golden eyes swelled. "*The man* was murdered, and we were blamed. He'd become part of this court. A friend, even. And we'd been accused of killing him, been given no recourse to defend ourselves."

"But I don't think that that's exactly what happened," I said without hesitating.

I reached over into the satchel and withdrew the leather folder. From inside, I retrieved a stack of paperwork. It was a full description of everything that the Elders had been informed of, with regard to the envoy's death.

Reid Barton, a Fire Mage, had been sent to Drakys to look after the mine, because his power allowed him to provide safety for the miners. It didn't hurt that his fire magic would allow him to fit in with the people of the land. I'd skimmed the details, and noticed how sparse they were.

The only information that the Elders had received from the Dyr was that Reid had been killed, and no foul play was suspected on the part of the Court. That his body had been returned to the EarthWorld via the portal in the cave, in pieces, hadn't featured in the report submitted by the Drakys Senate.

The Queen frowned as she read the file. When she looked up her eyes were filled with tears.

Queen Lyra and Reid?

Holyshit.

That would explain her emotional reaction to this whole process. That would also explain Andyr's arrogance. He was using her emotional lapse against her.

"But this isn't right," she whispered, her hand going to her pale throat. Her black painted fingernails were a stark contrast to her porcelain skin, even if you ignored the gold filigree nail caps.

I cleared my throat. "I assure you that is all the information received from your delegates."

She was shaking her head as I spoke. I understood now that there was more miscommunication regarding Reid's death than we knew.

"His death was suspicious." Her voice was a whisper. "The general had his men search the mines, looking for the killer. Reid certainly wouldn't have killed himself."

"Can you explain to me what exactly happened? Right now even the Elders have no idea how he was killed."

"He was killed in the mines. His body was found in the bottom of a ravine." The queen's voice shivered and she swallowed hard. Sienna cleared her throat. "Within the mines there are numerous ravines, and earth-holes that go deep into the ground. The miners are well aware of the dangers. And so was Reid."

Despite her words, her voice told me what she really felt.

"So you suspected foul play?" I said, more curious now than ever. "Why did you not explain that to the Elders?" A glance in Andyr's direction showed he was perfectly serene. Except for the swirling of his gray eyes. And the hint of a glow on his skin.

What the hell was he?

"Because we believed we would be blamed for his death," Queen Lyra said.

"But that's a ridiculous assumption. Just because he died on your soil doesn't mean you killed him."

"At the time that was the impression." Lyra's voice said that she disapproved. She sighed. "I admit that we were concerned about the circumstances of his death." She pushed to her feet and began to pace. "To be completely honest, I was worried that our relationship would come to light."

She turned and faced me, lifting her chin in defiance. "We cared deeply for each other. And often I wondered if he'd been killed because of his feelings for me. Or rather my feelings for him. Caring for an outlander is a dangerous thing, especially for the queen."

I'd suspected as much.

Love was usually at the root of all problems.

Andyr got to his feet, a vein now throbbing on his forehead. "You shouldn't allow yourself to think that way. His death was an accident." He seemed to be controlling the urge to say more and I was glad because, considering everything I'd just learned, I wasn't above telling him to shut up and sit down.

But Lyra shook her head. "To this day I do not believe that. No matter how hard I investigated I was blocked at every turn. Someone kept the truth from me because they knew I would have torn them limb from limb for what they'd done to Reid. Someone who also wanted to halt trade with the Elders."

"So whoever provided us with that information wasn't working on your behalf?"

She shook her head and took a seat again, straightening her spine, drawing her composure over her like a shroud.

"With that in mind, I think we will call a formal meeting to discuss reopening the mining efforts. I think it would be best for everyone. And this time I won't accept any arguments against it." When her eyes met mine, they still glistened with tears. "And I would like to request that the Elders give consideration to reopening the investigation into Reid's death. It would give me great joy to identify the killer and have him punished suitably."

I nodded. "Of course. I believe I speak on behalf of the Elders when I say that we will do whatever we can to apprehend the perpetrator."

"If I may, I would like to make a request," the Queen said, her voice hushed.

When I nodded, she gave Andyr a short glance, an almost belligerent glare, before returning her attention to me. "If we may be allowed to sentence him here in Drakys, I would most appreciate it. It would be better for everyone I think if the killer is given justice on our soil. I understand that Reid was a mage from your lands, that people there, his friends and family, would be seeking justice for his death too. But I formally request permission to sentence and punish the killer"

I nodded. "This particular part of the agreement, I cannot decide on. I will have to take that to the Elders."

Though I was afraid of an outburst, which I'd understand considering the subject matter, Lyra seemed satisfied. She sat back letting out a soft breath, suddenly deflated, weakened by the discussion.

She waved at Sienna. "Sienna will look after you. She's my assistant but to be honest she's more of an advisor to me. She has more smarts and tactical intelligence than many of the generals in the army." I noticed she never said *my* army or *my* court. "She will help you draw up the finer points of the agreement. We shall meet here tomorrow morning, after the Senate has time to discuss, to finalize the particulars regarding the renewed mining effort. In the meantime, the City of Dyr is happy to welcome you. We will hold a banquet tonight, and you will be our Guest of Honor. No better way to give a blessing to your visit and to the reopening of the mines."

I wondered if she was being a little presumptuous considering the Senate hadn't yet agreed, but it seemed the effort already had her blessing.

Maybe that was all it really took.

Rising, I gave a formal bow. "You have my deepest gratitude. I am most grateful that the proceedings are being taken seriously on both sides. And tomorrow I hope that we will all come to a mutual agreement."

Sienna walked toward me. "I will see you to your room."

Both the queen and Andyr got to their feet, and I didn't miss the glare that he sent in her direction. Nor did I miss the tight grip that he had on her upper arm, as if he wanted to thrust her to the private chambers but was controlling the urge. Her opinion clearly didn't sit well with him. And I wondered what kind of power the man really had over the ruling of this country.

And what stake he had in the mines themselves.

Sienna was already walking toward the double doors, and I hurried to follow, throwing my rucksack and satchel over my shoulder.

Killing demons were a damn sight easier than all this political talk.

CHAPTER 37

She led me up another flight of stairs, and headed down a western corridor, where the setting sun shed bloody rays of light in through the numerous balconies that dotted the way. Despite being open to the outside, the palace remained warm and I found myself wanting to shrug off the fur-lined coat.

The halls were wide and high, and I marveled at the workmanship, the smooth stonework, the sconces set high up on the walls burning fat candles.

Sienna remained silent as we walked, our steps dogged by her ever-present guards, until she pointed to a wide passage on her left. "I'm at the end of that hallway. The very last door. If you need anything, please come and see me. I will endeavor to be available as much as possible." She gave a sweet smile and continued to the next corridor.

Making a left she guided me to the end and we stopped in front of a large wooden door, adorned with the pattern I'd seen decorating much of the palace.

Sienna opened the door for me, and said, "I hope you will be comfortable in your quarters. It has two bedrooms, a sitting room, a bathing room and a reception area." She smiled as I entered, clearly proud of the place. And I was very impressed.

The floor was covered with handwoven carpets and the walls in beautiful paintings; landscapes and dancing maidens with elegant wings. The most impressive of them all were the paintings of the Drakyr, some depicting dragons breathing deadly fire, others Drakyr armies fighting each other. It was a room that celebrated the power of the Drakyr, and the expansive history of its people.

The furniture, here again, was rich and heavy, hand-carved and beautiful. The *reception area* was a small living room, with comfortable sofas covered in rich gold fabric and complemented by dozens of creamy soft cushions.

A low dark wood coffee table provided me with a place to drop my satchel. I turned to Sienna. "This place is absolutely beautiful. You're so fortunate to live in the palace. Are your rooms like these?" Questions that were questions about more than just beauty and palace accommodation.

Sienna lowered her eyes, but not soon enough to hide the darkness that flitted across her face. "My quarters are beautiful, but much more serviceable. I have a single room and a small waiting area to receive visitors. We leave the riches and the beauty for the dignitaries and the royalty."

I pasted a smile on my face and walked toward her. "I must thank you for treating me so well. I know it is probably just your job, but you made me feel welcome." My eyes flitted to the open door. And the guards beyond.

Sienna's cheeks bloomed with red, clearly she wasn't used to receiving compliments. She whispered a quick thank you and walked to the inner door, as if she knew I was about to launch into dream-related questions.

At the door she paused and put a finger to her lips, a clear instruction not to talk about sensitive matters. "There is a bell-pull above the mantelpiece if you require anything." Then she threw the door open and waved me inside.

A gigantic four-poster bed sat in the middle of the room. The wall on the right, like the one in the grand dining room, was a giant floor-to-ceiling window that looked out over the expanse of the city.

On the bed was an array of gowns.

"I took the liberty of having some garments sent up. I wasn't sure if you had anything to wear. It's not often that Queen Lyra throws formal events for visiting representatives of the Elders. I hope you will not take offense."

I smiled and shook my head. "Of course not. I more than appreciate it. All I have are furs and thermal undies. Not to mention clunky shoes. I'd expected the place to be cold. The palace is certainly *not*."

Sienna laughed. "The palace is built along the side of a volcano. Lava heats the crystal, and a system beneath the city uses the lava to heat the buildings. A natural underfloor heating, if you know what I mean."

"You know about underfloor heating?" I said with a laugh.

She walked toward the bed and picked up a deep red dress. "I'm well educated in the ways of your world. Part of my tuition was to study the technology there, so I am well familiar with everything, including your mobile devices." Her eyes were wide open with excitement and curiosity, and I lifted a finger.

"Stay right there."

I hurried back out into the main room and dug around in my satchel, retrieving my tablet. When I returned to the room Sienna was sitting on the bed holding the deep red dress in her hand, a faraway expression in her eyes.

I held out the tablet and said, "There are a few things that I need to do with it while I'm here, but you're welcome to have it when I leave."

Her eyes widened and her smile too. "I could not ask you to do such a thing for me."

I waved my hand at her. "Absolutely no problem at all. I have plenty more where that came from. Consider it a gift from the Elders."

She took the tablet and began swiping from screen to screen. For someone who didn't have that kind of technology in this country, she seemed to be quite adept. Then I was reminded that she did manage a visit or two to Sand Beach.

After a few minutes she got to her feet and passed it back to me. "Thank you so much for the offer. I won't abuse your time with it while you are here but if you really do think you could leave it when you go home, I would be most appreciative. Our country would benefit greatly from such technology."

"Well, once we're trading again, you'll have the funds to bring such technology in. I don't see why you couldn't buy tablets like these for everyone on the council, or even for the students in the school. Maybe even your general?"

She snorted. "General Vyrian is old school. Such frivolities would be a waste of his precious time." She spoke tenderly, as if she had a history with the general. Something I'd have to ask her about at another time. Then she smiled.

I was tired, drained from months of emotional stress, and at that moment, I was content. I very much enjoyed her company.

Sienna nodded, her face serious now that she thought about the possibilities of such devices. Then she took a deep breath. "Well, enough about state business. You can choose from these, but I think this one is the perfect one for you." She thrust the dress at me, looking so enthusiastic that I could hardly turn her down.

Red was so not my color, but it wasn't a blood red. Rather, the red of the sun, tinged with orange, which complemented my green eyes. That much I knew from my days as a teenager when I'd played around with dozens and dozens of different colored clothing. It was probably all those colors that made me give up in the end and choose neutral black-and-white.

Siena walked toward me and held the dress up against me, pushing me toward a full-length mirror that was edged in a gilded frame.

"There you go," she said with a big grin. She stared at my reflection and actually laughed out loud, enjoying how right she'd been.

I literally was a vision. The dress was stunning. Made of red scales, it clung to my hips beginning in a corset just under my bust, hugging my figure all the way to my knees where it spread out before touching the ground. If it weren't for the skirt it would look very comfortable on the battlefield.

I smiled at her. "It's beautiful. But I'm certainly not going topless."

Sienna giggled and hurried to a wardrobe in the corner. She opened the door, wincing as it creaked, and muttering about getting the servants to oil it.

From inside she withdrew a black silk blouse studded with red gems. It was a stunning combination. I took a breath and sighed. "I'm taking you back with me and you can be my personal wardrobe manager?"

She laughed. "I've always been good with colors. And this matches your eyes and skin perfectly." Then she gave a satisfied nod and hurried toward the door. "I have to go now. I have to bathe and dress and be done before anyone else enters the dining hall. So much to do." She gave a quirky smile and hurried off before I could ask any more questions.

Sinking onto the bed, holding the dress and the shirt in my lap, I stared at the closed door. So much had happened since I'd arrived in this land, and I prayed that everything would go according to plan. I was determined to ensure that the Elder's treaty would be accepted. This land was seriously in need of a boost in the economy, and deserved to have the advantages of modern technology.

If the Fae could partake of modern tech, then so could the Dragons.

I made a mental note to request a visit to the mine, to see for myself what technology was used and how efficiently. I suspected that if we did end up agreeing to lease their land for mining, we might need to use more advanced machinery.

Heading to the bathing room, I was pleasantly surprised to see functioning plumbing. And more than happy to see the gigantic bathtub that sat in the middle of the room.

I couldn't think of anything beyond just having a good soak for now. Business would come later.

$\mathcal{J}$ was dressed and ready when Sienna knocked on the door and called out my name. Hurrying toward the door, I flung it open, frustrated and annoyed. "What's the matter?" she asked.

"It's this damned hair," I said, pointing at the mess.

I'd washed it and had no way to dry it, or comb it, without a damned hairbrush. Naturally, I'd forgotten it.

"And these." I stuck my bare feet out from underneath the skirt. "My boots won't look good with the dress. Unless I want to start a new trend."

Sienna stared at the offending boots, and seemed to be considering my proposition. "We could provide you with shoes at short notice; our shoemakers are quite capable. But use your boots, and I will join you in that fashion statement. I will be right back."

And then she was gone, leaving me staring at the open door. I sat on the sofa to put the boots on. A few minutes later, after I'd managed to drag my fingers through my hair, Sienna returned, wearing a pair of gorgeous leather boots that looked like dragonskin. Which of course it wouldn't be. Not here in the land of the dragons.

I hid a smile as she handed me a brush and helped me tame my hair. She'd brought pins and styled it in a puffy bun arrangement that I wanted to comb out immediately. Except she wouldn't let me.

Ten minutes later Sienna and I made our way back to the Grand dining room, which had been transformed in the last few hours, as if for a wedding. More than a dozen six-foot vases spewed forth bouquets of flowers of every color imaginable. The enormous table was set with gold and obsidian place settings, and goblets and drinking glasses of glinting crystal. Half a dozen flower arrangements dotted the length of the table.

At each corner of the room and along the walls, twelve footmen waited, ready to serve in severe black suits.

Guests walked the room, mingling here and there, pairs and threes and fives. All looked up when Sienna and I entered. For a moment I wondered why I'd gained that much attention, but they weren't looking at me. All eyes were on Sienna for some reason. Many adoring, and just as many admiring.

Some glances were resentful, not so well-hidden behind the admiration.

Sienna had enemies within the court, and I made a note of each and every face that bore a negative expression. Among them was the all too good-looking Andyr.

He stood at the queen's side, no more than an inch from her, his bearing that of a guard. Or a jailer. The man had a strong hold over her and I had to find out who he was and where he'd come from.

As we walked closer, I slowed my steps and Sienna, looked over at me. She was stunning in a gown of white dragon scales, each connecting stitch adorned with gleaming crystals. The shocking white blouse was also fitted with silver thread and beaded with crystal. I could understand why she'd received the room's attention when she entered. She was a particularly stunning woman.

The beauty of it was that she had no idea.

She gave me an inquiring look, probably worried that I was uncomfortable. So I went with it. Without looking at her I said, "Your solicitor . . . Andyr. He makes me feel a little uncomfortable."

She laughed softly. "He tends to make a lot of people feel that way." Then she rolled her eyes. "At least those people don't have to worry about having to live with him the rest of their lives."

My mouth dropped open. "What the hell is that supposed to mean?"

She shook her head, amused at my anger. Sorrow bloomed in her eyes. "We marry on my 21st birthday."

"Why?"

"Because it has been decreed by the queen that we join the experience of the law of the country and the technology of the country. My knowledge has turned out to be quite a curse."

"But why him? What's so great about him that they have to force you to marry him?"

"He's rich and powerful. He chose me."

"Does that happen often here?"

"Kai, here in Drakys, you will find that women are no longer treated with respect, the way they are in your land. Here, the men prefer a patriarchal way now. Historically, all queens were seen as the mother of the land. Despite the queen being a woman, her right to rule was never questioned. More because she bore the burden of queen along with her brother. Thus the land was ruled by an equal pair. One closer than that of a mated couple.

"Since the death of Queen Shrya, much of the traditional ways have been put aside. The new queen tries, an example being me, a female tactician, in her court. But forces have worked around her, around us, every step of the way."

"I just can't fathom . . ."

She nodded. "Perhaps after two decades of having a Regent in control, one who isn't as powerful as a true queen, one who isn't as respected, the Senate have become used to finding ways to manipulate things to their own liking."

"That makes me think of someone else I met recently."

"Who?" she asked with a smile.

"Prince Elan of the Winter Court."

"You met a fae prince?" she asked, her eyes wide and sparkling with excitement.

I nodded. "Definitely destroys the stars in one's eyes when one meets a hot-as-sin, *sexist* fae prince."

She snorted and her excitement dissipated.

"Anyway, why can't you just refuse?"

"Because I am nothing. I'm a mere human servant. I bring nothing to the table beyond my knowledge and experience. I'm sure my brain is the only reason I am still alive."

"You trying to tell me that the queen will have you killed if you don't do as you're told?" I stared at her, aghast.

"Not the queen."

I knew what she was saying. The queen was a mere pawn. My gaze drifted around the room, pausing for a moment on a flash of white before I looked back at her. "And I'd bet every cent of that dowry I'll never have, that a certain influential solicitor is the one moving the chess pieces."

Her eyebrows rose. "You catch on fast."

"It's a privilege of being a woman. It's called instinct."

Sienna giggled and slipped her hand into the crook of my elbow. "Come. Before people start talking, let me take you to the Queen. He's been glaring at me."

"Yeah, I saw that. Let's go." I walked with her, then out of the side of my mouth, I asked, "You think it would cause an inter-realm incident if I were to punch him in the face?"

Her laughter turned into a choke, which she suppressed as fast as she could. She was good, because within seconds she'd removed all trace of amusement from her face. She drew me toward the queen and bowed before leaving us alone.

If one can be alone with having your every step dogged by the beautiful Andyr.

He took my hand and bowed low over it. "I believe compliments are in order, Kailin Odel, Emissary of the Elders. Your beauty is almost incomparable. You have turned a few heads and surprised many. The Elders have chosen wisely in sending you to us."

I raised my eyebrows and glared at him. "I believe you are implying that I will get what I want from you and the queen just because I'm appealing to the eye?"

Queen Lyra clicked her tongue. "That's exactly what he is trying to say. Andyr here believes a woman gets her way by using her looks and her body."

Her tone was bitter and angry, and even though he stared at her with fury, she didn't budge an inch. Her smile surprised me. Genuine, even warm.

"Come walk with me, Kailin Odel."

One does not deny a queen, so I walked with her.

CHAPTER 39

"**W**hat is his problem anyway?" I asked, trying hard not to look behind me because I knew he'd be standing there, staring at us.

"He thinks he has more say in the running of this country than I do."

"Does he?" The question popped out before I even thought to stop it. Terrified I had offended her, I gave her an apologetic smile.

Queen Lyra simply nodded, shocking me further. "To be quite honest Andyr has made inroads with many of the council members. Much of the Senate give him their support. Maybe it's his money, or perhaps he has a power we are unaware of, or maybe he is right, that looks get you everywhere." She sighed and stared off into the distance. "I'm outvoted at every turn, reprimanded at every opportunity. Every year that passes I grow more weary of it."

I felt strange. I'd come here thinking Queen Lyra was the bad guy, that perhaps she'd orchestrated her sister's death in order to ascend the throne, but it seemed that she was just trying to do her duty and was up against a whole Senate full of people who wanted to oust her.

"I'm really sorry to hear that. Perhaps you need a new solicitor."

"I fear we do not have much hope of ridding ourselves of our beautiful lawmaker."

I shook my head as we turned a corner at the end of the room. "Where is he from? He doesn't look like he's from Drakys."

She laughed softly. "You are beyond astute." Admiration edged into her voice. "He comes from your world. But sometimes I can't quite believe it."

"Why is that?"

"Just something about him. He seems magical, as if he can control the emotions of people around him. Not saying that he can levitate things or walk through doors, but there is an odd power about him."

I nodded. "I know exactly what you mean, I felt it the first moment he touched me."

Crap, Kai. Talk about oversharing.

I shouldn't trust her so easily. There was too much at stake.

She smiled and touched my shoulder. "It is a woman thing. Which is something that I most admired about my sister. She was powerful, yes. Her DragonFyr was like nothing anyone had ever seen. But beyond that, even beyond her intelligence, it was her instinct that I admired the most. She could tell a lie from a mile away, and I often wish I had that power."

"You miss her?" I asked softly, deciding to take advantage of the moment.

She nodded and then we took another corner, heading back along the other side of the room. People had moved around, combinations had changed and Andyr looked like he was heading Sienna's way.

"They would make a beautiful couple," I said.

Queen Lyra snorted. "If there was a heart somewhere in that

well-defined chest, then I would probably say she deserves to have him. But Sienna doesn't deserve a man so uncaring. I would rather she die an old maid than to see her marry a man like him."

The Queen turned to look at me. "Some would say that I'm against the marriage because *I* want him as my husband. But that is untrue. I have reigned for two decades. I have done my duty in the memory of my sister. But I grow weary. Weary of having no support, weary of men trying to push me out in order to gain control of a country that has no *leader*." Her tone was derisive yet still filled with hurt. All these years and those who were meant to support her were merely using her.

"The trade agreement would make you more powerful," I said. "*You* would have the full support of the Elders, and even though you're not the queen they want, you can be the queen they need."

She studied my face, her expression flitting from confused to relieved, and then to guilty. "I had thought of it. The moment you arrived I wondered if the Elder's offer would be my saving grace. But I don't deserve the help of the Elders," she said softly, turning to look out of the window. "There are things I have done that cannot be undone."

I shook my head. "What you've done in the past is just that - the past. You can always change your future. And you can always try to repair the damage."

She shook her head. "In this case there is no reparation."

"Then at least make a way forward that is better for your kingdom."

I smiled, hoping to temper my words but my audacity didn't seem to matter because Queen Lyra simply waved a regal hand at the table. "Come, it's time to eat. Our chef will not hide his displeasure if the food gets cold."

We both laughed softly and headed to the far end of the table. Andyr came to help the queen take her seat, before taking the place at her right hand. I slowed my steps, hoping I wouldn't end up looking idiotic having no idea where I was meant to sit.

But a hand on my arm saved me the worry. Sienna guided me to the chair at the left hand of the queen. "Here is your seat. As the guest of honor, your place will be at Queen Lyra's side. And I will be right here beside you."

As she sat, I let a sigh of relief escape. The grandiosity of the room and the decor was a little overwhelming and despite my rest, my body was rebelling. I was still healing after all.

I swallowed hard and sat as elegantly as I could as a light buzz of conversation began to simmer around us.

Andyr sat not six feet from me, his eyes drifting across the three women before him. The first course was served; a delectable ice which Sienna advised was made from *kish*, the fruit of a tree that was similar in taste to a grape. Unfortunately, it bore a striking resemblance to a clam.

Course after course appeared, thankfully each portion was only large enough to qualify as a few bites. Which was perfect for tasting the delicious variety of foods from fish to game to poultry. Drakys had plenty of meat and vegetables which resulted in an impressive table. As it happened I made it to the end of the dessert course with a mere bite to spare.

I'd been afraid that the tightly bound corset would stop me from enjoying the meal but it too had proved kind on my stomach. Just when I thought I could not put anything else into my mouth, Andyr got to his feet and tapped his fork against his crystal goblet. The sound sang through the great room, bringing everyone's smiling attention to his commanding gaze.

"Queen Regent Lyra of the house Yl would like to thank you all for attending this dinner, held in honor of the arrival of Kailin Odel, Emissary of the Elders of the Supreme High Council, Guardians of the Realms." Then he faced me, flicking a finger at the servants around the room, who surged forward with silver trays of tiny glasses containing what looked like port or sherry.

Dark and red were all I could tell.

They rounded the room, serving each guest. A separate server brought a platter with a single glass and handed it to Andyr. He passed the glass to me and raised his own, forcing me to stand in order to be polite. I never enjoyed being the center of attention.

He cleared his throat. "Kailin Odel, a toast in your honor. May your stay here be comfortable and fruitful."

A round of cheers went up and Andyr downed his drink. Others around the room, including the queen and Sienna, did the same so I followed suit, barely registering the sweet liquid as it made its way down my throat.

Once the toast was completed, the guests began to mingle again, slowly drifting to me to have a polite word. After the third delegate had shaken my hand and offered his high hopes for the success of my stay, I blinked as my vision began to blur.

I swallowed, my throat swelling making it hard to breathe. I blinked, searching out Sienna, only to find her on the other side of the room talking to the queen.

Tightening the muscles in my legs, I took a step toward her then stopped as the room began to spin. I wavered on my feet, my legs as fluffy as marshmallow.

A second attempt to swallow failed, my mouth thick and cotton-wooled, my lips and tongue numb.

Please don't drool. Please don't drool.

I grabbed the back of the nearest chair, blinking hard as I struggled to remain upright.

A voice beside me inquired as to my health, another could be heard calling Sienna to us.

But I passed out before she came.

I swallowed, my throat tight as I opened my eyes. The room was familiar; my quarters in the Palace of Dyr.

I sighed, relieved, until I heard the rustling of fabric. Expecting Sienna, I smiled and tilted my head in search of her.

Instead I found a man leaning against the open balcony door, staring down at the countryside.

My sigh drew his attention and he turned, pushing off the wall and gazing at me, his dark eyes filled with concern.

"Logan?" I asked, blinking fast, not quite sure what I was seeing.

How was Logan with me, in Drakys, when he was unconscious in my bed back in Tukats. Could it be that he'd recovered?

"Logan? How are you here?"

He sat beside me. Taking my hand, he kissed my fingers and I watched him, frowning as his lips touched my fingers and a spark flared. A spark that was the furthest from attraction or comfort of anything I'd ever experienced.

"How are you feeling?" He traced a finger along my cheekbone and I shied away.

"Awful. I have no idea what happened to me. I hope it wasn't food poisoning." I found myself conversing with him as if it was totally expected that he'd be here with me in the palace in Drakys.

It wasn't.

"I'm sure they'll find out it was the food." He sounded certain.

I watched him, listening as hard as I could as the volume of his voice rose and fell.

"How are you here?" I asked him again, my tone insistent, almost threatening, definitely suspicious. "You can't be here."

"What do you mean?" He leaned forward, his expression curious.

I frowned as the room tilted a little. Concentrating hard on my words, I said, "You're in Tukats, unconscious. Or at least that's where you were when I left home." I lifted myself onto my elbows battling the rising nausea and dizziness. "How did you recover so quickly?"

He smiled gently, his face wavering in front of me as he leaned closer. "Of course, I have recovered. How else would I be here?"

I frowned, staring hard as his face swam before me, one moment in focus the next an unrecognizable blur.

"How is that even possible? Darcy said it would take time."

I coughed and cleared my throat as I moved my legs over the edge of the bed. I had to get to my feet, had to make sure this wasn't just some food-poisoning-induced hallucination. And a larger part of me wanted to put some space between myself and this impossible apparition.

I cleared my throat and took a few steps away from him. But he followed, coming around to block my way.

Logan smiled, his expression making me slightly dizzy as I stared hard, trying to understand what was wrong with this picture.

I reached out and he took my hand, leading me closer to the window. He pushed the silky drapes aside and led me out onto a narrow balcony, protected only by a waist-high glass balustrade.

The wind gusted hard at this height and I wondered why they'd built a balcony when a person could easily get blown off it.

Of course, Land of Dragons.

Logan's arm went around me and I swallowed. I was here in Drakys, which meant Logan was at home in Tukats, which meant either this was a dream or I was in deep shit.

When his arm tightened I gasped, more at the proximity to the balustrade than his grasp. I glanced up and his face shimmered, as if a mirage was layered over his features, and then it shifted.

Just for the briefest second.

"You're not Logan." I barely got the words out before he grabbed me by the throat and began lifting me off the tiled floor, began to squeeze the air out of me.

I kicked out, grabbing at the lapels of his coat, my fingers burning as it scraped something dagger-sharp, but his hold was impossibly tight. Shadows crept in at the edges of my vision.

A sound caught my attention, the door to my room opening with a rush and a creak. Sienna burst inside, staring at the empty bed in surprise.

It all seemed to happen in slow motion. Sienna's hair shifting around her face as she turned her head to stare out at the open balcony door.

Her eyes going wide with shock as she caught sight of me, so dangerously close to the edge.

The glass dug into my back as my attacker pushed me back, further, closer to death. I considered the fact that I was feline and wondered if at such a height I'd be lucky enough to land on my feet.

Part of my brain registered Sienna surging into a run as she raced to save me. I tried to shake my head, to scream at her to stop but no sound or movement arose.

"Kai!"

Sienna's voice cut through my mind so sharply that I blinked, aware that I hovered a foot above the air.

"Stop. What are you doing?" she screamed.

Her body hit my attacker's, causing him to push me further over the edge. I choked, desperate to tell her to stop. Not to save myself but to warn her that she was now also in danger.

They struggled as Sienna screamed, "Let her go!" She slammed her hands into his arms and I felt the vibrations of the blow around my throat.

The loud crack of glass rang out and even at this altitude the sound echoed.

And then we fell.

Shards of glass pierced the fabric my dress, my ankle twisted, and something tore painfully at my fingertips.

We were falling.

Sienna's arms were around my waist and she was screaming. Wind flapped against our gowns and I bore a faint hope that they would act as parachutes.

Air rushed around us, and behind me Sienna was panicking, struggling for air. I couldn't see her. I was about to apologize for failing her when a sudden gust of wind hit us sideways and we were airborne, as if we'd become weightless.

The grip around my waist tightened and when I looked down I saw giant claws encircling my torso. Where Sienna's hands had been only seconds ago.

Air billowed past me, and I craned to look behind me, knowing already what I would see.

Sienna, the golden dragon.

CHAPTER 41

The great golden dragon held me gently, its wingspan thirty feet wide or more. It banked and made a gentle turn, then thrust its leathery wings. Wind rushed against my face as the giant creature skimmed the air currents before slowing in front of my balcony.

It angled its body, wings flapping high above, and lower legs stretched. The creature landed gingerly on the small balcony, only a tiny square of crystal, its giant claws clicking loudly on the smooth floor.

It unfurled its claws and released me, and before I could offer my thanks it began to shimmer. Gold and bronze light swirled while specks of sunlight sparkled within the haze of color. The giant form rippled, undulating into an even smaller shape and then it disappeared in a puff of bronze and gold light.

I slumped to the cool tiles, knees and hands slamming against the floor, my limbs too filled with the icy numbness of shock to move. Sienna lay on the floor beside me, her flaming hair fanned around her, her face pale.

Her clothing remained intact, not ripped to pieces like most shifters. Drakyr must have different magic from shifters.

She lay deathly still and I leaned closer, ready to perform CPR, but then her eyelids fluttered and she let out a soft puff of air. She frowned, groaning as she lifted her hands and pressed them to her forehead.

"What the hell just happened?" she mumbled.

"Don't you remember?" I crawled forward, my own shock forgotten as I worried over her.

She shook her head. "One moment I was fighting off your attacker and the next we were falling." She squinted back up at me, and gold flames flickered in her eyes. "How did we get back up here?"

"A dragon saved us." I didn't elaborate.

She scowled. "Who? Where did they go?" She got to her knees, reaching for the balustrade, and stared out over the city. Smoke curled from chimneys, and soft lights glowed from windows opened onto the dark streets.

Beyond, stars twinkled, silver and blood, in an inky sky. There was no dragon in sight.

I shrugged. "No idea." I'd never seen a dragon before today, much less been cuddled by one. Although the creature had been gentle with me, I had to admit I was a little freaked out.

Even though I knew that Sienna was the dragon, I decided that it was best not to tackle this new development with her just yet. Something was very wrong with her. Her memories must have been tampered with. It's what I'd expect from Omega so nothing surprised me now.

But as I studied her pale profile, her confused expression, I had to wonder how many other times had this happened. How often had she shifted into Drakyr form and then not recalled a thing?

The danger in this was unquestionable, and terrifying.

But it wasn't something I could just drop in her lap this minute. She needed time to process it all. I'd have to ease her into her new reality. And while doing that I had to understand what was staring at me in the face.

If Sienna is a Drakyr, then Logan is too.

It meant that Logan was no human fire mage. And Sienna was no human Drakyr slave.

Logan and Sienna, twins with powers that have been hidden even from themselves, watched over by people who don't seem to have their best interests at heart. Who would want to keep them powerless and ignorant of who they really are?

The Queen and the General.

My mind repeatedly looped back to the story of the powerful twins destined to sit upon the Drakys throne. Could Logan and Sienna be these twins? Were they caught up in some royal political power play? If so then that put Lyra's integrity in the spotlight.

Or was it more sinister? Perhaps an inter-realm power play with Omega at the head of it all? And considering Reid's death, was the mining of the Erulite of any importance?

And if all of this were true then were they the rightful Queen and General of Drakys?

I pushed to my feet, tracing a finger along my now throbbing throat. I'd have a bruise within a few hours. Would be fun explaining that to the Senate in the morning.

Sienna turned to me. She weaved on her feet for a moment then came to curl an arm around my waist as she helped me to my feet.

"What happened to you? Who was that man?" she asked as she helped me into the room. Her voice was tinged with uneasiness; she asked a question to which I suspected she already had the answer.

"Someone . . . Someone was in my room."

"I saw . . ." She sent a panicked glance at the empty balcony behind me. "He looked . . . familiar."

"It wasn't Logan." I said his name, even as I wondered how

wise it was to discuss him here, considering the invasion of my room. But a man had attempted to murder me, I should be far more careful about the real reason I was here.

The mention of Logan drew an unexpected reaction from Sienna.

She stiffened. "You . . ." She let go of me and put her finger to her lips.

I sat on the bed and took a deep breath. "I'm fine. I think it may have just been a hallucination." I stared hard at her and she got my drift.

She nodded, turning on her heel and heading out into the living area. She opened the door, then over her shoulder she called, "I believe that some fresh air would do you good. I know the perfect place."

I pushed to my feet. At least breathing was a little easier now, although it still hurt to swallow.

As I reached the door, she placed an arm around my waist, offering to help me out of the apartment and into the hallway. I steeled my muscles, taking my weight onto my own feet and gave Sienna a smile of gratitude before sending her a pointed glance at the pair of guards who bracketed the entrance to my room.

Despite appreciating her help, I didn't want either them, or any passers-by, to see me weak, and she appeared to understand, giving me a supportive smile and removing her hand.

We continued along the hall, Sienna's twin guard-dogs a dozen yards behind, Sienna herself walking slowly to ensure I didn't get worn out, but she didn't have much experience with Walkers. A mere five minutes passed before the ache in my throat subsided. I knew the bruises would have faded a little too, it was only bullets and arrows which managed to bring a walker to their knees.

At the end of the cavernous hall, we reached a set of stairs that led up and around, along a tower wall. The clanking and tapping of the guards' armor and heels drew to a stop as they contemplated our next move.

Without a glance backward, we followed the stairs up two flights, the tap of my boots on the stone risers echoing up and down the tower stairwell. Sienna's guards maintained a decent distance.

At the landing we were halted by a giant metal door and two fierce looking guards.

Fierce Guard One scowled. "Counsel Sienna."

He tipped his head the tiniest bit, as if deferring to her seniority, but there was a burning of some emotion in his eyes. Had it been malice, I may have been tempted to dispatch him then and there. But then, in my new position I wasn't allowed the privilege of doing as I wanted.

"Hello Fes." Syn's smile was at loggerheads with his icy demeanor. "The Emissary of the Elders wished to see the view and I told her the battlements here provide an incomparable one."

The two guards shifted away and Fes opened the door. He closed the door and attempted to follow us outside but Sienna turned and said, "We will be discussing private Senate and Treaty issues. I'm afraid you need to keep your distance."

He paused, then took up position beside the door without a complaint. Behind the slit it was easy to see he wasn't happy.

Sienna didn't seem to care. She took my arm and began walking me toward the parapet. Black gravel crunched beneath our boots, and a cool breeze fanned my heated cheeks; a welcome relief.

Safe at the edge of the parapet, Sienna faced me, her eyes showing the strain of our recent encounter.

I sighed. "I was poisoned."

"I figured as much." She nodded, a dark look in her eyes. Her profile was shadowed, light from the torches cast strange accents on her bone structure, and yet they couldn't erase her beauty. "Who?"

"Whoever it was used Logan's form to trick me." Anger strummed my vocal chords and I had to take a deep breath. "I don't know for sure, but I'm beginning to suspect it was Andyr."

Sienna's eyes widened. "What makes you think that?"

I opened my fist and revealed the diamond clasp in my palm. Sharply angled, it looked like a naturally formed crystal but from the workmanship it was easy to tell that the gem was Fae and hand-carved. "When I first laid eyes on it, I knew it was familiar. I'd seen it only two days ago, on Elan, the Winter Prince."

"The *Fae* Winter Prince?"

"That's the one. And when I met Andyr this morning, I felt something familiar about him. I didn't recognize the clasp. That was stupid."

"Why would he think nobody would recognize it?" Sienna shook her head, perplexed.

I made a face. "Elan is arrogant. I doubt he'd have expected to meet anyone that he knew here in Drakys."

Sienna tapped the black crystal of the parapet wall. We stood between two merlons, looking out at the dark valley. "This is too much. I think my head is going to explode." She moved her hand to cradle her forehead.

The transformation must have taken its toll on her, even if she didn't know it. Now, more than ever, I had to get her to leave with me.

I took her hand away from her head. "I'm here to help you."

"Logan sent you." She eyed me warily. "He said he would."

I nodded, relieved I didn't need to fight her.

"He made me promise to find you. To tell you about the danger you face here, and to ask you to come home to help him."

She frowned and faced me, fear lighting the flame in her eyes. "Help him? What's wrong with him? Is he okay?" Her hand was back on the wall, this time clutching the edge hard enough that the white of her knuckles gleamed.

I shook my head. "No. He's in a coma. We don't know how to save him and he wanted me to tell you to come to see him."

She stared at me. "That makes no sense. How does he speak to you if he's in a coma? How is he speaking to me?"

"His thoughts can still touch you, as long as you allow him in." I smiled. "We used a DeathTalker to communicate. He showed me where you were in Sand Beach. And he's in a coma, not dead."

"That *was* you. I knew it." She managed a brief smile. "The Goth look suits you. And I should have guessed considering goth had been my choice of disguise in Sand Beach."

I nodded. "We came hoping to find you, but why did you try to have us killed?"

"What?" She gasped. "No. I did no such thing."

"Someone did. After you left us at the diner, Lily was injured and I was too. Badly."

She shook her head. "I go to Sand Beach sometimes to think. Not many people know that I go. I doubt it would be received with enthusiasm. My guards understand. They take me, watch over the portal and me. They trust me."

"Clearly they don't trust you enough. Whoever we encountered in Sand Beach were prepared to protect you to the death."

"What do you mean?" she asked in a whisper.

"I killed someone there. A shadow mage."

She looked confused. "I don't know any shadow mages. Most human mages aren't even allowed into Drakys."

I frowned. "So if you don't know who is protecting you, then maybe they aren't protecting *you* as much as they're keeping people *from* you. They must have seen us together at the beach or the diner, then targeted us after you left. Eliminating possible friends that may lure you away."

She snorted. "I'm not that important. I advise the queen, yes, but I hardly warrant such drastic measures. Not killing, surely." Confusion simmered in her tone.

"But you warrant a twenty-four-seven guard?"

Her shoulder lifted in a dainty shrug. "I do have a lot of state secrets up here." She tapped her temple.

"And so does Andyr. You don't see him guarded all day, do you?"

"Good point," she said, her mouth twisting in a wry smile.

I sighed. "Something else is happening here, Sienna. Something we can't yet understand. But whatever it is, it can wait. Right now, the most important thing as far as I am concerned is Logan. I need you to help me save him." I stared at her, my voice pleading.

"How can *I* save him?"

I shook my head. "I don't know. He's a fire mage and you are brother and sister. Your fire is there somewhere, deep inside you." I didn't want to tell her that there was more than just fire lurking within her. But that didn't stop me from probing. "Do you ever dream of strange, unusual things? Magical things?"

She stiffened, and even in the darkness I could see her face pale. "Like what?"

I lifted a shoulder. "I can't be sure. Maybe fire? Being burned? Maybe you dream of throwing fireballs, or breathing fire."

She nodded but her neck was tight as she shifted her gaze to the city lights. "Even if what you say is true, and my dreams do mean I have the same powers as Logan, how can I help him? What can I do?"

I wasn't blind to the agony in her voice. Whatever bond she had with Logan, however tenuous, it was unbreakable. And filled with emotion.

"There are theories. That maybe your fire can help him heal. That just being with him will help him recover faster. Whatever happens, we will do everything we can to help you get back home and make this place safer for you." I touched her arm, and she glanced back up at me.

"You don't have to keep trying to convince me, Kailin. I will go back with you, if only to meet my brother." I nodded. "I will do what I can to help him."

I sighed with relief. "Thank you. You have no idea how happy I am to hear that."

She patted my hand. "We do have a problem though. As much as I'd like to go back with you, I doubt the queen will allow it."

"Then perhaps we don't give her a choice?"

Sienna raised an eyebrow. "Let the games begin."

CHAPTER 42

The next morning, Sienna fetched me early to grab a quick breakfast in the morning room before the Senate meeting. Although much smaller than the great dining room, the place was a miniature version, right down to the decor and the floor-to-ceiling window.

We'd barely swallowed coffee and a dark, almost black flaky pastry that reminded me of burnt croissants, when a guard entered and announced that the Senate was ready for me.

I held Horner's leather folder tightly as I entered the room, ready to do battle with these stubborn men.

But I needn't have worried.

The absence of Andyr was significant enough to confirm my suspicions, and inquiries as to his whereabouts received a number of vague and evasive responses.

The Queen Regent sat at the head of the table, a mere puppet to the gathered Senate, her skin pale and tight as she nodded and smiled, all the while exuding a quiet fury. Beside her sat General Vyrian, who I was surprised to see with a seat on the Senate. It would have made sense had he been the queen's brother, so perhaps he was family.

All points on the list were agreed to, the Senate stating that they required a paired management system for each mine, one overseer for the Elders and one for the Senate to maintain transparency.

Decisions of sale prices were deferred to a later date, but at the end, I thought the Elders would be happy with my progress.

I'd done my part.

As the General got to his feet, effectively dismissing me, I cleared my throat. "I do have one small request." He raised a bushy eyebrow. "I'd like a tour of the mine. Just so I can brief the Elders on what we need to help upgrade in terms of machinery. If that were required."

"I'm happy to show Kailin around, if that's okay with you?" Sienna asked. In the face of the table filled with mostly unreadable faces, I could feel her concern that they may decline.

The General cleared his throat. "I'm afraid the queen wishes to see you first. In private." He gave Queen Lyra a hesitant glance then met Sienna's eyes with what looked like fatherly sympathy.

Was nobody really who they first appeared to be?

The room emptied and I followed the men out, spending the next few minutes pacing the stone floor while Sienna spoke to the queen.

Less than five minutes later, she stalked from the room, her cheeks red. The look she gave me announced trouble.

"You may have to miss out on your trip to the mine." Her voice was filled with anger and frustration, her spine stiff as she grabbed hold of my arm and pulled me down the hallway.

"What's the matter?" I hissed.

Sienna looked over her shoulder. Her guards were about twenty feet behind us so she lowered her voice and said, "If you want to get me out of here, we need to do it now. Andyr moved up the wedding date. The Queen just told me to get my affairs in order. I will be married in three days."

My jaw dropped. "What the hell is he up to?"

Sienna shook her head, pulling me down the stairs. "I have no idea. He tried to kill you, and now he wants to move the wedding date up. Sounds to me like he feels threatened."

I snorted. "Sounds like he feels my growing connection to you is a threat to him."

She stopped in her tracks, on a stair halfway down the flight, and stared at me, confused at first until things clicked into place. "You think I'm the real reason he's here?" She frowned. Then shook her head. "I'm of no value to him. Why would he risk so much just because of me?"

"I think I know why."

She raised an eyebrow as if daring me to come up with a good one.

"Do you ever dream of flying?"

At my question, Syn's face paled, and she let go of my hand. "How would you know such a thing?" She inhaled sharply and continued her descent. I followed.

"Because what happened today on the balcony tells me that you are of more value then you realize."

Stopping at the base of the staircase, she turned sharply to me and asked, "What happened?" She sounded impatient, the words slicing through her teeth.

"We were falling, you and me. We weren't far from the ground, seconds away from being splattered all over the market square. And from nowhere a golden dragon appeared and carried me to safety." I kept my voice low.

"I thought we both fell. I'm sure . . . That's what I remembered," she whispered.

"We did both fall."

"But if the dragon saved you then how did I get back to the balcony?"

I met her gaze head-on. "How do you think?"

Sienna shook her head. "You think the dragon was me?"

I nodded.

"Dear Goddess."

CHAPTER 43

We agreed that we keep up the pretense of the mine visit and use it as a means to make a getaway. We returned to my room to prepare for the visit.

"By the way, how did you manage to get the queen's permission?"

She gave a firm nod. "I bargained for it so I'm damned well taking you."

"Bargained?" I asked as I packed my rucksack.

"It was one of my conditions."

"You gave her conditions?" I asked, smirking. I grabbed the leather folder.

Sienna handed me my satchel. "Yes. I agreed to the marriage as long as I can assist the Emissary of the Elders during their tenure in Drakys. And as long as I don't need to sleep with him for the first five years."

I choked and ended up coughing up my laughter. "You're kidding right?" Tucking my folder into the satchel, I sat it beside my rucksack, now ready to leave.

Sienna folded her arms and lifted her chin. "Not kidding. In

Drakys a woman can choose if, and when, she wants to bed her husband. It was a law that Queen Shrya's great-grandmother passed a few centuries back."

This time I did laugh. "No wonder the men want to control things. They're being deprived." I sniggered. Moving to the balcony I shut the glass door and pulled the drapes.

Sienna grinned. "I totally agree. Now, just give me a few minutes to pack a bag and arrange our transport, then I'll come fetch you."

I frowned. "I don't want to leave you alone. I'll come with you."

"I'm just a little worried about our bags. If someone suspects anything they may be inspected."

My turn to negate her words. I pointed to my chest. "Diplomatic immunity."

She smiled. "Ah yes, I forgot." A contemplative frown creased her brow "If that's the case then you may as well hide my stuff inside your bag. I won't pack too much." She grinned as we headed to her room.

True to her words she packed light, taking only a small silk jewel bag, and a single change of clothing.

With a nod Sienna smiled and headed for the door. "Let's get moving. It's a long way there."

As we entered the corridor I asked, "Surely we can get us a pair of wings? This city is full of dragons, isn't it?"

Sienna smiled, glancing over her shoulder at the guards who fell into step behind us. "I never said we'd be walking, did I?"

AIR RUSHED AGAINST MY FACE, pressing against my skin, pushing into my mouth and nostrils as I struggled to breathe without passing out. Sienna had been right. Her two guards had kindly provided us with winged transport, although I worried that we'd need to ditch them soon.

We were so high up the air felt like icicles in my throat. Below us the fields were a patchwork of greens and browns, not that different to back home. We followed the Red River almost halfway to the portal cave when the guard, or dragon, that I rode banked right and dove for the river. He aimed at the point in the river where it dove beneath the mountains, and I frowned despite the gusting of air against my face.

I'd passed this way and never known it was there.

The dragon reached for the ground with his massive hind legs, claws glinting in the afternoon light as they hit and scraped against the sandy shoreline.

His powerful, leathery wings flapped loudly around my ears, the sound drowning out even that of his companion, who'd also landed beside us.

Sienna slid effortlessly off, with all the confidence of someone who'd been doing this for years. I, on the other hand struggled, afraid to hurt him if I held on too hard, worried that if I descended carelessly, I would make him uncomfortable. It was a strange feeling knowing that the creature you are riding is a sentient being, as intelligent as you are.

My dragon lowered his body to the ground, angling his front leg in such a way that I could use it as a step. I placed my foot gently on his scaly knee, holding onto the spikes at the side of his neck, and jumped to the ground, my heart still jumping from the hair-raising ride.

As soon as I descended, he transformed back to human form and stood to attention, as if he'd not just been a gigantic flying creature moments before. The transformation was equally as amazing as that of Sienna's, except her dragon was magnificent compared with these two, and twice as big.

It was interesting to watch, the first dragon was an amalgamation of silver and gold where the second bordered on black and gray with silver sparkles. Beautiful, yet nothing when compared to the beauty of Sienna's gold transformation.

When I looked up she was at the edge of the water beside a set of dangerous looking rapids, waving me toward her. I hitched my satchel higher on my shoulder and hurried to join her. She pointed at the side of the rough face of the mountain where the river rushed at it and then seemed to disappear into solid stone.

"That's the entrance to the mine," she said raising her voice so that she could be heard over the rushing of the water. As far as I could see, the entry was invisible.

"Where exactly?" I asked, curious, not impatient.

"Come with me," she said over her shoulder as she strode along the edge of the river bank. The heels of her boots crunched against the black gravel and the longer we walked, the more I had time to notice the area around me. The river was wider here than at any other point that I'd seen since we left the city. The banks on either side were steep, almost vertical, and the water's edge was overgrown with plants.

Strangely beautiful and completely ominous black-leaved, midnight lilies had taken over the surface of the water, sending a pungent perfume our way.

Lilies.

I really disliked lilies.

Despite the rapids, the river ran slowly, probably dammed by the rock face.

Beyond the riverbank, the land on either side was barren, giant trees with bark as black as the lilies, almost scorched. And leaves that hung lifelessly from the branches, their colors overcome by rot.

My heart crashed against my ribs. The sights around me were far too familiar and my steps slowed. Even the sound of the clinking of the armor behind me didn't make me move. My ears were ringing, and I felt Sienna come to stand beside me.

"What is it?" she said softly beside me.

"I can't believe what I'm seeing," I whispered, swallowing the words that rose in my throat.

My mind was filled with a tornado of impossible thoughts. I was beginning to see a parallel between the condition of these trees, and the presence of a Fae in this realm. The very same Fae who could possibly be a traitor to my best friend.

Could Elan be the reason Tara's investigators had lied to her? Could the Fae Prince be behind the killing of our Ash Trees?

"What is it?" Sienna asked, her tone worried, urging me to answer.

But I just shook my head. The guards were too close for a conversation that could prove dangerous. We'd have time to discuss this soon enough. Once we were back home.

I gave a sheepish smile. "I've just never seen anything so unusual before." I pointed at the black petals of the lily.

Sienna smiled. "I understand how you feel. This black lily is one of the most deadly flora on the surface of this world."

I raised my eyebrows, falling into step beside her as she began to walk along the river again.

She pointed at the jagged rise of the mountain. "The mine is here, just beneath the surface. It's efficient, and uses little labor and time as possible. But the mining process produced a toxic sludge. It ends up back in this water. And the lily, over the years, has absorbed the toxin, transforming its very nature. Giving us this." She waved a hand at the flowers.

I shook my head, frowning. "And mining will continue to poison the river?"

I was quickly beginning to doubt the intelligence of the decision to begin mining again.

"It will continue to poison the river, yes. And the surrounding areas. But that's where it stops. The black lily absorbs the toxins, cleaning the water and allowing it to continue on its journey. It is one of the reasons why we don't mind mining the Erulite. We have a perfect natural method of ensuring our water remains unpolluted."

I stared at the flower and then back at the trees that surrounded us.

The dead trees.

Trees dead like the Great Ash.

CHAPTER 44

shook my head. "I'm not sure that the toxins are being cleaned." I pointed at a collection of trees whose species I could not identify, but whose affliction I understood completely. "That shouldn't be happening."

Sienna paused before a rock that curved outward, hiding a large archway inside. She looked across the river at the thinned stand of trees. "Unfortunately their root system reaches too close to the river, and some of the toxins have leached in through their water supply. It's unavoidable, but I can assure you that it is restricted only to this area. The poison does not reach the city's water system. Our people and our crops are safe. Of that we have been extremely careful."

As she began to walk off, I hesitated. I knew what I had to do. "Wait up," I called.

I spun on my heel and hurried back to the batch of lilies, kneeling beside the water as Sienna drew up beside me.

"What are you doing?" She crouched beside me.

"I just think they're so beautiful," I said, my voice an octave too high.

Sienna's eyes widened before she glanced quickly over her

shoulder. She rolled her eyes at the two guards who laughed between themselves at the silly outlander going nuts over their poison lilies.

While they had their fun, I picked a couple of lilies, and carefully slid them into two separate plastic bags. I slipped the bags into my jacket pocket and nodded at Sienna.

Aware of the guards behind me I gave her a nod as if I were satisfied with her explanation, but the look she gave me told me that she knew I wasn't done with this conversation.

She glanced over her shoulder at her guards and pointed to trees further back up the hill that were green and alive, and actually did provide shade. "Set up camp there. I will give Kailin a tour of Sector One. And we'll stop at the viewing platform for Sector Two. Don't worry. I won't go any further than that."

The guards both nodded, their expressions somber yet unconcerned, as if convinced that there was nowhere else that she would, or could, go. They both turned and walked off without even looking back.

"So much for shadowing your every move," I mumbled.

She huffed. "It's boring and tiring for them to dog my every step. My life is uninteresting."

I shrugged. "Me, I'd fire them this second for incompetence."

Sienna laughed. "The General would like you." Then she gave me a surreptitious glance and pulled on my elbow. "Come, we have to be quick. It takes about an hour to inspect Sector One, so we have a head start. If we're not back by then they will come looking for us."

I followed closely behind her. "Lead me to the back door."

She laughed, the sound echoing against the rock face before us. "Follow me."

Inside the tunnel, the sound of rushing water enveloped us, so loud that it even dulled the echoing noise our boots made on the obsidian floor. We walked through a long tube of jagged black glass.

Beside us a rickety looking cart sat on a track, the metal and wood old and cracking.

"So how exactly is the Erulite mined?"

She paused and pointed to a hollow gouged from the wall; a crater with the center much deeper than the side. "We use heat. DragonFyr. An initial indentation is made with a chisel. The problem with metal tools is that they shatter the Erulite, making it difficult to transport."

I nodded, understanding what she meant. Solid rocks were easier to move around as opposed to bags and bags of ground up crystal.

"The rocks are transported along the mines rail system beneath the mountain. Sector One is where the rocks are mined. They are processed in Sector Two."

"Processed?"

"More like 'graded'. Before they are sent out for sale, they are sorted manually. A dedicated, experienced technician studies each and every rock that comes through here. They guarantee only the highest quality of Erulite."

I stared around the tunnels as we walked. I would have been concerned for our safety but we were both fully capable of protecting ourselves, even if Sienna still didn't know exactly how to.

I cleared my throat, aware that what I was about to suggest may not go down well with Sienna. "I'm beginning to suspect that Reid was killed because he found out something sensitive or potentially dangerous to the city."

Sienna nodded. She glanced over her shoulder before saying, "I agree." She kept her voice to a soft whisper as we hurried along the path and veered left. Into almost pitch blackness. "I discovered something about the mines two years ago. About the time that your fae prince arrived."

"*My* fae prince?" I was offended.

She giggled. "He isn't mine either."

"Pretty sure it's *you* that he's marrying."

She cleared her throat. "So I was coming back from the portal when I stopped here one night. It was late, and just after the Rebirth Ceremony Day. As you know, without a queen the rebirth ceremony is merely a date, but there are small bands of acolytes who make a pilgrimage to the Life's Blood."

"Life's Blood?" I asked, intrigued. "Is that the special egg that the queen must imbue with her power?"

Sienna nodded, her look of approval amusing. As if I really was here as an Emissary. "The Hollow of the Life's Blood is located on the other side of the mountain. Below it runs a stream, and I believe some of the life of the egg leeches into the water as the stream runs by. In the old times, the priests believed the egg was magical and that the water contained healing properties. Anyway, while I was there I noticed a strange glow in the water where the lilies grow. I followed the side stream all the way to the egg where it originated. Since then I was convinced Reid probably discovered that the flowers were more than just poisonous. And someone wanted it kept a secret."

"Why?" I already suspected I knew the answer.

"The magic of the egg combined with the toxin on the Erulite makes the lilies a super-powerful plant."

"And yet they're still sitting there on the water, as if they were any old lily?" I was incredulous. The freaking plant was deadly. "I'd bet they are somehow harvesting the plants. And Reid must have found out."

We came to a sharp turn, the incline steep now. We were going up. And hopefully out of the mine.

"The outside of the mine is maintained in much the same way as it was five years ago. I suspect it's to ensure that everything looks fine. If, all of a sudden, the lilies disappear that would cause questions to arise."

A gust of icy air hit my cheeks and we exited the tunnel onto a shallow ledge.

"Whatever they are up to, Reid paid the ultimate price."

"Don't worry. The Elders will do what they can to put things right. Someone is taking advantage of your land. And if it's the fae then I'll do everything I can to stop them."

We struggled, keeping our backs close to the cliff-face, moving a foot at a time.

"What can you do to stop them?" Sienna asked, her voice raised so I could hear her against the rushing wind.

"I know the Queen of the Fae." I glanced down the mountain-side. We'd come out further south and across from the guards who'd build a small fire and were ignorant of their escaping charge.

"You know the Fae Queen?" she asked, shocked.

"Yup," I said with a grin. "She's my best friend."

"Oh. Of course. Your best friend," Sienna mumbled as she scrambled up to the ridge and sank to her knees.

I scurried behind her and she glared at me.

"Is there anyone you don't know?"

I shrugged. "I know the important people. That's what counts."

CHAPTER 45

We arrived at the portal on the ice shelf in Alaska and fell straight into the freezing cold water.

Thankfully I'd made a last-second grab for the key as we hit the icy surface and managed to save it.

We, on the other hand were soaked and frozen, and feeling very far from safe.

Sienna's teeth chattered and I matched each clash with my own. We sat side by side on the dock, barely able to get a word out.

"I'd shift if I thought it would help." I said. Then I shook my head, which didn't really matter because I was already shaking my head so hard that my neck hurt. "But I'd just be a wet, freezing cat. My body mass is higher in human form."

Her eyes were wide and I couldn't read them. Was she surprised? Amazed? Incredulous. Who knew.

I pushed to my knees and hobbled to my feet. "We have to get out of this wind or we'll die before Larsson comes back for us."

Sienna's groan was swept away by a gust of snow-laden air. She coughed as she inhaled the iciness then doubled over and swallowed hard.

As we hurried around the dock I stopped so suddenly that she walked right into me.

"What?" she yelled over the gusting wind.

"You?"

"Me?"

"Yes. Do your dragon thing and make us a fire."

"Are you insane?"

"No. We need the warmth or we will die. Either go all scaly and breathe me some fire or at least give me some protection so I can try making one. But just bear in mind the fine print indicates I can't build a fire to save my life."

Sienna was shaking her head. "I can't do either of the things you're asking. I only dream of flying. I can't even remember being a dragon. And as for fire, that's just something I've never done before."

We got to the snow-covered bank beside the river and headed to a pair of trees that offered a tiny harbor against the wind. I rounded on Sienna.

"Quit complaining and help me." I ignored her shocked expression, dropped my satchel on the ground and began to search behind the trees for branches and wood and leaves. Anything that we could use to make a fire.

She left her bag beside mine and followed my lead in silence.

When we had a small pile, I stood beside it and began to stamp my feet to get some blood flow going.

"Well," I yelled at her over the pile of wood. "What are you waiting for?"

"I can't," she screamed back and I could barely hear her.

I shook my head. "Stop making excuses. You can. Your twin is a Fire Mage. Which means you are too. Either make fire or make peace with your spirits because we are going to die."

She stared at me, anger now pooling in her eyes. "It's not my fault we fell into the water."

"Do I look like I'm responsible for the location of the portal?"

I shouted, feeling a twinge of guilt at what I was doing. But the fire of anger in her eyes urged me on. "If you don't make a fire I'm going to die. Try explaining that to Logan when they find you."

"We'll both die."

"Have you not been listening to me? You are a fire mage. You can't die of the cold. Your body will generate enough heat for you to survive. So no fire, I die. You live."

I glared at her, stepping closer as she shook her head. When I shoved her backward she let out a shocked gasp. "Thanks a lot, Sienna. After all I did for you, coming to Drakys to save you, this is how you thank me."

I turned to the fire and stamped harder. I should just shift and run away but I couldn't because I'd lied to her. Her fire wouldn't save her from freezing. She'd have to generate a low ebb of it inside of her body so that she could survive the snowstorm. If she failed to make fire she'd die too.

I spun around and yelled at her. "Just one freaking spark. That's all we need."

She took a step closer, shouting now too. "Why are you doing this to me?"

"To you? I'm doing this to *you*? You're the one too weak to try to save us."

"Don't you understand that I can't just do something I've never done before?"

I laughed even as the sound was snatched away. "You have made fire before. You just don't remember it."

She shook her head, shivering harder now. Her lips were blue and I was sure mine were too. "I can't."

"Logan believed in you." I pointed at her, marveling at how still my finger remained even when my entire body shook with cold. "He protected you when you were children. Even now, dying in a fucking coma, he's protecting you. He'd die if it meant saving you. But it seems you won't do the same."

"Don't say that,." she screamed, tears gleaming in her eyes. "I'd do anything for him."

"Liar," I spat back and began to pace. "Tell that to him when they come for my body."

Then she screamed, so loud that I was afraid the snow-laden branches above would release their cargo on our heads.

Fire sparked within the pile and I rushed to it, unzipping my jacket in a swift swipe to provide as much protection as I could. Sienna did the same, her face still projecting her fury and her hurt so much that she hadn't yet registered what she'd done.

Protected, the weak flame caught onto the twigs and branches, then wavered before flaring and catching onto the rest of the branches.

I looked up from beneath my lashes. "Well done."

She frowned, confused. "What?"

"I knew you had it in you," I said, warming my face in the heat of the fire.

Looking up, I met her eyes as they narrowed, as awareness bloomed behind them.

And I smiled.

She leaned closer, flames flaring within her glare.

"Bitch."

CHAPTER 46

*L*arsson arrived two hours later, during which time Sienna had gotten over her fury.

Mostly.

She'd attempted to practice her fire magic, unable to control the curiosity, or to hold back the temptation.

She'd failed most of those times, much to her renewed fury.

But there was a passion in her eyes that reminded me so much of Logan that I wanted to burst into tears.

Instead I filled her in on Logan, his youth and his work or Omega. She'd stared shocked when I revealed that the agency was under investigation, furious that Storm had betrayed us all and hurt Logan.

And heartbroken when I told her about Anjelo's death.

Then I gave her a shortened version of Darcy's memory deletions and reminded her that she could have been subjected to much worse considering she'd been so far unable to recall memories.

I didn't mention that she'd been the one to call out to Logan in the first place. There was so much to tell that we went from one thing to the next, jumping around from topic to topic, to talk to whatever occurred to us next. But I didn't touch on the subject of her parents' death.

Thankfully, Sienna hadn't asked.

Larsson, with his tall, imposing and comfortingly silent demeanor, deposited us in the front hall of the Elite Headquarters.

"Hey Larsson?" I said, holding out a bag containing the lily. "Can you take that straight to Ash and have her run some tests on them?"

"Will do." He nodded and pocketed the bag making me sputter in horror at the disrespect to evidence.

He stepped away when I said, "Larsson?" He turned, a question in his eye? "What's your first name?"

He studied me for a moment while I tried hard to stop my teeth from chattering. Then he smiled. "Bjorn."

"Thank you, Bjorn," I said. Sienna echoed my gratitude.

Larsson nodded then proceeded to hurry off fetching blankets and ordering rooms and baths while we defrosted on the handmade carpet. It came as a surprise to me, despite my knowledge of the house, that the building contained real rooms, with baths and beds.

Neither Sienna nor I questioned Gerda when she herded us to the top floor and waved us into adjoining rooms, giving stern instructions to warm up. She left with an assurance that food was to follow shortly.

After a long hot soak in a deep claw-footed tub, the steaming water coming to just beneath my ears, I felt rejuvenated. To feel my fingers and toes was truly a wondrous thing.

My clothing had been collected and tossed into a drier while I'd bathed, and was there waiting, folded neatly at the foot of my bed, perfectly dry. The speed implied the work of a mage but I didn't question my good fortune, or the fact that another agent had gotten up-close-and-personal with my undies.

Dressing quickly, I knocked on the internal door that joined the rooms and entered when I heard Sienna call out.

"How are you feeling?" I asked, taking in the sight of her sprawled limply on the four-poster bed, staring up at the canopy.

She stared at me as I walked in, her expression not entirely free of accusation. Then she sighed, and shook her head. "I'm not sure how I feel. For some reason I'm drained. And I'm sure that makes some kind of sense. I haven't used this power, this power that you seem to think I've had all my life. And now that I've used it, it feels more like a burden than a blessing."

I swallowed hard, wondering how she was going to react when she discovered that *she* was the reason her mother had died. It was hard enough for her now, so taxing on her body and her mind, to practice using her magic.

I hoped that she would be strong enough to get through that grief when the time came. And hopefully she would have Logan by her side. The fact that she had regained some of her firepower, gave me the confidence to hope that she could help him get better.

"Most gifts feel that way."

I sat on the mattress, keeping a safe distance. I didn't want to encroach on her personal space. She was still angry with me, I could see from the narrowed look in her eyes, and thin line of her lips.

"What do you know about it?" she asked, challenging me.

I shrugged. "For a long time, I was at odds with my panther. I didn't want to accept who I was. I even went almost a year without shifting. Then, years later, when I discovered my mother's true blood, I wondered whether the hybrid nature of my DNA had affected me. I certainly hadn't behaved like a proper Alpha's daughter."

"Hybrid nature?" she asked, sitting up. Her color was slowly returning.

"Yeah. My mom is a human mage. Tracker. Dad's the Panther Alpha."

"Wow." Her mouth rounded. "You must have had a pretty interesting life growing up."

"Sometimes I wish I could have skipped it altogether. My mum left us when I was five." Sienna's eyes hardened and I waved at her. "Don't worry. She had a good reason, all of which I understand. I probably would have done the same thing. But it's easy to sit now and look back at her choices and understand why she did what she did. The thing that I can't change is how I felt back then. All those years of missing her, pining for her, hating her. That's a lot of pain for a kid to grow up with. Add to that the pressure of being an alpha's daughter and that's a barrel full of C4 ready to blow."

She'd shifted up, and was now resting against the pillow behind her. "I understand; I grew up without a mother too." She frowned, her brow creasing as she looked off into the distance. "Sometimes I dream of her, and then sometimes I wonder whether my dreams were of a mother, or of a figment of my imagination."

"Did anyone ever explain to you where you're from?"

"No. They always seemed ignorant of my past. All they said was that I was brought to the Drakyr as a child, sold to General Vyrian by a human mage who wanted to pay off a gambling debt. No one ever told me who this man was, or how he had come by me. For all I knew he could have been my real father."

"So. General Vyrian is a father figure?"

Sienna nodded, and I got the sense that she didn't want to discuss it further. I'd have to continue the conversation at a more appropriate time. But right now, we had to get moving.

"Right, if you're feeling better, I think we'd better get back. I sent a message to my dad, just to let him know that we're okay. If we don't get back soon, they'll probably send a search party."

She smiled, "Must be nice to be so loved by someone that they'd boss you around."

Funny thing was, I'd never thought of it that way. I waited in my room while she finished dressing, and we left moments after.

Horner provided us with the vehicle, stretch limo of all things. The driver drove us all the way to my father's house up in the mountains. Both Sienna and I fell asleep for most of the ride.

WHEN WE ARRIVED HOME, Dad and Baz helped us inside. The twins were asleep, and though I'd wanted to see them, especially sweet little Alina, I resisted the urge to ask Baz to fetch her.

Sienna paused inside the doorway, hesitating on the threshold only a second before Dad put his arm around her shoulders and drew her into the living room.

Darcy was setting down a tray of hot chocolate and the fire was roaring and crackling. It felt like a homecoming, but one without Logan.

Sienna smiled shyly as she entered the room and sank onto the sofa beside me. She gave Darcy an inquisitive glance and I introduced them. At the mention of Darcy's name, Sienna flinched.

"You don't have to be worried about Darcy. She's a friend."

Darcy laughed and leaned forward. "Despite what I've done in the past, I'm only here to help."

Sienna nodded, then glanced at me before returning her attention to Darcy. The one look said that she'd trust Darcy only because I trusted her.

Relieved, I got to my feet and went to Dad at the fire.

"You seem to spend a lot of time here," I said warming my hands over the heat.

He sighed. "Not nearly enough." He sounded tired.

"How did it go?" I asked. "How's she reacting?"

Dad looked away from the fire. His eyes were dark as he said,

"Let's take every day one at a time, okay. Right now, I haven't seen much progress and my disappointment is making me want to throw in the towel."

"It's all or nothing Dad. That's what Lily would want." I spoke softly, listening to the murmur of conversation behind me.

Darcy probably taking both emotional and mental stock of her.

"Is she conscious?" I asked.

He shook his head. "No. It's been painful. I have her sedated right now."

I nodded, sadness tugging at me. I'd harbored a silly hope that she'd be all healed and perfect by the time I got back home. "Let me know when she wakes up."

Dad rubbed my back. "I will. You just concentrate on the drama at hand." He gave my uninjured shoulder a squeeze. "I'm going to check on her." In his absence I drank hot chocolate and texted Tara, letting her know I'm home and that we needed to talk in private. Then I watched Sienna's face as she responded to Darcy's subtle probing.

Although it could be considered an invasion of her privacy, we only wanted to ascertain her mental health. Not make any changes.

And yet I still felt guilty. But I'd have to deal with Sienna when we told her.

Which wouldn't be today.

A few times the MindMelder glanced in my direction giving me an encouraging nod. From that, I understood that Logan's sister was healthy. Though her mind had been wiped, her brain was still in good condition. I'd been terrified that whatever they'd done to her mind, would not be able to be undone. Thankfully from Darcy's expression she seemed confident that there was hope.

The moment I entered the house all I want to do was to run upstairs and check on Logan. But if he wasn't okay, my father would have told me. I knew he'd be asleep, resting. Yet, that kind of assurance never did work for me but I didn't want to cause a scene and go running upstairs like some hysterical lover.

I'd given Sienna enough time to settle down, and now I glanced at her. "You ready?"

She nodded and got to her feet, dusting down the front of her pants. She gave Darcy a grateful smile and joined me as I walked to the door. We left the warmth of the living room and hurried up the stairs.

I headed to my room and stood on the threshold waiting for Sienna to catch up with me. At the doorway, I watched her as she caught sight of Logan for the first time. Tears filled her eyes and then ran unchecked down her cheeks.

She looked at me. "Is it okay if I . . .?"

I nodded vigorously. Hoping the tears that burned behind my lids would not fall. "Of course. You go right ahead. I'll give you some privacy."

She reached out to me. "You sure it's okay?"

"Absolutely." I patted her hand, feeling an overwhelming sense of affection for her. "I'll come back in a little bit. You two get acquainted."

She gave me a wry smile and went into the room and I left the two of them alone.

Brother and sister, reunited at last

I left Sienna and Logan to get acquainted, although I wasn't sure exactly how they would manage it. Even watching his unmoving form from the doorway, it was obvious to me he'd grown weaker, paler. He didn't look any better.

Was that why Dad had failed to mention his condition when we spoke?

I shook the thoughts from my head, preferring not to think about it. Right now, there were other issues that required my concentration. Funny how the two main things in my life, the two things that hurt me the deepest, were the dead and the dying.

I headed downstairs to the living room, welcoming the warmth of the fire against my skin. For the first time in my life I felt ice right to the bone. I was grateful that the room was empty, and I sat beside the fireplace and leaned my head against the warmed stone.

Retrieving my phone from my pocket, I rang Nerina and asked her to come. When I had something to ask her, I never told her over the phone. Probably my distrust of her high priestess making me paranoid.

Nerina materialized beside me not long after, in a swirling

blizzard of gray. She looked so serene, standing there all gray eyes, gray hair and gray cloak, and yet I knew more about her than I'd ever known about the DeathTalkers. They used to be creatures of the OtherWorld to me. Now that I'd made friends with one of them, I knew the truth. Deep down we were the same.

And our fates were intertwined, whether by prophecy or mutual need.

"How'd it go?" she asked, taking a step toward me.

She knelt beside the fire and touched my arm, her fingers cool against my warm skin. The fabric of the clothing beneath her cloak peeked through and I was surprised to recognize a pair of jeans and a cable-knit sweater. Weather appropriate for sure, but death talker appropriate?

The longer Nerina spent with me the more she broke free from the chains that bound her to her Order. Lady Kira would never forgive me if she discovered her daughter's transgressions.

Hopefully she never found out.

I nodded and marshaled a smile, one that was much weaker than Nerina deserved. I lifted my brows to the ceiling. "She's here. I brought her back with me. But we left a whole lot of problems behind."

Nerina nodded. "Nothing more than what we'd expected." She looked serious, but unconcerned.

I sighed, the air coming out of my lungs in a tired gust. "The Prince of the Winter Fae wants to take over Drakys. Someone is killing emissaries of the Elders. Someone, either the same or an entirely different someone, is actively poisoning the Black Lilies of the Blood River and harvesting them for some nefarious reason. Someone else, or maybe even the same someone, is using the very same poison to kill the Ash Trees of the EarthWorld . . ."

I looked away, reluctant to continue because if I did I'd end up mentioning Logan's condition and then I may or may not release the floodgates of tears that had been taking all of my strength to hold fast.

From Nerina's silence I knew she was shocked. When at last she took a breath, she said, "Ok. That's certainly *more* than we expected."

She shifted and soon she was sitting on the floor, her legs crossed yoga style. "Now, tell me what you need from me."

I tilted my head and looked at her. "You think that our friendship is based solely on my needs for your services?"

She smiled at me, her expression serene. "I think perhaps that is the way our relationship began. Which was a long time ago. A lot has happened between us. And I have the utmost trust in you." She reached out and squeezed my fingers. "There is nothing to be ashamed of because you need my help. We are all here to help each other. Perhaps someday I will be in need of yours." She gave a cheeky smile.

I laughed. "Not exactly sure what I can bring to the table in terms of talent. I don't speak to the dead, I don't jump through the veil, I don't read minds."

Nerina laughed. "Ah well. We'll cross that bridge when we come to it."

I snorted, trying to school my features. "Right, so I need your help to get in touch with Anjelo."

"Huh?" She raised eyebrows. "What is it with you and the Graylands?" She didn't sound happy.

I shrugged. "Everyone keeps ending up there and then they need my help."

She pursed her lips. "How do you know Anjelo needs you?"

"It's not Anjelo who needs me. It's Lily that needs me to fix what's going on with Anjelo."

Nerina's frown deepened. She did not understand the intricacies. Nor did she know the depth of Lily's problem, her insecurities and her inability to shift. Only I knew the burden she carried now, the burden that was Anjelo.

But she seemed to understand that this was a personal thing. Getting to her feet, she waved me toward the sofa. I rose in one smooth move, reluctant to leave the warmth of the fire. Nerina sat down on the sofa, plumped up the cushions behind her, leaned back and got comfortable.

I sat on the carpet beside her. She looked tired, smudges of shadow gouging the hollows beneath her eyes. "You know the drill," she said.

And I did.

Before too long, her lashes fluttered as she opened her eyes, now gray and pale and looking like death.

I leaned forward, watching Nerina's face closely. "Anjelo?" I asked softly.

Nerina tilted her head, her eyes still and unseeing, although her expression was confused and curious, and her lip curled in a familiar way.

"Kai?" came Nerina's voice, although now it contained a roughness that reminded me of Anjelo as much as that smartass smirk of his.

"Is that you?" he asked, his voice edged heavily with disbelief.

"Yes, it's me," I said gently. "I'd ask you how you are but . . ." I stopped talking, wondering if I was just going to upset him with my wisecracks.

But he just laughed. "Yeah. I'm not exactly in good *physical* condition." He fell silent after a while, then lifted his chin. "How are *you*?" he insisted.

"I'm fine. Just a lot going on right now." I didn't want to go into it all.

"I can understand that."

"Lily told you?" I wasn't surprised.

"A little."

I sighed. "Lily *is* the reason for this . . . meeting."

He laughed. "I knew you had to have a good reason."

"Of course, I did."

Now his laughter was a little bitter. "And of course Kailin Odel's feelings would be the last thing *you'd* consider."

"What's that supposed to mean?" I asked, my tone a little too sharp.

"Don't get your panties in a bunch." He snorted. "All I meant was that you'd arrange this seance or whatever the shit it is you're doing to contact me, and you'd do it only because someone else needs your help. Not because *you* may need it."

"What? Are you trying to imply that I should be talking to you for myself? Because I'm not dealing with my own grief?" I was beginning to get annoyed.

"Are you?" he asked simply.

I let out a sharp breath. "Look. I won't pretend that I'm fine. We failed to apprehend Storm in time. We failed to save your life. And it may well be possible that we will fail to save Logan too." I swallowed hard. "So, no. I'm not fine at all. I'm struggling to deal with your death. I miss you and I blame myself and I see the pain that Lily is in, and all I want is to yell for someone to stop this insane ride so I can get the hell off and get some peace. But this is my life and my life never goes the way I want it to, so I'm sucking it up and moving on."

I came to a barreling stop on a rush of air.

"Then why make contact with *me*?" I could have sworn that where he was, he was smiling.

"Don't flatter yourself, dude," I said, choking on a laugh. "It's Lily that I'm worried about."

Nerina's body stiffened, her features tightening and Anjelo grew worried. "Is she okay?"

"Yes," I answered. Then I sighed. "No."

"Kai-"

"Yes, I know. Stop talking in riddles." I groaned and held my forehead, forgetting for that moment that I was talking to Anjelo through Nerina. I was getting way too used to making contact via a DeathTalker.

I really need to get out more.

I inhaled harshly. "Look. I was worried about talking to you about this. That's why I took so long to make contact. But, to be totally honest, there isn't any other way to say this." I paused, taking another quick breath. "You need to leave Lily alone."

Silence was all I got for a long while. Then Nerina bent forward and Anjelo said, "Now, why in the name of Ailuros would I leave her alone? She needs me."

"That's where you're wrong."

"What do you mean?"

"She doesn't need you. What she needs is time to heal. To get over you. And right now she can't, what with all the late-night ghosts-of-christmas-pasts visitations."

"Geez, can you get any more dramatic?" He was annoyed but there was a hesitation in his voice, like my words had made some sort of unexpected sense to him.

"Anjelo, listen to me. When people die, those they leave behind take time to heal their hearts and their minds. There's anger and grief, fear and frustration, all rolled in with regret and longing. Right now you aren't giving her the space to feel these feelings. You're still around, however transparent you are. Next thing you know the two of you are going to break out the pottery wheel and get all muddy together."

Nerina snorted on Anjelo's behalf and I couldn't tell who was truly responsible for that amusement.

"What I'm trying to say is this . . . isn't healthy. You're not helping her."

"So I'm the problem?"

Defensive much.

"Yes, you are."

"So what do you want me to do?" More defensive.

"Leave her alone. Move on to the Afterlight. Shoo." I even made a shooing motion with my hands before realizing he couldn't see me.

Another snort.

"She's not strong enough to handle this, Anjelo. You're killing her slowly."

"But . . . I thought I was helping her."

"So how long were you planning on sticking around?"

He didn't respond.

"Months? Years?" I sighed and rubbed my forehead. "What happens if in two years you can't hold on anymore and you have to go into the light? Then what? You're going to break her heart all over again. How is she going to live her life, meet someone to love, have a family?"

More silence.

"She can't do any of that with you hanging around," I said softly. "As much as I love you and want to spend time with you, even I know that the Graylands is only a temporary stop. You'll leave again and then break her heart twice over. She's too fragile for that."

"What do you mean? Fragile?"

"She's still having problems with being Pariah. My father's giving her some treatment. And what if it works? What if she gets better and can move on, don't you think you're going to hold her back then?"

Anjelo sighed. "Guess I didn't think about that." He was silent for a few moments and Nerina's face remained unmoving and pale. "I didn't realize . . . All I wanted was to comfort her. I was terrified that she'd blame herself for my death. You know how she is. But . . . I guess I was wrong."

"I'm sorry." I really was. This was so hard to do, getting him to let go of her and move on.

"It's okay."

"It's not as if I want you to go."

"Come on, Kai. I know you want me to leave."

"Yes. I do."

"See?"

I shook my head and smiled. "You need to move on. Find peace. Figure out whether you're going up or down. Then do it. You can't live in limbo forever."

"But I thought I could help you." He sounded earnest now.

I sat back. "Help me how?"

Nerina shrugged for Anjelo. "Liaise between the worlds. Help you with information. We hear a lot from here. It's like a network of crossed wires all concentrated in one place. We hear things."

I took a chance on him. "Hear anything about the ash trees?"

"Nothing about ash trees but something about planes."

"You been talking to Agent Chou?"

"That's the one."

While on a case, our paths had crossed with Chou, whose misguided grief over his father's death made him join an off-the-books CIA project that injected subjects with paranormal DNA. We'd been forced to kill him and I'd ended up meeting him in the Graylands when I went to look for Anjelo and Lily.

"I remember him mentioning planes in our last conversation but I was a little out of it."

"Yeah. He's not one to trust. As it happens, it's not airplanes you should be worried about. It's something to do with a poison."

And things just got more interesting.

"A poison?" I asked, holding my breath.

"Not sure what it's about or what type of poison it is. All I know is I overhead him talking to someone and mentioning that he sent you on a wild goose chase with the planes suggestion."

"He didn't. I haven't had time to pursue that, thank Ailuros."

"He's one of the reasons I didn't want to just up and disappear. I can be of help to you here. Even if it is for a short while."

I was beginning to see his point but I didn't want to concede so quickly.

"Fine."

Apparently, I have no self-control.

"But no more visitations with Lily," I said firmly. "If you want to talk, come find me. Just leave her alone until she heals."

Another long silence stretched painfully between us. "Okay. I will." He sounded like he'd just cut his heart out of his chest with a blunt knife. I knew the feeling.

I sighed. "You also need to accept that you're no longer part of our world. I don't want you hanging onto some pretense of helping us just so that you can retain a grip on your old life. It's over."

"You're hard, Kai."

"Someone has to be." I smirked.

"I hate it when you're right."

"I'm always right."

"Don't I know it."

And don't I wish that I wasn't.

CHAPTER 48

Logan

The air beside Logan's bed shifted and he felt it move against his skin. Someone was in his room. Or rather, Kai's room. Which didn't matter in the least since he'd taken it over.

A part of him was already expecting Kai, but he knew something was different about his visitor. She smelled different.

Kai smelled of cinnamon and fresh cold air. The person standing beside him made him think of pink bubble baths, and toasted marshmallows over a hot fire.

He blinked, his eyes moving beneath his lids. He couldn't see a thing, and the inability to look around was extremely frustrating. He wasn't entirely sure how much longer he had left before he went crazy.

The woman shifted, the fabric of her clothing crinkled loudly in his ears. These past few days, lying here in the bed unable to see a thing, sounds had grown sharper. The tapping of footsteps, the creaking of the house, the beeping of the machines in the room. Even the low rush of water within the pipes in the walls. The mattress beside him tilted as she sat next to him.

"Logan?" she said. He could feel her leaning closer toward him, her warm breath drifting over his cheeks.

He tilted his head toward the sound. "Can you hear me?" she asked again.

There was a note in her voice that suggested she knew that he couldn't hear her.

The problem was he could hear her only too well.

He waited until she shifted, wriggling little. At last, she spoke again. "You told me to come." Logan's heart began to beat faster. "Kai fetched me. I have to admit all the cloak and dagger of it was quite exciting. But we left in a bit of a rush. I knew I had to come when I heard you were in a coma."

Logan could barely breathe. Could it really be her? As much as he had wished, no prayed, that she would come, a large part of him didn't believe it was even possible.

Even when he'd sent Kai off to look for her, he'd suspected she'd fail, that he'd die before he ever set eyes on his sister again.

And right now, he wished he could open his eyes and see her face. It wasn't enough that she'd come. Logan wanted to see her, talk to her, watch her smile.

But it wasn't like he had much of a choice.

She sighed, and he wondered whether it was fatigue or sorrow that weighed her down. "Right. I'm here now. What do I do?" Her voice was soft and filled with fear. When he didn't answer, she leaned forward and took his hand in hers. "I'm here. I'm not leaving. You need to tell me what I must do. How can I help you?"

Logan shifted, knowing that whatever movements he made would not transmit themselves to his limbs. Here, lying on the bed these past weeks, he'd found himself in a strange mental state. He moved all the time. Shifted his legs, and waved his arms, but all those movements were confined to his imagination. A result of stupid hope.

The people around him, the people that came to visit him had made an effort to spend time with him even when, as far as they knew, he was as sentient as a carrot. He wanted to assure them that he was fine, he was well, albeit frustrated and angry.

He wanted to tell Corin Odel that he appreciated everything the Alpha was doing for him. The man has shifted his duties from his Alpha responsibilities, to research and tending to Logan. He'd been attentive, caring, determined to help Logan however he could. Any other man would have left Logan to waste away. He certainly wasn't good enough for the Alpha's daughter. Even Logan knew that.

Probably one of the reasons Justin Lake had begun to pursue Kai. *He* knew what was coming. Logan was nobody, and Kai was Walker royalty. That he was human complicated the matter further. Not that it was so bad, what with Kai's mother being human herself.

But Logan was well aware of the problems that the alphas had with the Walker High Council and the new treaty.

He wanted to tell Kai how much he appreciated every single moment that she spent with him. He knew that she made time to see him, no matter what her work schedule was. These past weeks she would deal with her cases, then come to sit at his side and tell him everything she'd done. Sometimes she sounded eager, excited and other times her voice was filled with desperation. All he wanted was to sit up and tell her everything was okay. That he was fine.

But he couldn't. As hard as he tried, he couldn't.

Movement beside him reminded him that Sienna was there sitting in silence, patiently.

There was nothing he could do right now other than listen to her listen to him. Then she moved, short sharp jerky movement. "I just realized something," she said with a confiding tone. "If I could meet you in my thoughts all the way from Drakys, then can't I do the very same thing here and now?"

Logan would have smiled, had he been able, and he would have done so proudly. She was smart, and he'd expected nothing less. His sister had always been brilliant.

It didn't take long before he felt her touch his mind. Gentle probing, that made him welcome her searching mind.

Inside each other's minds they were both comfortable, and they fell into their routine; the small period of silence in which they absorbed each other's emotional state. An unconscious attempt to achieve a sense of peace before they traveled down emotional roads that could prove painful.

"Tell me what to do. I want to help you," she whispered.

"I'm not sure what you need to do. Maybe start by trying to use your fire."

"Firstly, I'm not sure I can do it again, and secondly, do you really think that's wise?"

Logan frowned. "Why would you think it's not wise?"

"You certainly don't want to burn the Odel family home down to the ground."

Logan wanted to laugh. "I wouldn't want to do that, that much is true. But I don't think you have anything to worry about. My fire is well and truly stuck inside me. I'm not sure what I can do to release it."

Sienna shifted beside him, her body tilting back and forth, and he could picture her shaking her head. "I've only used my fire for one day. The last thing *I* want to do is to burn the Odel house down."

They were silent for a few moments before Logan said, "Maybe instead of trying to generate fire, you can try taking mine out of me."

"How in the world would I do that?" she asked, puzzled.

"Clear your mind, and concentrate. Then take hold of my

hand, and use the energy in your fingers to reach into my body and look for the fire."

"You make it sound easy."

"That's because it is easy. You're a fire mage, and using your power to create magic and manipulate fire is in your blood. You should be able to do it in your sleep, and even while you're unconscious."

"Guess I won't be able to do it in a coma though would I?"

"Smartass."

Sienna cleared her throat. Gripping his hand tighter, she said "And what do I do next?"

"Close your eyes and think of what fire feels like, then use your mind and your nerves to find anything in my hand that feels like fire. My energy is within my body. I feel it surging beneath my skin all the time. So it shouldn't be all that hard for you to find it and pry it from me."

"Won't that be dangerous?"

"The buildup of the fire within my body and my mind is enough to cause spontaneous combustion. And that's more dangerous."

"Okay, let me try." The silence lengthened and a few minutes later, she said, "I can feel the rushing heat inside you, as if your blood is on fire."

"That's exactly how I feel." Logan smiled wryly.

"Okay. I'm going to try and draw some of that heat toward me."

Another few moments passed and Logan could feel the heat inside his arm begin to travel toward the surface of his skin, seeming to seek out Syn's energy. It was working, he had no doubt of it

"Ow," Sienna shrieked, jumping up and patting something solid. She groaned and Logan could smell scorched fabric, and wanted to smile.

She'd managed to set his bedclothes alight.

"You really should try not to set me on fire," he said dryly.

"Shut up. You told me to pull the fire from you. Not my fault that it jumped out before I could catch it."

If Logan could smile he would have. She was just as he remembered. Exactly as he remembered, even the smart mouth too.

For the next half hour, she continued to drain the buildup of fire from inside his body, giving him a peace that he hadn't felt in weeks.

At last she sighed and sat back. "How does it feel? Is it any better?"

Logan smiled and knew she'd feel his happiness. "Much better. And see, I told you you could do it."

"Now you sound just like Kai." Her tone was annoyed and dry, making Logan smile more.

"What did she do?" he asked, knowing Kai would have had to do something impressive to deserve this reaction from his sister.

Logan listened as Sienna replayed the events on the glacier, her reluctance to believe she had it in her to create fire, the distraction of being soaking wet and ice cold and the fury induced in her by the woman he loved with all his heart. Kai was impressive, and despite her tactics he was grateful she'd taken the chance.

But beneath his sister's words he sensed something else, something that was worrying her.

"What's wrong? There's something bugging you, Sienna. You can tell me."

She got to her feet and began to pace. "There was something that happened. I couldn't believe it at first because it made absolutely no sense. But now . . . After the whole making fire thing, and this . . . Helping you? It's made me understand that there is so much I don't understand." She sighed and stopped moving.

"What was it that you couldn't believe?" Logan asked, not

wanting to push her. Whatever troubled her, it didn't seem like it was something she'd easily accept.

She sat again, shifting rhythmically and he could almost picture her crossing one leg over the other and swinging it back and forth as she frowned.

"So there was this incident." She hesitated. "With a dragon."

"What happened? Did it hurt you?"

"No. Actually it saved Kai. One of our Counsels was attempting to kill her when I walked into the room-"

"What?"

"Don't worry. She's fine. It's one of the reasons we got out of there fast. Things were getting dangerous." She spoke quickly. "Anyway, I ran toward her. I'm not sure what the hell I expected to do but when I grabbed him I could have sworn we both fell over the balustrade."

"As in over the side of the building. Like, plunging-to-your-death falling?" Logan asked, his heart thudding faster now. He tried to assure himself that Kai was fine because had anything happened to her he would have felt it in Sienna's emotions. She'd never been one to hide her feelings and it already seemed like she liked Kai. So he breathed slowly and waited.

Sienna laughed. "Yes. We should both be dead. But we were saved by a dragon."

"Sounds cool."

"Maybe." She sucked in a breath. "I don't remember anything about the fall. I fell, then I woke up on the floor of the balcony. That's the extent of my recollection."

"And the dragon?"

"That's the freak-show part of the story. Kai said the dragon was me."

Blood rushed through Logan's ears, loud enough to color his thoughts. "Why would she think that?"

"Because she said she saw me transform from a dragon into me before I passed out."

"And you can't remember any of this?"

She shifted in the seat, probably shaking her head.

"If Kai says she saw it, then she saw it."

"I'm not doubting her words. What I am wondering is how this is possible. How can I be a fire mage and not know it? How can I be a Drakyr and not remember shifting into one?"

Logan swallowed then took a deep breath. "There is something else we need to consider."

"Which is?" she asked, sounding disinterested. He didn't need to probe her feelings to know she was exhausted, from the events of the last few hours and from the conversation.

"If *you* are a dragon, and *we* are twins…"

"Holy Goddess."

CHAPTER 49

Sienna returned to the living room, her expression revealing her uncertainty. She looked like a woman hovering somewhere between excitement and disappointment. I wanted to drag any information from her that I could get, but I controlled the urge.

We'd been waiting patiently for Sienna to come downstairs. Darcy wanted to test Logan's mind to see if Sienna's arrival and interaction with him had helped.

I cleared my throat. "So?"

Sienna shrugged. "We talked about what happened in Drakys. And about my fire."

"Did you try using it with him?" I asked, still unsure what she was meant to do.

But Sienna nodded and I felt a lilt of hope. "He guided me, and I tried pulling some of his energy from him. It was easier than I expected."

"It would be," responded Darcy. "The magic of a mage lies in their spirit, their essence. It's a totally natural thing, easily accessed once the bearer of the power accepts it. And you have accepted your abilities. Perhaps that is why it wasn't difficult."

Sienna nodded, looking relieved at Darcy's explanation. "I think it helped. He said he felt less stressed with the constant buildup of energy."

Darcy let out an audible exhalation. "Thank God for that. I was so hoping you could help him enough that his body stops laboring under the strain."

"Is that why he couldn't recover?"

Darcy nodded. "Yes. His fire was in constant flux, unable to dissipate. So his body had to spend far too much energy to fight to recover as well as fight to contain the energy in case it explodes."

"And this will help?"

Darcy nodded, her eyes exuding a confidence which made me breathe easy. "Definitely. I'll go in a bit and have a look at him, but I'm sure I know what I'll see. Even if you helped him only a little, it still means you've given his body a chance to fight back. You may need to repeat the process a few times."

Sienna nodded vigorously. "However much it takes, I'll do it. I'm not going anywhere until he is well."

Her eyes sparkled and held no trace of her more recent fury with me. When she met my gaze she was smiling, the look of someone filled with joy. It amazed me that she'd feel this way despite risking her life to run from Elan and the queen of Drakys.

"Kai. I need to thank you for what you did."

"What? I didn't do anything except royally piss you off."

Sienna laughed, the sound tinkling and echoing around the living room. "That you certainly did. And it worked. But you realize it was extremely dangerous. I could have killed you if my fire had been volatile."

I shrugged. I'd expected that and was grateful at the time that she hadn't incinerated me on the spot.

"How did you know I wouldn't kill you?"

"I didn't," I replied, lifting my chin. "But I'd do anything if it meant giving Logan a chance at surviving."

Sienna studied me, tipping her head to the side. "You'll make a good sister-in-law."

I choked on my laughter. "Now, don't get ahead of yourself. Let the man get well first before you start pressuring him to propose."

She stilled. "And you'd say yes?" she asked eagerly, as if all I had to do was to nod and she'd be flying up the stairs to convince him of that.

"Of course I would," I said, finding my words echoing deep within my heart. Despite my feelings for Justin, and I'd be a fool to deny them, what I had with Logan was just as strong, if not stronger. I was his as long as he wanted me.

I smiled and got to my feet. "Speaking of which, I have a date with Sleeping Handsome."

Sienna giggled as I hurried up the stairs to Logan's room, a bundle of nerves.

Just before I entered my cell phone began to buzz in my hand. The screen announced Horner and I headed back into the hallway and swiped to accept.

"Yes, Boss."

"I hear you've returned. Sorry I wasn't able to check in on you earlier."

I assured him I was fine and filled him in on much of what happened in Drakys, except for Sienna going all scales and wings on me. That he didn't need to know yet. Like me, Horner was concerned about the toxic pollution, and the potential to use the Black Lily's for bio-terrorism. Ash was probably testing the lilies right this minute.

"And you're certain Counsel Andyr is really Elan?"

"Absolutely no doubt in my mind."

"Fine. I'll speak to the Elders."

I hesitated, then decided I had nothing to lose. "Could you hold off contacting the Fae regarding our suspicions?"

Horner fell silent. "Why?"

"Because I'd like to tell Tara this myself. I don't want her surprised when the Elders contact her. Whatever Elan was up to, it wasn't done at her behest, nor was it actioned with her knowledge."

Horner cleared his throat. "I hardly think either of us are in a position to make assumptions-"

I cut him off. "I'm not making assumptions. Trust me. I know Tara. And she'd already been investigating the poison. She was the one who suspected the Winter Court of having a hand in the killing of the trees. At least now we know how they're doing it, and why they find Drakys so valuable."

"Fine. You have twenty-four hours. In the interim I shall speak to the Elders and we will decide where to go from here."

I took what I could, thanked him and rang off.

My stomach was tight, and I suspected I needed food or something stronger. Maybe a brandy. But alcohol didn't work for me which totally sucked.

I pocketed my cellphone and took a deep breath. Things were all happening too fast. But I'd knocked a few things off my list. Anjelo was sorted, and Logan and Sienna were together.

As I turned to enter the room and check on Logan, a cloud of golden light appeared down the hall. Tara materialized and beckoned me to Greer's room.

I followed in silence, and closed the door as softly as I could.

"How did it go? Did you find anything?" Tara asked. She'd pulled a glamor around us, hiding our conversation which was good thinking considering our hacker-vamp who may hear what we said. I nodded and dug into my pocket for the second lily I'd plucked. "I brought this. I sent a sample to our lab but this one is for you."

She nodded, glowering at the black petals.

"It's a poisonous plant from Drakys." She was nodding again, now with recognition. "I use a powdered form of Black Erish to amplify the toxins in your ammo."

"Erish?"

"The Drakyr name," she supplied. "What does it–"

"The magic of the Life's Blood has leeched into the lilies. Together with the toxins from the Erulite mining, this is a particularly potent poison that works in a way that I've only seen recently."

Tara's eyes widened as she stared at me, slowly putting pieces together. "This is what they used to poison the Ash trees?"

"That's what I suspect. The lab should verify it."

"Thanks, Kai. I'd better get this back– "

"Tara?" She stopped, a little startled at my second interruption. "There is something else. Or rather someone else that I met in Dyr that would be of interest to you."

"Who?"

"Councilmen Andyr Dar-ys, Royal Solicitor, fiancée to Sienna, and attempted murderer." I held out my fisted hand, and Tara hesitated, glancing at it, then back at my face. She raised her palm and I dropped the diamond clasp onto her pale skin.

Her mouth hung opened in shock as she stared at the shimmering jewel. "I . . . Elan. I should have known he'd be capable of something like this." Fury and disgust raged on her face and finally she took a deep breath and regained some calm. Then she looked up at me with concern. "Who did he murder?"

"Attempted murder." I smiled, still furious at the attempt he'd made. I pointed at my chest. "Me."

"What?" Tara was paler than I'd have thought possible. About as pale as the opalescent gown she wore today.

She staggered to the bed and sat heavily on it. Then she stared up at me. "I knew I should have stayed away from you. Now he's going to go after you."

I shrugged. "He tried. And he failed."

"He's relentless. Nothing will stop him, Kai." She gave me a sad look, then her features hardened and she got to her feet. "Let me deal with this. I won't alert him just yet. But I will try to uncover his plan."

I said, "Why would he want to kill the tree?"

She shrugged. "Destabilize supernatural faith. Absorb power from the tree?" She sighed. "Some of the Fae live off the power of the ash trees. The much older ones for whom the Elements are not sufficient. Maybe he wants to eliminate the Ancient Council of the Fae? Who the hell knows what's going on in his psychotic head?"

I sighed and beckoned her. "I have to go. At any rate, that's as much as I know. I only managed to buy you a day. I'm sorry, I tried but all I got was twenty-four hours. Then the Elders will be paying the Fae Court a visit." Tara got to her feet and drew me into a crushing hug. "Thank you, Kai." Then she squeezed me harder. "And I'm so glad you're okay. I'm going to get that bastard."

"Not if I get him first."

CHAPTER 50

At last I entered Logan's room a little preoccupied.

My part in the case was closed now, of course. Elan was behind the poisoning of the trees though his end game was still supposition. Even if he wanted me dead, I wasn't about to live in fear of him. I'd wipe him off the face of the DarkWorld if I had to.

Besides, the next move in this hideous game would be more political, and that was the Elder's problem. And so was their mining effort in Drakys. They'd have come up with a good explanation for their missing emissary and the queen's vanished handmaiden. I was only too happy to give the Elders the task of smoothing over that political disaster job.

And I wasn't blind to the fact that the Elders would soon come to me for an explanation. Soon enough, we'd have to come clean about hiding Sienna and Logan in my father's house.

Our ice prince was likely already back at the Fae Court, probably pretending he hadn't just tried to kill me, totally oblivious to the fact that we were on to him. And to the fact that he'd almost married the true Dragon Queen.

I smiled.

He'd known me, beneath the goth makeup. I had no doubt of it. Why else would he have attempted to murder me? And he'd know that he'd failed. I could only imagine his fury. I felt a rush of pity for the people in his vicinity. Things would be mighty cold for them for a while.

Of course, I hadn't forgotten the shadows. I'd killed the Shadowman, but whoever sent him was still out there. And I'd soon be able to verify if my shadow stalkers were in league with the shadow Mage.

Life was definitely going to be interesting what with princes wanting me dead, shadows stalking me, and dragon queens probably wanting my head for stealing her slave.

I still had Lily to worry about. The treatment simply had to work. I knew how devastated I'd be should it fail. The depth of my emotions made me all too aware of what Lily's feelings would be on the matter.

The treatment had to work.

It simply had to.

My thoughts returned to the twins. Fire mages? Definitely not. Although, as a cover it was a brilliant choice.

Sienna and Logan were the rightful heirs to the Kingdom of the Drakyr. As soon as Logan was well they could return and retake their throne as was their right. And in the end Omega, and whoever else was involved in the plot against the siblings, had failed.

Sienna was safe with us for a while. She seemed overjoyed to be able to help her brother. And if Darcy was right about the process then Logan would slowly get better. He'd soon be well enough to find out how to release his dragon.

The thought sent a shiver down my spine.

Logan was a Drakyr.

A real, honest-to-goodness, in-the-flesh, sexy man-dragon. Who'd have thunk it? I couldn't wait to hear what he thought of it all.

I'd come to accept it slowly. I'd lived with his fire, and his nightmares.

What's a giant scaly alternate personality thrown into the mix?

Now, as I watched my dragon lover lying there so peacefully, I prayed to Ailuros to guide him safely back to us.

I'd gone to Drakys, found his sister, almost been poisoned by the Ice Prince, almost been strangled by the same, almost plummeted to my death, been saved by a golden dragon, and almost died on the glacier, and I was tired.

And before that I'd been reunited with my best friend, been impaled by wooden stakes, and been saved by a magical dagger.

I was so very tired.

Tired and a tiny bit afraid that everything had been for naught. His condition hadn't changed.

But I had to have hope.

I lay down beside him, and traced my fingers across his cheek. His eyes remained closed, his long eyelashes fluttering with the slightest of movements.

He was in there somewhere.

And he'd said he was sometimes conscious. That sometimes he knew we were around.

I bent closer and kissed his lips, probably a little harder than was necessary. But right now, I'd take any amount of intimacy that I could. Even a chaste kiss would satisfy me.

I rested my palm over his heart, absorbing the beat of his heart into my veins, feeling the comfort of having him alive. No matter what happened I'd wait for him. And he knew that.

Settling my head on his shoulder, I listened to the soft thudding of his heart, yearning for his arms to close around me.

I fell asleep there, with his warmth against my cheek, a soft smile on my lips.

And Logan's arm curled around my waist.

CHAPTER 51

Logan

Something warm and heavy lay on his shoulder.

His first instinct was to move, to lift his head and see what it was that weighed him down. But he knew.

He knew because that delicious weight belonged right there, against his heart.

Her scent enveloped him, cinnamon and wine. In his mind he could see her green eyes glitter, he could feel the softness of her skin beneath his fingers. Her breath was sweet as it drifted across his cheek.

His fingers traced her hipbone through the fabric of her pants.

Logan stiffened, his fingers searching the planes of her hip frantically. He was holding her, his hand curled around her waist.

He felt her warmth all along the left side of his body, felt her chest move against his as she inhaled.

But he couldn't open his eyes, nor could he move any other part of his body. But he wasn't blind to the fact that progress, even that which seemed minuscule, was still progress. Sienna would help to heal him.

And then they both had a job to do.

He'd lived in his sister's thoughts for weeks now, and knew the lay of the Dragonland. And he was beginning to understand the role that both he and Sienna played. He was beginning to remember things. Things from his past. Fragments that were a combination of his past and events from his sister's memories.

A Queen, dead before her time.

A mother tall and regal, her hair as red as the sun of Drakys

Twin children destined to take the throne and rule the land.

Twins that should have been dead but weren't.

Siblings stolen and hidden, but by whom? Why had they not been killed along with their mother? Had someone saved their lives out of kindness by hiding them off world?

Or had they been taken for another reason?

And why had Omega sent Sienna back into the royal court, hiding her in plain sight?

Memories drifted to him. Realities he couldn't avoid or deny.

Sienna's name, her true name was Synestra of the House of Yl.

And Logan, like Sienna, had been given a human name. Holding Kai's warmth close to his side, he breathed the first peaceful breath he'd taken in the length and breadth of his memory.

His name was Lyandr, Son of the House of Yl.

When he recovered, and he *would* recover, he'd have to go home.

He had a land to look after, people who waited for the return of the rightful rulers. A land which needed their mother to return and infuse life back into the sun.

He'd have to take Sienna and return home.

And the brave, fearless woman beside him would lose him again.

Even though he was unable to open his eyes, he felt the burn of tears beneath his lids. Their relationship was turning into a long-distance one of epic proportions.

It would never survive both his responsibilities to his realm, or hers to her Alpha blood.

He knew what he had to do. He had no choice.

It was, after all, the right thing to do.

Logan would leave Kai. He'd have to leave, and never look back.

He was going to break Kai's heart.

~ TO BE CONTINUED ~
The SkinWalker Series continues with Fate's Edge.

ACKNOWLEDGMENTS

To my editor, JC Hart, my publicists Rachel Marks and Brina Courtney,
thank you for your constant support and encouragement.

And to my readers - Keep on turning them pages…

ABOUT THE AUTHOR

I have been a writer from the time I was old enough to recognize that reading was a doorway into my imagination. Poetry was my first foray into the art of the written word. Books were my best friends, my escape, my haven. I am essentially a recluse but this part of my personality is impossible to practice given I have two teenage daughters, who are actually my friends, my tea-makers, my confidantes… I am blessed with a husband who has left me for golf. It's a fair trade as I have left him for writing. We are both passionate supporters of each other's loves – it works wonderfully…

My heart is currently broken in two. One half resides in South Africa where my old roots still remain, and my heart still longs for the endless beaches and the smell of moist soil after a summer downpour. My love for Ma Afrika will never fade. The other half of me has been transplanted to the Land of the Long White Cloud. The land of the Taniwha, beautiful Maraes, and volcanoes. The land of green, pure beauty that truly inspires. And because I am so torn between these two lands – I shall forever remain cross-eyed.

Stalk Tee here:
www.tgayer.com
tee@tgayer.com

facebook.com/TGAyerAuthor

twitter.com/TGAyerAuthor

bookbub.com/profile/t-g-ayer